Also through TANSTAAFL Pr

Toy Wars

Flung to a remote world, a semi-sentient group of robotic mining factories arrive with their programming hashed. They can only create animated toys instead of normal mining and fighting machines. One of these factories, pushed to the edge of extinction by the fratricidal conflict, attempts a desperate gamble. Infusing one of its toys with the power of sentience begins the quest of a 2-meter tall, purple teddy bear and his pink, polka-dotted elephant companion. They must cross an alien world to find and enlist the aid of mortal enemies to end the genocide before **Toy Wars** claims their family—all while asking the immortal question, "Why am I?"

Demon Holiday

Torval, Demon Third Class, Layer Four Hundred Twelve of the Eighth Circle of Hell, has been in the business of chastising sinners longer than he can remember. Delivering punishment is the only job he's ever known—the only job he's ever wanted. After Torval witnesses something unexpected, his demonic Overseer demands that he take time off to resolve this personal crisis. And so Torval, the demon, finds himself sent on vacation...to Earth, the proving ground of souls!

To Colleen—for always believing

An Eighty Percent Solution

CorpGov Chronicles: Book One

Thomas Gondolfi

And again ... subtly is not my strong suit.

Thomas Gondolfi

TANSTAAFL PRESS

If you purchased this book without a cover, you should be aware that it was an unauthorized sale. All books without a cover have been reported as "unsold and destroyed." As a result neither the author nor the publisher received payment for the sale of this "stripped book."

TANSTAAFL Press
1201 E. Yelm Ave,
Suite 400-199
Yelm, WA 98697

Visit us at www.TANSTAAFLPress.com

All characters, businesses, and situations within this work are fictional and the product of the author's creativity. Any resemblances to persons living or dead are entirely coincidental. TANSTAAFL Press assumes no responsibility for any content on author or fan websites or other publications.

An Eighty Percent Solution

First printing TANSTAAFL Press
Copyright © 2012 by Thomas Gondolfi
Cover illustration by Tony Foti

Printed in the United States
ISBN 978-1-938124-00-6

Define Objective

Tony edged his oversized body out of the ever-present Northwest drizzle onto a lift-bus more crowded than *E. coli* on an agar plate. He ran his sand-colored hands absently through his thick, shoulder-length black hair. Flicking his wrist, he broke The Rules as the dislodged dampness sprayed across several of his neighbors. Several commuters gave him a hard glare. Unwritten TriMet Transit laws included staying in one's own space. He half-heartedly smiled an apology.

"Mondays," Tony whispered through a hangover that bothered him only enough to know he'd once again been drinking too much—the tenth time in twelve weeks. And for the same number of weeks he thought about breaking his own personal commandment not to use any drugs, even over-the-counter hangover cures. Too many burns started out that simply. He wanted to keep his personality.

To take his mind off the pain, he stared out the partially fogged windows at the passing miasma of gray. Another exciting day of running tests for a product that won't do much for anyone, for a company that cares only about the few credits it sells for, he thought grimly.

A departing commuter offered a diversion as Tony forced himself between several other passengers like they were two line-backers to capture the empty seat. Two other hopefuls gave him the angry looks often accompanying someone else's victory. Ignoring them and the hushed but omnipresent sounds of 218 commuters crowded against him—not to mention the press of 2.3 billion in the Portland environs—Tony wiggled his hips enough to get fully seated between his neighbors.

As comfortable as one could be on the TriMet at rush hour, he reached for the news chips floating near the ceiling, missing his first two

1

attempts. Working really hard to focus his eyes on the task, he finally snagged one. He snapped the seal as if breaking a cracker and waved his prize near the neural implant under his left arm.

As he dropped the chip's now-useless, biodegradable cellulose capsule to the floor, the headline screamed "Unemployment Plummets to 27 Percent!" through his neural connection. Despite the newsman's pleasant baritone, Tony winced and wiggled the muscle at the back of his ear, muting the audio. He then harrumphed at the headline's very concept. Only a gullible fool would believe news that optimistic.

Tony absently flicked his eye to change the solido page, but nothing caught his attention until the sports news popped up in front of him. Attention, but no relief. "Spiders Trounced by Packers in a 41-14 Rout." Tony read enough to realize the league would use his Aussie Spiders as a punching bag this season. The loss of their star quarterback to a neck injury three weeks ago had put the Aussies into a tailspin, and nobody, least of all Tony, expected them to recover.

He fondly remembered his football days in high school, but only in a child's dreams could he play beyond that venue. Lacking the size or talent to play tight end professionally, he would've needed massive implants or genetic drug therapies just to compete—both against league rules at the time.

"BREAKING NEWS" flashed across his view. "Third Greenie Bomb This Week!"

Tony's shoulders straightened. In lurid detail, the article explained how a small explosive device killed at least thirteen people and maimed scores of others when it detonated within the BioNetix home offices. Even before the first screams of the injured pierced the air, the Green Action Militia took responsibility for the act. "Violence will escalate until the world is no longer exploited by the megacorps!" ranted an unidentified GAM spokesperson.

In a sop to equal time, a midlevel VP at BioNetix denounced the act as nothing more than "the brutal ruthlessness of cannibals." As a commentator interviewed eyewitnesses to the explosion, the article played some poor amateur solido footage of the bomb's debris cloud engulfing a group of workers as they entered the building. The image didn't interest Tony much and he flipped to the scrollbars that summed up the sixty-seven other acts of terrorism attributed to the GAM, including eighteen direct assassinations, multiple bombings, product tampering, and many more.

The newsies, Metros, and even the pundits painted the Greenies as a "black necrosis," but the rabble considered them modern-day heroes. This dichotomy resonated on every gossip ring, coffee klatch, political mindshare, and bull session across Earth, not to mention most everyone in the solar system.

Tony absently wondered why anyone would fight order. His life balanced. It held order. It comforted him in a dismal and gray way. He knew from one moment to the next where his next meal and entertainment would come from. He wondered how an unwinnable, pointless war against the entire system could even be considered sane.

The romance of the GAM still attracted him like the Merry Men of Robin Hood fame, but the thought of leaving his reasonably comfortable life to kill people made him absently shudder.

Engulfed in the paradox between his heart and head, he didn't notice when the eyes of the woman seated next to him went wild and she spasmodically clutched her package to her chest. Oblivious to Tony, she gasped, eyes rolling back into her head. He glanced in frustration when someone bumped into his legs, only to find the woman collapsed on the floor, leaning against him.

Until just that moment, the ancient-looking grandmother with a streak of gold down the center of her curly hair had been just another insignificant cog in life to him—just another obstacle to negotiate and placate in his day-to-day life. She jerked spasmodically in place against his legs, unable to even fall over decently in the tightly packed lift-bus. Later, Tony remembered with shame that his first act was to push her away. She collapsed bonelessly to the rubberized floorboard. The only sound came from her head landing with a dull thud.

"Leave her alone!" shouted a man wearing the yellow vinyl tights of a bodyguard.

"Please step back from the victim," the automated TriMet emergency voice finally offered in a smooth, pacifying voice designed to calm any panicky witnesses.

The year his parents sent him to live with his grandparents in Queensland all came back in a rush. Tony remembered Granther hobbling around on his peg-leg. He also remembered, with some throbbing memories in the seat of his pants, how Granther's rattan cane forced him to learn. The war taught Granther many things, all of which he felt the need to cram into his grandson in the space of that single year.

Tony's thoughts returned to the old woman on the floor. Kneeling next to her, Tony tried to remove a badly misbalanced box she still managed to clutch to her chest. It took two tries and a jerk to free it so he could place it on the seat. With an ear to her chest, he muttered to himself, "No heartbeat."

He remembered the stings Granther delivered whenever Tony dared to err. "Lay the victim down. Make sure he/she is on a hard surface," Tony mumbled, mimicking Granther's thick Aussie accent. As he talked, he followed the instructions like an obsessive-compulsive, or one of Pavlov's dogs.

"For your safety and hers, please move away from the victim," ordered the lift-bus's pleasant voice. "We have been diverted to Seattle General. The Metro Police will meet us upon arrival in six minutes and twelve seconds."

"First, tilt the victim…" Tony's back flinched, awaiting a cane too many years and kilometers away. "No, no, first I have to make sure the airway's clear!"

He obeyed his grandfather's teachings automatically, without thinking. A mottled orange goop dribbled down the side of the old woman's face. "Don't be surprised by the taste of vomit," came Granther's drill-sergeant voice. "It's common for heart attack victims to regurgitate."

Tony tilted her pale face to one side and used his fingers to scoop out a clump of stinking goo the consistency of cottage cheese. With a strong flip of his wrist he sent the mess spraying across the small open floor area, adding to Sargasso Sea of discarded gum, ink stains, news capsules, and cigarette butts—and simultaneously decorating a number of shoes, trousers, and hose.

"Now tilt back the head and blow in her mouth," Granther's disembodied voice ordered in Tony's mind. He took the precaution of wiping off her mouth with his sleeve before bending over and placing his lips on hers.

A wet slime sprayed up through her nose across his cheek. The taste of sour milk and stale cookies filled his mouth. "Oh, yeah, pinch nose." This time he succeeded in expanding her chest with his breath.

"THINK!" Tony shouted out. The packed TriMet commuters managed to back away slightly, giving him a few more centimeters of room. "Is it two breaths and thirty chest compressions or the other way around?" Everyone looked dumbfounded. "QUICK!" he barked, looking directly into the dyed green-and-yellow face of an Oregon University student.

"Please stop, citizen. Your activities may be legally actionable."

Tony didn't hear a word, totally focused on his own question. The racing in his chest gave him the answer. More beats to his heart than the number of times he breathed.

"Lace your fingers together and push hard on the chest directly between the nipples." The sharp multiple reports of the woman's ribs dislocating carried through the bus, while everyone watched in morbid curiosity. A man in the front row fell over in a faint, caught and held nearly upright by the press of the other bystanders.

"Stop that! You're killing her!" one passenger insisted.

This time the lift-bus came to Tony's defense. "Negative," came the pleasant voice, still trying to instill calm. "There is no murder taking place."

"The first compression will almost certainly crack the victim's ribs. Don't despair, because repairing broken ribs is much easier than restarting a heart which has been stopped too long."

One large man looked menacingly down at Tony. "Leave her," he insisted. "The doctors will take care of her—if she has medical, that is."

Tony paid no attention, slowing his compressions. "After thirty full compressions, each about every half second or so, you need to give two breaths of air, assuming your victim isn't breathing," Granther said through him. Tony's ear moved right next to the woman's face. He still heard nothing.

"Continue your thirty chest compressions followed by two breaths until help arrives or the victim's heart starts. This should be checked every compression set."

Tony continued his physical lifesaving. Many wouldn't even look. Others stared with the same sort of fascination as if watching someone put their head in the mouth of a lion.

"Yes, I know," he mumbled jerkily during one chest compression session. "Everyone says don't get involved. Stay at arm's reach. It's not my problem. But I can't sit here while someone dies."

Time lost its cohesion for Tony. He muscles burned and his own chest ached with the unusual labors. Thirty. Two. Thirty. Two. Thirty. The repetition kept him going. Whether one minute passed or sixty, Tony's heart leapt when he detected a pulse—faint, but definitely there. At last, the woman began to breathe on her own.

Tony all but collapsed against the seat, still straddling the old woman's torso. Spots danced before his eyes and his ears rang. He coughed heavily between desperate drags of air as the bus gently settled down on a landing pad. A pair of red-suited medicos waited along with a Metro cop, completely sealed in his blue suit of armor showing no face to the world.

The trio slowly filed on as soon as the doors opened. The Metro, in a rare instance of friendliness, helpfully directed civilians toward a waiting replacement bus.

"Hurry," Tony urged, barely having enough air for a few desperate words. "Has pulse," he gasped with his last possible breath. The medicos, not bothered by Tony's pleas, casually lifted the woman's wrist and scanned her DNA from her epithelial cells.

"She's got full medical. Get the life capsule in here on the double!" Haste replaced the formerly lax efforts. A high-tech gurney floated in.

"Out of the way, civilian," one of the medicos all but yelled at Tony. Still winded, Tony didn't respond, instead crawling a few feet out of the way. The doctors lifted her quickly into the golden coffin-like device and closed the lid. The life capsule would sustain any spark of life left in her.

"I did it! I saved her!" he gasped breathlessly, as his chest gradually felt less and less like he'd spacewalked without a suit. "It feels good! Did you see what I just did?"

"Sir, are you a relative?" the policeman asked, snapping him back to reality like the first yank of a bungee jump.

"Huh? No, sir. She was just another passenger. She was sitting there and then her face went white and—"

While the policeman's fully armored face contained no clues, Tony still detected a sense of disappointment or resentment. "I'm going to have to ask for your ident," came his voice, colder than before.

"Certainly, officer," Tony said, offering his own wrist for a DNA sample. The officer scanned it with a device built into his left index finger. "First time I've ever had a policeman scan my ident. Is that a fourteen-seventy-five Merrick Scanner?"

The policeman ignored the question. "You aren't a trained medic."

"No, sir." While Tony paid his police protection money promptly every month, he saw no reason to antagonize this officer. Who knows who might've paid them more? And paid or not, police could and would arrest you for anything they might feel like. "But my grandfather was a paramedic in the Australian Civil War. He taught me—"

"Then why were you attending to her? You could be in a great deal of fiscal trouble. This lift-bus carries all the proof she needs to convict you of malpractice."

"I understand, sir. But I couldn't just stand there and let her die."

"You could and should have. I suggest you go home and think this over. I'll notify your work, Tony Sammis."

"Yes, sir." Tony exited the bus back into the gray wetness of the day with extreme emotions simmering—excitement, happiness, fear, and dread. He walked absently toward the replacement transport when he felt a tap on his shoulder.

"Sir, your box," offered the Metro. The emotional stew boiled over. Having a policeman's attention never boded well. Without thinking he took the proffered box from the cop's blue-clad arms.

"Thank you, sir," he said, stepping onto the bus. In retrospect, Tony never knew why he took the box.

* * *

The subtle scent composition "American Beauty," by the Master Composer Beatrix Smith, wafted jasmine and cinnamon across the room.

"This October meeting will come to order," called an unamplified voice.

The décor's pure simplicity proclaimed the occupants' wealth. A simple mahogany table, the wood alone valued as much as a large home, dominated the room, with matching straight-backed chairs added as a garnish. Manufactured-diamond glasses and decanters with ice water sat next to pads of actual wood-pulp paper, where a lesser organization would've used computer screens, or perhaps even synthetics. The steel-gray depression that coated Portland nine months of the year artificially filtered in colors through a stained-glass mosaic that ringed the one-hundred-ninety-sixth floor penthouse. Fittingly, it depicted the purchase of Manhattan from the natives for a handful of trinkets.

Ten of the richest individuals in the entire Sol system calmly took their seats around the table. For all their wealth, they still wore almost identical charcoal-gray suits, differing in cut only for physical size and sex. They'd been the cogs of the great megacorps too long to fully embrace the individuality they'd earned the right to express with impunity.

Almost as one they turned on the recording mechanisms nearly transparent on their left sleeves. Even by meeting in this loose association, these people of power defied every antitrust law in every country or merchant association in the system, but this transgression would come as no surprise to anyone, anywhere.

"Old business?"

"France hasn't been forthcoming with the devaluation of the franc as our lobbyists decreed."

"So you're pushing for punitive measures?"

"Yes. I believe we've been too easy on the statutory authorities of late."

"I second that."

"Any objections?"

No one spoke.

"So do we have options for these punitive measures?"

"I suggest a four-week transit strike."

"In France it'd be a miracle if there wasn't a transit strike."

No one laughed. "Percomm Systems is out of order."

"Energy embargo. No energy in or out of the country. Our projections show they have enough for a three-month reserve. I suggest we withhold energy from the Palpon Station for a minimum of four months, but in any case until compliance."

"This will be a good visible lesson."

"Good, and we can piggyback that with some profit-taking against our energy reserves in the country."

"Objections? No? It is carried. BirskTek, would you please implement this action immediately. Any new business?"

"I'd like to propose a solution to the Green Action Militia's recent depredations on each of our organizations," Nanogate announced.

"A solution?" spouted Percomm Systems, as he shifted to try to get more than sixty percent of his personal bulk into his chair. "Preposterous!"

"The member from Percomm Systems is out of order again. Proceed with your proposal, Nanogate."

"As you all know, we've seen an alarming increase in the actions of the group known as the Green Action Militia." Several of the executives nodded in agreement. "Each of our corporations has suffered the attentions of these terrorists. I'd like to propose a course of action to bring these losses to our gross profits and personnel back in line."

"How?" the pudgy man interrupted again. "We've all tried. They're like wily feral animals. Oh, occasionally we get one or two, but never enough to even cut into their recruiting."

The chairman raised his walnut gavel to control the Percomm Systems' executive officer, but Nanogate caught his eye and waved him off.

"Too true. Our actions have not only been ineffective, but going even further, they've added to our own troubles."

"That sounds a bit farfetched," commented the chairman, breaking his own rule.

"May I have the indulgence of the panel for a few moments to prove this?" Nanogate, the newest addition of the group with only six months of tenure, didn't have the clout of the others. His peers often outvoted his pet projects. A solidographic projection atop the table tabulated the results.

"The member will proceed," announced the chairman.

"One of our conglomerates' major products is arms. We sell to any group that can pay the price. As a result, we have good modeling systems for the interactions that take place below the purview of the system government. I'm speaking, of course, of the black market. We've applied that modeling to our current crisis. In short, the data I'm projecting over the table shows that our actions have only removed the less successful members of their movement. Worse, their failures—our successes— only bring them more sympathy and attract recruits to their cause.

"The models project a range of outcomes that at best case show within sixty months, even with our chokehold on the media, fifty-eight percent of the public will be behind the GAM. This would lead inexorably to a requirement for major and costly concessions, cutting profits nearly eighty-three percent."

While no sound uttered from any member, eyeballs clicked in Nanogate's direction. Attentions that had wandered to thoughts of sexual conquests, hobbies, and other business immediately refocused themselves directly upon him.

"Remember, I'm talking best case here," Nanogate added for emphasis. Two members actually turned in their seat to face the most junior member of their august company. "Worst case, our projections show their support growing exponentially. If not checked, this would result in the breakup of this committee and the destruction of business as we know it."

No one said a word for nearly a minute.

"How is that possible?" Pudgy demanded, the first to break the shocked silence that permeated the room. He stood, a breach of unwritten etiquette, to emphasize his next question. "How do we know your simulations are accurate?"

"I'll be more than happy to have my experts talk to yours. Our databanks on this matter are open to all." The significance of that gesture, in an age where knowledge equates to wealth and power, wasn't lost on the other members. Not one of them would have the information checked.

"So is there a solution?" asked CNI, one of four female members.

"We need to eliminate the GAM as a significant force."

Even the chairman couldn't let this inconsistency pass unchallenged. "But didn't you say that attacking them would only make them stronger?"

"No. I said our current methods were less than ineffective."

"Then what more than trained troops and police could possibly suffice? We all spend a small fortune keeping forces trained, informants paid, and an army of field operatives trying to sniff them out, not to mention bounties offered for key members."

"If I might digress for a moment to basics taught to us by the late *zaibatsu* of Japan: eighty percent of any problem can be solved with twenty percent of the resources needed to solve the entire problem. I'm suggesting only solving that which is cost-effective. I only ask the required effort from each of you as you have the ability.

"This is the eighty percent solution I offer." A small stack of bound wood-pulp papers slid around the table, with each representative pulling off the top copy. Nanogate waited as they each scanned the four widely spaced pages. When each of them looked up, he continued.

"I call for a vote."

"Before the vote," remarked the chairman, quickly scanning the pages before him, "I'd like to point out that there'll be an initial increase in losses on the order of twenty-three percent over the first quarter."

"What's the schedule for reduction?"

"My team's simulations show that by the end of the second quarter, our losses will be down by forty-five percent and eighty-two percent by the end of the third quarter.

"As a whole, the GAM is probably a necessary evil. They provide an outlet to the populace that will, at the end of our campaign, be relatively harmless."

"Please place your vote." The computer tallied ten "Aye" votes.

"The next item on the agenda is planning the reduction of the food supply next year…"

* * *

Smoke wandered liberally but leisurely up from a tiny clay pot in the center of the almost barren room, filling the top of the chamber like a ghostly inverted bathtub, even to the dirty rings of previous gritty fills. In a perfect lotus position, a young Latina blended into the serenity room near the smudge, only the barely audible sounds of an ocean surf interrupting the silent tranquility. Even the most open-minded physician would be concerned about the slowness of her breathing and heart rate, if anyone so lofty would deign to enter her world.

The twenty-something *chica's* long, crude-oil-colored hair hung down over her right shoulder in direct contrast to the bare skin on the left side of her head. Buttoned only in one place, her white lab coat, bearing numerous random stains, fell loosely over her legs, partially hiding the glyphs tattooed directly into her caramel-colored skin.

From the outside of the room's only door came the tiniest of scratches. Her breathing increased and her body languidly unwound from itself as she stood, showing even more of the ebon symbols against her evenly tanned skin. Her knees locked, and with legs clamped together she bent in half at the waist, placing her palms flat on the floor. Without moving from this position, her long aristocratic fingers lifted a lid and placed it over the smoldering pot. A quick exhalation doused the tiny flame beneath.

Unrolling back to her full height, her gaunt form rose over 180 centimeters. Only the barest crest in the upper part of her smock gave any indication of sex. The black runes covered every visible centimeter of her skin below her neckline. She walked with a gliding grace toward a small mechanism in the far corner. A spring-wound conveyor lifted a trail of sand, pouring it over a series of wooden and metal plates. Turning off the motion, she silenced the ocean's simple cadence. Opening the door, she repatriated the sounds of Portland's bustling city into her sanctuary.

"Good morning, Plutonia," Sonya said in a soft soprano to the tiniest wisp of gray fur that wound around her ankles. A large orange and white tomcat joined Plutonia in praising their human companion. The mewing chorus of seventeen other felines, plus the shrill barks of one small Pomeranian, joined the admiration. Live pets, banned everywhere on Earth for the last fifty years, were her only roommates.

Sonya started a pot of boiling water over a simple gas grill, yet another of her illegal activities. As she waited, she spread five kilos of homemade pet food into a wooden trough on the floor. Plucking three broad leaves from a mint plant in a window box, she laid them into the top of a tall wooden drying box and took a similar number of dried leaves from a slit in the bottom. Between her palms she ground the brittle leaves to a near powder into a tiny metal bulb. The old-fashioned teapot worked hard to develop its shrill, piercing cry after starting from a low, lonely note.

As Sonya dipped the tea bulb into a petite porcelain cup, Plutonia jumped up to the beaten and scratched white polymer tabletop. The cat stepped over and around bags of nitrogen compounds and detonators, and a stack of incomplete pipe bombs to sit unconcerned amongst the potential destruction and clean her fur.

Sonya pushed aside a plastic bag of gunpowder, set down her teacup, and eased herself into a patio chair whose green color clashed with just about everything nearby. Sonya took a moment to stroke her tiny friend and croon encouragingly at her in a low, raspy voice. She knew a customer waited in her living room. She sensed him arrive during her meditations, but her morning tea took precedence. Her customers often suffered much longer waits than this man would endure, especially as his tabby only had a minor chest cold.

She sipped her hot tea with both hands firmly around her cup. It brought back fond recollections of her mother. Sonya could see her sitting in the kitchen brewing some potion or another—this one for wart remover, that one as an AIDS cure, the other one as a love potion. Her mother, an aging woman even in Sonya's earliest memories, lived in a one-bedroom slum apartment. The reek of cooked cabbage and raw salmon pervaded all of Sonya's recollections. They were the smells of home, however revolting to most. She could remember helping her mother simmer sauerkraut for use as a poultice against baldness. The day before the Metros murdered her, she said to her daughter, "Girl, you are equal parts empathy, knowledge, and magic. You'll be a formidable witch one day."

* * *

The dreary little man swayed back and forth from one foot to another in front of the big obsidian desk. He held his hands together so tightly that his skin broke into a pattern of blanched white and angry red.

"So we discovered the books didn't balance if we did them on independent machines. They did balance when we did it on the network," he said, trying hard not to back away.

Nanogate sneered. A small bit of his mind enjoyed his subordinate's discomfort. The staff psychologist designed his office for the purpose of intimidation. The slanted floor and huge desk made people feel small. The slate-gray walls chilled the entire room with an untouchable distance. Even the faux waterfall in the corner added an icy mist reaching far across the visitor's area.

"How much?"

"Fourteen point six million over the last two years." The little man couldn't help it this time, and backed up almost ten centimeters as he reported.

"These books include our combined conglomerate dealings?"

"Yes, sir." The accountant's shoulders slumped. Nanogate could read his vassal's eyes. His employee felt two pieces of bad news might finish him. "Without it you get an incomplete picture."

"Who could be responsible?"

"I'm sorry, sir, but for that breadth and the areas it doesn't touch it can only be Kensington, VP of accounting."

"Thank you for bringing this to my attention, uh…"

"Rupert Wingley. Accounting grade four."

Nanogate didn't feel like shooting the messenger today—but only today. "You are promoted to grade six, Rupert. I thank you for your diligence."

"Thank you. Thank you, sir!"

Nanogate nodded and waved his hand in dismissal. The accountant beat speed records out the massive granite doors in spite of his great fortune. Nanogate pushed a hidden button under the surface of his black stone desk.

The rush of the waterfall provided the only sound as a slight man glided in. He stood barely 140 centimeters tall, with Nordic features of blonde hair and blue, sleepy eyes. His muscles always drew attention. They didn't bulge on his body, but protruded unexpectedly, because places where fat should pad the flesh to fill the hollows, it didn't. He looked like an old-fashioned medical dummy with only bones, muscles and a coating of skin.

He wore a pair of body tights so formfitting they looked more like toe-socks poured from yellow vinyl up to the waist, with nothing covering his hairless chest. Everything about the man screamed *KILLER*, even without a visible weapon or body modification.

"Mr. Marks, I have a job for you," Nanogate said from behind the darkness of his desk.

"Of course, sir," his visitor offered in a quiet, calm voice.

* * *

From a distance, Tony's condominium looked indistinguishable from the seven thousand other upper-middle-class dwellings in his building. Against the condo's covenants, a small metal plaque, "Valhalla," forced his door to stand out amongst the multitudes that appeared otherwise identical, save the oversized silver numbers on each.

Tony entered and tossed the large box onto his dining room table. "I really feel great about saving that old crone," he remarked to himself, "but what if she sues me? What if I lose everything? I'd hate to have to move." He needed something to soothe his mind and murmered, "Music—mellow classic rock." Strains of "Hotel California" by the Eagles filled his tastefully decorated home. Tony flopped down on one of his imitation black vinyl sofas and kicked at what appeared to be a white bearskin rug.

"Percomm Carmine at work." The solido of a flowing brook filled the middle of the room, until a few moments later the face of a beautiful Pacific Islander replaced it. Her dark skin contrasted the white brilliance of her long hair and white lace bodice. "Nice lightning bolts," Tony playfully commented about the pattern of blue over each of her just barely hidden areolas.

"Hi, baby! What are you doing at home? Playing sick? I can't come and play nurse today." Her tone implied that her nursing would have very little to do with the medical profession.

"I wish. No, I had some trouble on the TriMet. I helped an old woman survive a coronary."

Her smiling face transformed into a frown that showed a harsher side of her beauty. "Why did you do that? She might sleaze you and I don't scope having a bluecoat bibling me to rodent your mental state. If they spent the dime and didn't just Nil you." Anger brought out the gutter in her speech. Carmine, despite her limited intelligence, had pulled herself up from the streets from a Nil—a person outside of the databases who could be killed by anyone just for fun—to a respectable member of society.

Tony smiled to put her off guard. "You mean you wouldn't lie for me, Mink? Nah, don't worry. You know I can always land on my feet."

"Don't you 'Mink' me! I'm only your mink when you behave! Her family might send a Private Enforcer. I'm not mixed up enough to think that's behaving. I don't want a corpse for a sweetie. Hell, they may even box you."

"Enough. I got the point. Shall we meet for lunch?"

"Nope. Betty's taking me to Powell's bookstore for a romp in the stacks."

He smiled. She often joked about her liaisons. She probably only planned a shopping trip of some kind, or a visit to the manicurist for new nail implants. "Don't wear her out too much. She's due to come back here tonight."

"Tease!" she said, sticking her tongue out at him, flashing the blue lightning bolt tattooed there as well. "Wilted Rose?"

"Tomorrow night, half-dozen. I have a late appointment tonight. Later, Mink."

"I'll 'Mink' you," she said in mock anger as she switched off the per-comm.

* * *

The rich, musty smell of autumn harvest filled the Rose Garden Arena as Sonya, wearing only her tattoos and a loose brown chemise that went down to mid-thigh, wandered around through the milling swarms of people. Despite how people packed themselves in between unlicensed hucksters and questionable food stalls, a zone of emptiness 2 meters across flowed with her. Random decisions and free action always seemed to keep that zone open with Sonya in the center. No one noticed the gap.

She breathed deeply to draw in the spicy draft of roasting chilies, bruised thyme, garbled lavender, and simmering mystery stew heavy with the stink of cabbage. She stopped at a stall with dried herbs in plastic containers and an Hispanic proprietress. The pots encircled her four layers deep. "*Te de diosa*," Sonya said.

While pivoting around, the woman grabbed leaves and pieces of bark out of seemingly random bins and stuffed them into a loose plastic bag. With her bare hands she gently stirred the dry concoction before sealing it with a plastic tie. Sonya handed her a credit slip in exchange, dropped her goddess tea fixings into her woven marketing bag, and moved on.

Two Metros, decked out in full assault gear—the only way a policeman would be seen at street level—strolled by with their own radius of emptiness around them. The members of the throng would take one look and decide to visit a stall in the opposite direction. The two toughs walked right by Sonya without a second glance, even as she passed through their own safety zone. The pair ambled up to a small food vendor, whose face went ashen.

"*Pagueme el seguro*," one of the cops ordered in a no-nonsense tone.

"I don't speak Spanish."

"You spoke it well enough last week, bitch. Insurance now or we'll remove this unlicensed stall from the premises."

Sonya stood behind and watched, nibbling on some dried tomatoes from an earlier purchase.

"I only have half," the proprietress complained, quickly handing them a handful of small plastic bills. "Business has been off."

The taller of the two tongued his mic. "Dispatch, I have a forty-three sixteen, illegal merchant without a permit. Our twenty is Rose Garden Arena, grid fourteen. We are removing it now."

The smaller of the two Metros tossed over a huge boiling pot, spilling the contents all over the ground. Several unfed urchins scampered around, licking the bounty off the cracked floors. They scooped up chunks and put them inside their filthy clothes to eat later.

"Please don't!" the vendor screamed. "This is all I have! I can't feed my children!"

"Stand aside or be destroyed with it." Both men took up lasing weapons and aimed at the fuel source, an old propane container.

The woman moved around to shield the tank, begging desperately. "Don't. I can't..."

The first one struck her with his right fist, bowling her over onto the wet ground. Both reached for their triggers, but something stopped them. They couldn't squeeze. Sonya closed her eyes and muttered ungrammatical Latin to herself before the two officers put away their weapons and moved on.

No one saw anything. No one heard anything. Later that evening the two officers would probably have a splitting headache and wonder why dispatch thought they'd removed an illegal vendor.

The Metros' own statistics showed crime at the street level—minus their own thuggery, of course—at two murders, sixteen rapes, eight robberies, sixty-four assaults, and eighty-four muggings per city block per day. Those stats vastly understated the true numbers by at least a factor of two, if not three or four, because Nil victims don't get counted.

Being the white knight could suck you dry doing it each and every day. For every one you saved, you lost seventy or more others. Sonya knew that being the hero didn't change the world. It never had and it never would, but in this case it made her feel better.

Sonya didn't wait around. No one noticed her involvement. No one noticed her leave.

* * *

Despite his Metro-assisted excuse to skip work today, Tony couldn't avoid one related responsibility, much as he might want to. After a quick check of the guest list, the Kendry's doorman, a substantial Hispanic with no obvious body modification, invited Tony in.

"May I take your coat, Mr. Sammis?"

"Yes, thank you." Tony slipped off his full-length, faux mohair coat and offered it without a thought. He brushed his cobalt blue suit to smooth the wrinkles and checked his ruffled blouse.

"If you'd step through to the parlor, the other guests are gathering there."

"Thank you." Tony wandered toward the general murmur of conversations and muted music.

Knots of people meandered around the large, open room, breaking and reforming in the classic manner of all cocktail parties throughout history, swaying to the classical strains of Enya. The women each led a trail of fabric from their dress like the tail of some prehistoric beast, while the men, like Tony himself, straitjacketed themselves in an ancient suit called a tuxedo, all determined by the current fashionistas for this season. One of the most famous, Simone, had decreed that dresses in the front barely cover half the thighs and carried high-necked bodices, ruched up tightly against the throat. The color and details on each person seemed to indicate individuality, but Tony saw only a sea of conformity.

A serving girl came up, breaking Tony's ruminations. She wore a bar prosthesis like a tiny miniskirt flared wide around her waist, plus a skimpy black lace top—neither of which covered much. "Drink, sahr?" she asked in a thickly accented voice.

"Rye on bare cubes, please." Tony dropped a pair of credit chips into the tip bowl dangling beneath her ample charms.

"Thank you, sahr."

"Tony!" called out Lindsay, an attractive cougar from the accounting office, as she bolted over toward him. Her iridescent silver evening dress accentuated the mischievous glint in her eye and the glitter spray in her dark black hair. Without giving him the opportunity to answer, she pulled him toward a small group of people by one hand as he grabbed for his drink with the other. "You just have to meet Raymond, the new level four manager in Cosmetics Development!" she insisted. "Also, he's dishy as hell. Better take me before he gets me," she whispered directly into Tony's ear.

Tony managed not to vomit.

Heedless of the quiet conversation being interrupted, Lindsay busted in to a small group. "Raymond, this is Tony Sammis."

"Mr. Sammis," came an immediate reply.

"Oh, just Tony, please. This is a party, after all," Tony said, sipping at his drink while trying hard not to duck the smoke from Raymond's narcostick.

"Tony it is, then. So Lindsay says you're interested in cosmetics and perhaps moving up with it."

Lindsay smiled obsequiously as she not-so-secretly fondled Tony's ass.

"Who isn't looking to move? Up, that is."

Tony worked hard to ignore the groping as he and Raymond, a rather pleasant man in his forties, chatted meaninglessly. They found a common ground with their mutual enjoyment of the Aussie Spiders, but stood opposed on politics. After ten minutes, Tony felt he might've made an important contact for his career advancement, but at the cost of developing permanent bruising on his gluteus maximus—and probably his gluteus sinister as well. In payment, he whispered indecencies in Lindsay's ear for the next hour, promising a repeat of their dirty weekend of Easter last.

Once free of his shepherdess's clutches, Tony breathed a heavy sigh of relief. He knew that politeness insisted he remain for at least another hour, soaking up even more of the artificial atmosphere created by the players in this production—identical in all but dress and locale to hundreds of others he'd attended throughout his career.

He wandered around the room, listening to snatches of conversations and occasionally nodding his head to another colleague as he let the ice cubes dilute his drink. He avoided further entangling conversations with others by pointing across the room as though expected by another knot of people. Instead, he made his way to the ersatz balcony. Projections from the rooftop, the right mixture of air circulation, and carefully concocted scenting made him feel as though he actually looked out over the massive borough of Portland. Tony breathed in deeply, as if the air didn't hang heavy with narcostick smoke.

"Nice, isn't it," said an unidentified male sitting in a chair across the patio.

"Should be, for what Chris and Michael paid for it," Tony answered, turning to regard the speaker with an air of indifference.

The other man smiled affably. The black suit he wore contrasted with a massive codpiece, but the high-necked gauze blouse with a ruffle of black lace around the top gave a hint. His lipstick rivaled the color of Tony's suit and the earrings glittered brightly. Tiny solido vignettes within the jewelry proclaimed his proclivities.

"Yes. I actually thought of getting one myself until Chris told me what he paid."

"I couldn't…" Tony felt a slight tremor in the floor interrupting his train of thought. Moments later a flash turned his attentions to the "outside." A rising fireball, the size of a grapefruit at this distance, illuminated a gaping hole in the top of a building several kilometers distant. "What was that?"

"Oh, my," the ambi said, holding his manicured hands up to his mouth. A bass roar cut through the din, stopping all conversations. Many of the guests came over to the balcony to peer out. Chris called for CNI. Tony preferred to look at the real thing, forgetting for a moment that even this view was nothing more than a visual illusion, nonetheless listening carefully to Central News and Information.

"We have received reports that an incendiary device detonated on the loading dock of Gimbals just moments ago. We are shifting live to Barbara Moorcock. Barbara?"

"Ben, the destruction is horrific. Body parts litter the scene. I can't even begin to estimate the death toll here. As you can see, here's what looks like part of a hand, and I think that over there is an eye.

"There's a physical crater in the roof at least two hundred yards across. Flames continue to race out from it. The heat is too intense for me to get close enough to estimate the depth. The scale is just incomprehensible.

"Emergency crews are racing about now trying to put out the flames. I'm receiving reports now that the pumps aren't functioning and the emergency reservoirs are completely empty, despite having been inspected just yesterday."

"One second, Barbara, we're receiving additional information. We have another manifesto from the group called the Green Action Militia." A certain twisted part within Tony jumped in fascination. "The Greenies claim…"

* * *

"Good evening, Mr. Kensington."

"What! How did you get in?" The blond Kensington sat straight up in bed between two well-endowed young women. From the thick smell in the air and their shared dreamy expression, all three suffered from the self-infliction of some type of narcostick and one too many sexual adventures.

"Actually," came the nonchalant reply, "I slipped in through the plumbing crawlspace."

Kensington's eyes focused somewhere behind the short, slight intruder. "How dare you invade my home!" Mr. Kensington demanded.

The tiny whipcord of a man lifted one of the butts of a narcostick and sniffed it closely, with some disdain.

"Wait a minute, this isn't even my home," Kensington mumbled almost inaudibly. One of the girls rolled over with a moan, cuddled up next to her benefactor, and fell back to sleep. He looked around with wide eyes sporting the quick, jerky motion common to his vice. He didn't notice the intruder's bodyguard-yellow pants.

"Do you know who I am?" Kensington all but shouted.

"Very certainly, good sir."

"Then you know you are dead!"

"We all bear that curse, Mr. Kensington. Unfortunately for both of us, you are going to lose to that curse first."

"Huh?"

"I'm here to kill you, Mr. Kensington," the man said without bravado or rancor.

With remarkable clarity and speed, especially for someone so intoxicated, Kensington pulled up a small machine pistol from beneath his pillow. "Really? Now tell me just why you're here and who sent you."

"You mistook your company's money for your money."

"How did you find me?"

"Satellite tracking of your tie-tack. I enabled it twelve hours ago."

"Who sent you?"

"Your CEO asked me to deliver this message…" In a blur, the tiny man rotated out of the line of any possible fire and smacked the back of his hand across the bridge of his victim's nose. Bone and cartilage exploded forcefully up into the former VP's brain before it could even send a signal to pull the trigger. "You're fired."

Mr. Marks nodded as the life left his victim's eyes. With great care and deliberation, he put a mask over each woman's face and released enough narco gas for the pair to overdose in the space of twenty seconds. Carefully, he posed one kneeling over Kensington's body. Using the young woman's fingers on the trigger of Kensington's own machine-pistol, he fired two bursts into the nasal cavity he had just destroyed. The dead woman slumped forward, one of her augmented breasts spilling obscenely to one side, streaked in blood.

As he examined his handiwork, Marks tapped his right foot three times. Trillions of submicroscopic nanites swarmed out of his yellow shoes, programmed with the sole purpose to find and destroy his own DNA anywhere they might find it. Thirty minutes from now they'd quite obligatorily render themselves into inert components indistinguishable from the multitudes of other organic compounds that make up ordinary dust. The assassin faded out the front door, confident that he—or more importantly, his employer—couldn't be implicated in the justice he'd just imposed.

* * *

Home, Tony thought, pouring himself a stiff drink of rye over ice. So many different emotions lashed at him, but one stepped up to dominate his thoughts. How could he be happy about the deaths of so many?

He sipped gently. Could it be that he just wanted anything different? Maybe he felt he witnessed a little piece of history. Maybe he despised the political games he played to get ahead and wanted someone to get rid of it all? Perhaps more specifically, he wanted to get out from under the attentions of his over-amorous mentor? No matter what caused it, he couldn't deny he felt good.

His mind pondered for several more minutes before it just went blank. He downed the rest of his drink and put the glass down, catching sight of the half-cubic meter of gray plastic box sitting innocently in the center of the table.

"And what's in that box?" he asked himself. "I probably shouldn't, but what the heck. What's a little more trouble?"

Carefully lifting the lid, he peered inside. What stared up at him wiped away any questions of sexual advances or terrorism.

A tiny calico kitten, barely bigger than a shot glass, sat patiently in one corner, looking up at him with head slightly cocked. The creature let out the tiniest of mews and stood on its hind legs, batting at the air as an obvious plea for playtime. Without thinking, Tony scooped up the tiny ball of white and brown fluff in his hands and rubbed it under the chin while it batted at the gold and silver star hanging from the necklace in amongst the ruffles of his dress shirt.

"How adorable you are, little miss," said Tony idly, "but kittens and cats are against the law. Maybe I should turn you in."

Despite his outward calm, he'd never been so terrified in his life. Before this little bundle of fur, the worst he could reasonably expect to

suffer from his little life-saving adventure would be temporary inden-
tured servitude. Possession of a live pet carried a capital sentence.

Despite the heart beating in his throat, Tony made purring noises
and wiggled the necklace charm around for his houseguest. His grandfather had won the Silver Star in defense of a Chinese village in the
Aussie Civil War. "You like your toy?" Watching the charm gave Tony
courage.

After a predictably short time, the brown and white feline tired of
her new plaything. Looking up into Tony's eyes with uncompromising
trust, the tiny kitten mewed. He brought the furry creature up for a
closer look, and the kitten seized the opportunity to brush up against
his face. Tony sputtered and tried to wipe the residual downy hairs from
his mouth and nose with his free arm. Undisturbed, she buzzed with
pleasure, jumped from his hand to the tabletop, the chair, and finally to
the ground.

"What am I going to do with you? The law's quite clear. All proteins
must be collected for food distributions. You, my cinnamon-colored
friend, are protein."

With the vast majority of the Earth barely avoiding starvation, food
often seemed sacred. The laws were selectively enforced, but the punishment for tampering with the Emergency Subsistence Act of '26 was
execution by starvation.

"I don't want either of us to die," he said, absently watching the kitten poke its head under one of his dirty shirts on the floor, "but if I get
caught with you, there isn't a thing in this world that's going to save
me."

The object of Tony's dilemma stalked an errant dust-bunny with a
wiggle of its bottom and tail high in the air. "I just can't imagine pushing
you into the calorie reclamation bin. You'd be ground into paste and
flushed into the city's food return. It'd be the lawful thing, but not the
right thing.

"With that said, I guess I better take the appropriate precautions."
Tony securely locked and bolted his front door and switched on the
active security measures. The kitten bounced across the floor and sat in
the middle of the room, looking up at its new owner. "I haven't a clue
how to take care of you, but we'll learn together.

"What are we going to name you, hmm?"

Establish Plan

Coffee (no longer grown anywhere on Earth), fresh cranberry muffins, and living servants—genetically engineered deaf/mutes, of course—attended the corporate heads to the faint strains of Mozart lilting across the room in time to a medley of mint scents.

"As you know, we needed a human weapon," said Nanogate, the plan's progenitor. "Someone who isn't in the critical path of any of our programs. I want to thank all of you for access to your personnel files. In this case, we didn't need them. I think we have the one we want. This one is exceptionally qualified for the task."

The room dimmed and a solid projection of a large, swarthy man floated above the table. Thick black hair spilled over his back like tar pouring from his head. Curly pubic and chest hair were his dignity's only protection as the solidograph rotated. "Born in Corvallis, Oregon, in 'twenty-eight, he's a second-generation Turkish refugee of the Chinese Amalgamation. No genetic manipulation of the birth, save the standard subdermal cybernetic implant. Left hand replaced with a Dec model five-dot-three cosmetic when the original was crushed in a lift-car accident at the age of five. In his teen years, he worked for Downput Demolition Company and learned how to handle and manipulate shaped explosives.

"He obtained a master's degree in Molecular Mechanical Engineering. He has an aptitude of eighty-fourth, physical of ninety-first and an individuality quotient of ninety-sixth percentiles. He possesses first-aid skills and leadership ability, both officially unrated but present—our sims say above eightieth percentile in both."

23

"He's currently employed by Nanogate Dental Products Division and thus at our complete disposal per our standard binding employee contract," offered another of the executives.

"In short," the plan's owner continued, "this is the perfect rebel and skill set for our GAM targets. Per the plan, I suggest we make certain he isn't wasted within our corporation but rather finds a new home with our target."

"Any known medical issues?"

"None. Standard childhood diseases: mumps, measles, and Martian sand lice. No known immunities and his only allergy is to eight of the old antibiotics, level four—annoyance only."

"Family?"

"A one-year term marriage at eighteen that both walked away from without looking back. Parents have been dead for over a year as the result of an industrial accident in the water purifying plant where they worked. His current girlfriend's profile reads, in short, pliant to our needs.

"Gentlebeings, I've covered his life in great detail. He's an underachiever who thinks he's better than he seems willing to produce. He tends toward loquacity—"

"Excuse me. Loquacity?" asked Taste Dynamics, a gaunt woman devoid of outward sexual characteristics.

"Talkativeness, inability to keep his mouth shut."

"Thank you."

"To continue, he had a three-point-two GPA through high school and college and not a single one of his teachers seems to be able to remember him. He never joined a fraternity."

"Simulations?"

"The models we've built show a seventy-eight percent chance that our subject will be taken into GAM and a twenty percent chance that they'll destroy him outr—"

"Wouldn't his destruction impact our overall goal?" interrupted Pudgy.

"Even if they kill him, there's a sixty-three percent chance our plan will succeed anyway."

"Sixty-three? Planning on sixty-three percent seems on the weak side to carry any action forward," commented Percomm Systems.

"We aren't planning on sixty-three percent, but rather seventy-eight percent plus sixty-three percent of twenty percent or a total of ninety point six percent chance, or less than a ten percent of failure," he said directly to Pudgy. Nanogate's eyes then cast about the rest of the membership. "Let me add that the worst thing that can happen with a failure is that we've lost one insignificant employee. We can then choose to either pick a new pawn or we can look at a new plan."

No more discussion presented itself. Several attendees physically as well as mentally closed their folders on this topic. Not one of these individuals clawed their way to the pinnacle of power without using people. Only one had yet to directly order a person killed. None even hesitated at the use of one more. The choice passed without debate.

* * *

Sonya opened the door to the outer foyer. A tiny, weasel-like man, impeccably dressed in a tailored three-piece Kao Brothers suit, held a caramel-colored Chihuahua in his lap. The tiny dog, no larger than a dessert plate, shivered constantly. The situation wasn't right, but Sonya motioned them into her examining room anyway. The seemingly sterile room looked like something out of an old medical flattie, with an examination table, removable paper covers, a small and uncomfortable chair, a swivel stool, and all manner of antiquated, shiny, and manual-oriented medical equipment.

"You do know that owning an animal in the state of Oregon is a felony? And a capital offense at that?" Sonya asked these questions of all her new customers as a matter of policy.

He hugged the dog tighter to himself as it squirmed in place. "Yes, but I've bought the police in my precinct."

She nodded. Anyone who could own a Kao Brothers suit obviously held some clout. This one obviously swung his with abandon. "A different solution than most of my clientele, but completely acceptable. Payment is due now. I take actual credit slips, plastic money, proteins, plants, medicines, charcoal, or chocolate." Her customer looked up sharply at that last. She smiled brightly. "I have a weakness for chocolate, but finding a supply is difficult." Cocoa was another plant which no longer grew on Earth.

"I can pay with any of those you wish in the future, but would prefer electronic credit."

"No. I have no electronics in my home. No motors, no computers, no vidlinks, no technology I can do without."

"Greenie?"

"I'm a member of the Greenpeace organization, but I don't participate in any of their foolish extreme actions."

"I'm sorry. I didn't mean—"

"Don't be sorry. I'm not. I just wish the world were a slightly different place. I was born in the wrong age. Two hundred years ago, there were no prohibitions to keeping animals and there were only a handful of creatures on the endangered species list." Sonya paused, looking thoughtfully into space. Her customer remained politely silent. "Anyway, enough of that. So I won't take electronic credit. Hell, I don't even have an account."

"Everyone has an electronic account. You have one programmed from birth."

"You're assuming my birth was recorded."

Enlightenment showed in his eyes. Sonya had all but informed him that she belonged to that expendable minority known as Nils. They had no existence. They were in no way protected.

"As you were unprepared, I'll examine your pet for free."

"Thank you." He stiffly handed the dog to her, both arms outstretched and both shaking nearly as badly as the tiny dog.

Her hands didn't hesitate. From under the examination table, she pulled up an antique, silenced Berretta, pointing it at the man's head and pulling the trigger. For all its age, the gun delivered a quiet pop that efficiently deposited his brains in a red mess across the back wall. She caught the dog as the corpse's arms stopped receiving commands and flopped down with the rest of the body into a heap on the floor.

The tiny dog yipped at her, more in surprise than any outrage at the man's death. Sonya knew he wasn't the dog's master. The man didn't know how to handle an animal and this one certainly didn't belong to him. She tut-tutted to herself for the growing red puddle and the mess she'd need to clean up sometime later.

Shifting the dog to the crook of her left arm, she opened her victim's jacket with her right and searched for some identification. The expired Private Enforcement license for one Auzel Small confirmed her suspicions. Someone wanted her out of the way. Knowing PEs, only the person who hired him would care about his disappearance. Her only concern involved the patron's intent for finding her—either her clandestine work as a vet, or even more clandestine membership in the Green Action Militia.

Sonya shrugged. It didn't matter either way, except for any follow-on attempts. In the meantime she'd inherited another dog and, she thought as she looked down at the body, more food for her animals.

* * *

Their Rose Quarter expeditions had started as a lark between himself and Carmine. They hobnobbed with the lower class, getting a vicarious thrill at being so close to the edge. Over the last year Tony's outings had become more and more frequent, with or without his companion. Tony fidgeted with a tiny scrap of infamous blue TriMet seat fabric that had come loose. He all but leapt from his seat as the lift-bus landed.

The thickening of a rising fog, typical of the lower deck ghetto of Portland's Rose Quarter, added a dingy feel to the air. In spite of this, Tony's steps grew livelier as he walked out the TriMet doors. The slight wrinkle above his thick black eyebrows smoothed out as he relaxed.

Throngs of the poor, wretched, and homeless scurried by outside heavily armored doors and the many open, gaping holes in the abandoned lowest levels of the city. Garishly signed tube hotels, with their two-point-five meter long plastic coffin-shaped sleeping quarters for those lucky few who could afford even their modest prices, provided an eerie, if erratic, illumination.

A token girl, her State of Oregon prostitution tattoo prominently displayed over one shoulder, wriggled her barely clad and unnaturally firm breasts against Tony's arm as he wound his way past her beat. Next to her, a man without a left leg hobbled on the other and a crutch bearing a filthy plastic sign claiming "Veteran. Praise God. Please help." Tony didn't even register either of them as individuals, but rather part of the background one endured to attend the hottest clubs.

The transition from barrio to city hot-spot came without a marked delineation, yet the line definitely existed. No mugger passed a certain crack in the sidewalk, no bum caged a drink outside any club, no welf paraded her children past that unseen barrier. Here an armored Metro cruiser glided slowly past, punctuating the amount of money circulating in this tiny section of street level. One block in either direction, and the anarchy of the-fittest-will-survive reigned.

A glaring solido of a red rose slowly dying marked Tony's favorite watering-hole only a few doors down. The doorman cum bouncer, with two massive, silver-colored prosthetic arms, nodded deferentially to Tony as he entered.

"Hi, Jock. You get your arms readjusted?"

"Nope, still got that flutter in one. I almost broke a jug's skull with it yesterday."

"I know a good mechanic."

"So do I, Mr. Tony," the big man said with a grin. "Carmine's waiting for you."

"Thanks."

Typical of any night, the biomass of people in the Wilted Rose threatened to burst the building like an overripe plum. While not an olfactory bar, the bittersweet smell of lilies, probably two or three OU_E higher than comfort level, tweaked his nose. Ignoring it as irrelevant, Tony wedged, bumped, and shoved his way to the bar amidst the vocal stylings of the Communist Bananas, twenty decibels above the level that would cause harm to most deaf rocks.

"Bloody Mary," he shouted at the bartender. He cast about to find his girl. For once his height came in handy, for he could look above most people. He spotted her behind a pair of nude girls interlocked in a trib so sexual as to edge on even the loose moral codes enforced by the Rose's establishment. Carmine decorated a booth on the other side of the writhing pair with her long, silver hair contrasting with her loose, neon-green dress. She frantically waved and yelled to get his attention. "Make that two. And two scotch and sodas," he screamed, correcting his order.

Tony desired a partner to take his lead without much question—a difficult find in a world of "Do first before done to." He always knew Carmine's charms amounted to something more ornamental and empathic than intelligent.

Holding four drinks high above his head, Tony wound his way to the booth, ignoring three blatant passes, one from an ambi. He managed to only stain his floral print shirt with a moderate splash from one glass or the other on his way through the crush. He parted the booth shield—a layer of charged air particles held in a matrix of electric white noise—with his elbow and moved in. He silently praised Carmine for keeping the sound shield up. It lowered the racket and press of the room to a minimum whisper. Carmine greeted him with a bright smile of blood-red teeth and complementing lipstick.

"Weeble, but that band is loud tonight," he said a bit too loudly, depositing the drinks on the table.

"Yeah, I heard the Rose staff paid the Metros a bit extra so they wouldn't show," said the lithe woman in a voice barely louder than bedroom-talk.

"Now, that's a job. I should've been a cop. People pay you when they want you to do something and they pay you when they don't. I hear the protection money in The Hills alone quadruples your pay."

"Quit yipping. You had your chance like all the rest of us to take the Civil Service test in high school. I remember your friend, Bill, quoting you as saying, 'I'm not going to sit around for twelve years at some diddly-paying job until I can earn the real credit. I want it now!' Sound familiar?"

"It does. But I said it when we graduated Oregon State, not high school. But the offer from Nanogate just seemed too good to pass up. Now I'm not so sure."

Carmine got one of her I'm-right-now-shut-up looks on her face. "Velcro your mouth and enjoy the music. At least pretend you'll miss me from your bed tonight."

"What? Where will you be?" he said, trying but not really succeeding to keep the three-year-old whine from his voice.

"Sorry, business trip to Tycho City. I told you about it a week ago."

Despite the incredible beat of the music, Tony decided that his evening just tumbled into the gutters with the rest of the burns and filth.

"Yeah, and what happened to that frumpy old baggage you helped in the TriMet?" Carmine questioned, deftly changing the subject.

"I don't have a clue. No one called, so I might be in the clear."

"Good. That scare should teach you not to try to be Mister White Knight. It doesn't line the credit account."

"Probably right, but you wanna hear something even more strange?" Tony leaned forward over the table. He looked surreptitiously around. The volume of his voice dropped at least in half before he said, "She was carrying a box with a cat in it."

"Eww!" Her face wrinkled up in disgust. "Can't stand the things. Saw one at a zoo once. Filthy creatures. Fur everywhere in its cage. Should grind them all up for sausage. You ran it into the recycle, right?"

Carmine's unexpected reaction stopped Tony. He fully intended to tell her the entire story and now she frightened him. "Uh...right." Perhaps Carmine's unanticipated trip profited him more than the loss of his bed companion suggested. Certainly tonight, of all nights, he'd have his hands full with Cinnamon, the name he'd chosen for his new charge.

For the next two hours he drank sparingly, unusual in and of itself, and listened to the band's reverberations. Tony took the time to examine Carmine in a new light. Since fifteen she'd painted his life in some way. She sympathized with him while he lived out the letter of the contract to that bloodsucker, Pricilla. She stuck with him through the six years of his bachelor's degree, another three for his master's, his apprenticeship at Nanogate, and three years of seventy-hour weeks trying to make manager.

They shared fluids and beds anytime they could manage, but he didn't love her, and she repeated, as often as he'd listen, that she didn't love him, either. Tony never considered offering even a temporary marriage contract. They kept each other comfortable in bachelorhood as friends with many privileges.

Carmine's prejudice now colored his views of her. Her normal warmth suddenly carried the heat of an icicle and her jocularity sliced like a knife edge. Tony couldn't understand how she could even begin to harm anything as cute and loving as Cinnamon. A parsec of space suddenly warped in between them.

Anyone who paid attention from the outside could easily spot this one-sided gulf. Tony moved with the music without hearing it. He hardly said two words in as many hours. Carmine spent her time too engrossed in the band and watching the antics of the patrons to notice Tony's lack of banter.

About eleven, Carmine turned abruptly and planted a bright red kiss on his cheek. The self-heating lipstick stained and warmed his flesh. "Gotta run, honey-bunny. Just enough time to get to Black Field." Carmine parted the curtain and jumped down from the booth.

For the first time, Tony realized her beautiful body hid something callous. While she might not know it yet, this time she'd walked right out of his life. He grimaced as he wiped the still-warm lipstick from his face.

The Bananas finished their set. Tony looked around. While several acquaintances danced to canned music, for the first time none of them, male or female, could erase the cold emptiness he felt inside. He climbed down from his booth, to the pleasant surprise of a latecomer that just happened by the choice club real estate.

"Going home so soon, sir?" Jock asked as Tony exited into the relative quiet of the street.

"Yeah. Carmine had to run off to Tycho."

"Yes, sir. I saw her leave."

"Yeah, I'm just not feeling in the party mood tonight."

"Well, you be extra careful tonight, Mr. Tony. There's a level three riot just beyond the TriMet stop."

"Thanks, Jock." Absently, Tony wondered if Jock gave Carmine the same information. He gave his head a little shake of irrelevance.

"You might also want to avoid the TriMet Hub tomorrow morning."

"Oh? What's up?"

"Dunno, sir. But I wouldn't want you to get hurt. Duck, sir." Tony ducked just as a large metal projectile bent on mischief sailed over his head. Jock deflected it with his arms, not giving it another thought. Tony looked back to see three young kids running away into the darkness followed closely by two Metro officers. Just punks trying to get their kicks and maybe make a name for themselves.

"TriMet, eh? Where do you keep getting this information, Jock?"

"Oh, I hear things," he said with a shrug that accentuated the biomechanical interface.

"Well, I won't press. You have a good night, Jock."

"You, also, Mr. Tony."

Tony avoided the small riot, probably over food rations, only twenty minutes later to encounter a mugger at his condominium door.

"Give me everything!" shouted a man sporting an unkempt beard and wearing clothes that should've been condemned. He carelessly waved around an old Sony Blackburn laser pistol. Tony barely broke stride as he pointed his left hand toward the man. A trio of tiny dart-like projectiles burst out of the end of his index finger at just below the speed of sound. The would-be assailant collapsed into a pool of filthy rags, bleeding out of a 16 centimeter hole in his chest. Tony nudged the pistol away from the reflexively jerking hand, shaking his head sadly. Another welf decided he couldn't make it on the welfare rolls and tried to augment his pathetic income by murder, home invasion, and robbery.

"Just because you can't see a weapon, doesn't mean your victims don't carry one," Tony muttered in a derisive tone.

Without a second look at the horrific mess or the fecal stench that now arose, he opened his door to hear Cinnamon's tiny scratches from the bathroom, where he'd kept her during the day.

"I'm coming, Cin." As he locked and bolted the entry, he had a stab of fear.

What if someone had heard her? They could've called the Metros or maybe even Interpol! His trepidation lasted all of about three seconds. He checked the entry log and his personal security measures, finding no evidence that his privacy had been invaded. Nope, nobody was here. We're safe.

"What a day!" he said. "I'm so—" he yawned wide, "—tired." He kicked off his shoes, stripped his socks.

Tony released Cinnamon, playfully nicknamed Cin, from temporary prison. The tiny cat stropped his ankles, followed quickly by licking his bare toes. "Stop that, Cin. It tickles."

Cinnamon looked up at him as if she understood. She lifted her tail and bounded off to some mischief.

"That's right. I'll make supper. Maybe you need some food." Tony walked into the tiny kitchen and put a meatloaf, peas, and potato dinner from the freezer into the flash oven.

"Percomm Condo Association, Body Removal." The solido of a heavily muscled woman came into view over the counter in his kitchen as he pulled out a replacement for the shredded finger-cap in a miscellaneous drawer amongst spare Velcro straps for his shoes.

"Body Removal. Oh, hi there, Mr. Sammis."

"Hi, Adriana. I vaped another welf on one-fifteen."

"Fourth this year. You might get the association Top Gun award if you keep this up."

"I'd be happy if they just left me—" another yawn took him, midsentence, "—alone."

"Well, you get some rest and I'll send someone up to clean up. No Miss Carmine tonight?"

"No, Adriana. She went to Tycho City."

"I could find you some companionship, if you're interested."

"Thank you, but I'm just…so tired." Another yawn tore his sentence apart. "I'm going to tube out in bed. Been a long day."

"Understand, sir."

"Off." The meatloaf slid out of the flash, steaming. "Mmm, but that smells wonderful." His mouth watered even as he took it into the living room and plopped onto the sofa. Cin showed up, sitting by his side and looking pitiful. "You hungry, too? I wonder what you'll eat. Here, have a bite of potato." The cat licked at the tiny steaming morsel on the end of his fork, but didn't eat it. "Picky thing you are," Tony said, eating it himself.

"How about a bit of meat." Tony tore off a tiny chunk and set it in front of Cin. She licked it three or four times before picking it up in her mouth and eating it very daintily. "Maybe a pea?" He placed a single pea on the couch. Cin sniffed at it for a second before gobbling it down with all the subtlety of a Nil on a real steak.

"Peas and meat, eh?" Tony quickly found that while she'd eat the meat, she definitely preferred the peas.

Another huge yawn hit him in the middle of his meal. "I need some sleep, kitten." The drooping of his eyes and the fatigue pulling at them cut short his meal and the camaraderie shared with his guest. "I'm heading for bed. I guess the day had one too many shocks."

He put a tiny bowl of leftovers down on the floor for Cin and tottered off to fall into bed fully clothed. Cin found a way to the top of his bed and curled up under his chin. Without waking he wrapped his arm around her.

Implement — Phase One

Five teams worked in concert. The subject's heart rate, respiration, and alpha waves all dropped significantly. His eye movement increased. The Intelligence Team's state of the art medical monitors observed every major bodily function. All of them reported the same thing: "The subject is asleep."

To ensure no neighbors accidentally responded to any movements or inadvertent noises, the Cover-Up Team released a colorless, odorless gas into the condominium complex's ventilation system. Within fifteen minutes, everyone within two floors of the subject's one-hundred-fifteenth level home slept. Other members disengaged elevator access to those same floors. The Intelligence Team duly noted the subject's change from normal slumber to a drugged stupor.

The Continuity Team moved in next, ensuring no perceptible trace remained of the teams' outing. They needed seventeen seconds to open the subject's door without detection, deactivating all the electronic and physical security devices. A solido recorder, with its three huge eyes, floated into the door, registering the location and smell of everything, establishing a baseline in order to later return the flat to its original state. The recorder's sweep took seven long minutes.

After exactly seven minutes and one second, the eight-person Medic Team and four-person Vet Team, each clad in self-contained, yellow biohazard suits, passed through the condominium door with an equal weight of equipment and personnel.

As the team erected a field laboratory, the envy of any mad scientist, the resident feline received a dose of an additional sedative. The human had already imbibed his in the alcohol. Each of the teams closed on their respective charge and began a series of complex manipulations. The blood of each unwitting subject filtered through separate large garbage can–sized devices, injections were given in unusual places, and countless handheld scanning devices irradiated their skin. The teams completed all of these tasks over five hours, fourteen minutes, and sixteen seconds—well within mission clock parameters, and all without speaking a single word.

The two medical teams carefully packed their implements, forgetting not the least cotton swab, and departed out the front door, their evil done and irreparable.

The twenty-person Continuity Team, equally clothed in biohazard suits, moved in with replacement sheets, of the same manufacturer, prewashed with a placed pale orange stain, nearly identical to one present on the original cloth before any of the interlopers entered the home. One pillow had to be replaced due to a tiny blood stain. One team member returned a lamp, inadvertently moved by six millimeters, to its correct position. Another technician carefully replaced the sleeping cat within the human's arms in exactly their previous locations. Two others repositioned clothing slightly nudged amongst the random sprawl upon the floor in this obvious bachelor's home. A tallish member combed the human's hair and rearranged his leg by several centimeters. A glass sphere floated through the eerily silent room, occasionally expelling a fine mist to change the air's smell by some tiny fraction of an OU_E.

Team members faded from the scene as each completed his task. Finally, after the last left, a tiny, blond man wearing only yellow vinyl tights made one final pass through the home. Absently, he sprinkled a tiny canister over a clean surface to add just the right amount of dust. He left quickly, quietly and professionally, locking and reinitializing the subject's electronic alarms and protection devices.

Six hours, seven minutes, and thirteen seconds after its intrusion, the team might well have never been there, except for the damage they'd caused.

* * *

Tony awoke feeling stiff, but better than he had in years. None of the vodka's effects still lingered in his system. Mentally, he attributed this to the fact that he'd drunk much less than normal last night.

Oddly, he noted that he hadn't moved more than a few centimeters, despite sleeping all night long, and Cin hadn't moved far from his side either.

"Good morning," he said with the sunshine he felt coming out in his voice. The troubles of the previous day seemed to sublimate like dry ice. "Shall we get something to eat?" he asked, stripping down and slipping into a dressing robe. A huge yawn, for such a tiny cat, and an insignificant meow were the only responses he got.

A cheese omelet with bacon substitute put both Tony and Cin in even better moods. Cin cuddled within Tony's arms. She visually stalked a dust mote drifting at the whimsy of the air currents as if it were some edible prey. Tony leaned back and rubbed at the base of Cin's right ear, right where a patch of black fur began and seemed to pour down her right foreleg and chest.

"Hey, are you a boy cat or a girl cat?" he inquired curiously. The kitten, no longer interested in the dust-bunnies, tried to climb Tony's robe to some unknown destination, its claws making tiny punctures in the robe's delicate fabric. "Come here, you." Tony leaned the kitten onto its back. "A girl," he said, releasing her quickly because of her struggles.

"Goodness, I'm running late, Cin," he said, catching a view of the clock. "Race you to the bathroom." The cat didn't race, but Tony hustled toward the shower anyway. On the way, he managed to step on a small pile of kitten feces within some of his clothes littering the floor. He scowled a bit.

"A kitten's gotta go when a kitten's gotta go. Right, girl?" Cin looked at him and cocked her head and then dashed into the closet as she found something else interesting. "I don't know what we're going to do about that, but we'll manage." He jumped into the steaming hot shower trying to come up with a solution. As he dressed and shaved, he couldn't think of anything except sand. He'd get some colored sand and make some excuse about using it as a decorating accent.

"Bye, Cin. Sorry about keeping you in the bathroom," Tony said, scooting the kitten inside, "but it's for your own safety. We'll work something out soon." Still thinking of a way to make it more comfortable for her, he dashed out the door.

* * *

Stripping off the smock, to prevent even more blood staining the white fabric, she revealed that only a small patch around her curly pubic hair and an area about three centimeters wide over her spine remained virgin to the ink-bearing needles. The cryptic symbols still bore no obvious meaning to the uninitiated.

She used the blood-spattered apron to wipe her face before tossing it into a sink full of soapy water. She returned to the exam room with a cleaver, a cutting board, a large glass punch bowl and a plastic garbage bag. Several of the cats joined her, but the two dogs waited at the threshold. The cats arrayed themselves around the room on any horizontal surface available.

A slit in the victim's jugular allowed the body's remaining fluids to drain into the punch bowl over several minutes. Jointing the limbs took the better part of an hour, and eviscerating the torso took another thirty minutes. When she'd completed her grisly task the garbage bags almost overflowed with a protein bounty for her pets—after suitable adulterations, of course.

After storing the meat, Sonya put on a pot. Covered in blood, she tilted back in the plastic chair to savor her goddess tea. She yearned to be clean, but her pathological need for a tidy environment meant she couldn't stop quite yet. Her normally pristine examination room needed to be returned to its semi-sterile state.

She spent the rest of the day scrubbing, sanding, and disinfecting blood, bone, and brain tissue from the walls and floor. As Sonya meticulously scrubbed the hardwood floors with a stiff wire brush, she sang quietly, "That old black magic has me in its spell, that old black magic that you weave so well…those icy fingers up and down my spine, the same old witchcraft when your eyes meet mine…"

The three cats that remained with her throughout the entire process sat on the examining table crooning with her *a cappella*.

Implement—Phase Two

"Nanogate Building Four, Level one-hundred-fifty-one," came the soft, computer generated, pseudo-female voice over the bus PA. Even the voices were designed to keep the sheep of mankind at rest. Tony mumbled his standard apologies as he got his 190 centimeter height and 150 kilo mass out through the tightly packed commuters.

He jogged through the 6 meters of uncovered sky and perpetual drizzle to the covered entrance of his personal purgatory—the Dental Division of Nanogate Corporation. "Wet day today," he said to no one in particular. "Hope we'll see some sun soon."

He brushed at the rain clinging to his gray imitation-tweed suit and shook his long, loose hair. A quick check in the reflection of the great glass doors allowed him to straighten his burgundy tie before joining the rest of the throng entering yet another day as an insignificant cog in the megacorp machine.

The atrium stood 30 meters high, bearing a genuine Thaddeus sculpture filling at least 70 percent of that height—a grotesque and misshapen representation of a human worker floating over those starting their workday. It reminded Tony of the commissions Stalin made back in the Cold War. Some might call it art, but Tony chose to think of it as not-so-subtle intimidation. He couldn't decide if it symbolized what the megacorps did to those that worked for them, or if its sheer size indicated how little significance the megacorps placed on each worker.

Tony's cube, comprised of one-point-three-meter-high carpeted pseudo-walls with a desktop and computer workstation built in, held only one bit of uniqueness—a single climbing ivy decorated the otherwise sterile environment. One of the benefits of his grade level was an office on the floor of the Tri-Met drop. "No more climbing stairs," Tony muttered to himself, nudging one of his peers next to him as they watched the multitude of drones climbing the bank of stairs. His mind, however, darted back to Cin—her playfulness, the softness of her fur, and how expressive the tiny face and large eyes could be.

He squeezed his eyes shut and tried to focus. "Time to hit the grindstone," he said less than enthusiastically. The coworker mumbled his agreement.

His rear barely had hit the seat when a solido appeared on his desk. The less-than-honorable Mitch Anson's face turned directly toward him. Having no innate engineering talent of his own, Mitch adeptly wormed his way into other people's accomplishments and took some or even all the credit. From what Tony knew, Mitch could accept a bribe with one hand and the reward for betraying the briber with the other. Neither of these methods stood as particularly groundbreaking in history, but that's how Mitch managed to become Junior VP of Research so quickly. Mitch even now lustfully looked forward to removing the "Junior."

Even in these days of backstabbing and backroom deals, Tony felt his boss held a position one ecological step above a tapeworm without morals. The counterargument was that he knew his boss felt him to be the equivalent of a rabbit who existed only as an intermediate step in the food chain. Those were the words Mitch had spoken to a mutual friend. As a result of this mutual admiration, or lack thereof, Tony's assignments often reminded one of beef jerky rather than caviar.

"Sammis, report to my office at once," ordered Mitch. While the voice normally felt chilly, Tony recognized an abnormal brusqueness. The solido winked out as quickly and abruptly as it had materialized.

"Looks like Anson's in an ass-kicking mood today, gang," he announced over the low partitioning walls. A few snickers floated up from behind the anonymous facade. "Be on your best behavior." Several more chuckles followed, but not too loudly, for fear of reprisals.

Anson's office sported a 30 meter-wide view of the 170-acre Nanogate Botanical Forest. As the third largest open natural area within twelve hundred kilometers, and within the top four hundred largest in the world—moving up if the Yosemite Prison Bill passed the UN—it required eighty full-time gardeners.

The décor could've been copied out of any up-and-comer's office, with an oversized desk, antique leather chair, plastic straight-backed chairs for underlings to sit in, private bathroom, wet bar, and a red-headed, buxom secretary who shot Tony lasers as he entered and she left. The two Nanogate security officers, in body armor not dissimilar to that of a Metro, on either side of Anson's desk didn't exactly fit the image. Nor did a short, blond man wearing only the yellow vinyl tights of a bodyguard. He stood idly nearby with arms carefully folded behind his back.

"No, don't bother to sit down, Sammis. I'm going to make this short and sweet. You're fired. You have one hour to collect your personal belongings—under the watchful eye of our security forces, of course—and get out."

"Why?" Tony sputtered, barely even able to comprehend this disaster.

"You've been charged with practicing medicine without a license, possession of a personal vehicle, and resisting arrest. We here at Nanogate don't need that type of publicity.

"Personally, I didn't think you had it in you, Sammis, but the prime rule is 'Don't get caught.' You are through in the corporate world."

"B-but I've never done anything like those things!" Tony protested weakly.

"Doesn't matter, Sammis. We don't want you around. You'll give Nanogate a bad name just by association. As far as the government goes, they'll probably never get around to trying you for your crimes, so we here at Nanogate will take the appropriate action as defined by corporate precedent. You're to be cut out like a cancer.

"If you go quietly, the parent company is willing to give you the following: one year's severance pay, an equal length of full medical continuance, your accumulated retirement funds to date, and pay in lieu of accumulated vacation.

"By inference you can deduce what will happen to you if you fight."

Tony shook in place. For years he'd felt ambiguous about his place as another bit in the great megacorp machine. Now, without his consent, he no longer even carried that insignificant distinction. His muscles and gut willed him to some action, however futile, and his mind somehow kept them both under control.

"Granted, I think this offer is overly generous for someone who's violated the morals clause in their contract, but it wasn't my call to make. Take it and get out. Cause the slightest trouble and I'll strip you of even that crumb."

* * *

In his butter-mellow baritone, Nanogate spoke. "*Alea iacta est,*" he stated—rather succinctly, he thought. He received nothing but blank stares despite the broad range of education and mental implants represented in the room. "The die is cast. Phase one completed without incident. We discovered an added bonus in time to make use of it. The subject has recently obtained a feline."

With a scowl, Taste Dynamics, the only one at the table currently in a skirt, looked up. "How can that be a bonus, unless you eat those kinds of proteins?"

"Not at all. It has multiple benefits. It allays the fears of the members of the Green Peace organization, and the cat itself has already been set up as an additional weapon." There were several knowing nods around the huge wooden table.

"Phase two is underway as we speak," Nanogate went on. "We'll continue to increase the pressure until our subject has no other choice."

"Are there any indications of suicidal tendencies?"

"None for over seven generations. Mental profiles show no H-seven indicators of depression, no Cannon indicators of self-hatred or self-destruction. As an additional precaution, we added a deep-programmed block against suicide. If—no, when—he is probed, the terrorists won't find it unusual. As you know, such blocks are standard practice to infants in over twenty-four percent of Earth and seventy-four percent in colonies."

"What is the timetable for this next phase?"

"Phase two should last no more than two standard days. Phase three we theorize to take between seven to nine days. Gaining their trust, phase four, is variable, but we anticipate no more than two weeks."

"And the weapon?"

"Phase five is timed to begin replication at T plus twenty-one days. This will give him time to become a valuable member and no longer under suspicion. Evaluation of results should tally shortly after that."

"I suggest we move to the next topic of discussion then," the chairman offered. "I turn your attention to the new anti-cloning legislation in front of the UN…"

* * *

All Tony's personal belongings save one fit into his satchel. Under the careful and watchful eyes of the two Nanogate security officers, he packed the wedding solido of his mother and father and the boudoir solido of Carmine. Two plaques for completion of one course or another lay flat against his diplomas. He carefully folded a first-place T-shirt for longest softball hit at the Nanogate Sports Day Picnic and packed it in beside a toothbrush, a used tube of toothpaste and a Project Neptune mug.

"I guess that's it," he said sadly, wrapping his arms around the pot of green and white striped leaves. The spiderwort's presence so often made such a nice counterpoint to the sterility of the corporate nature. His mom called it a Wandering Jew plant when she took the original cutting from a large healthy vine she grew over most of her living room. He'd been diligent in keeping it alive.

"I'm sorry sir, but the plant must remain," said a scratchy voice from behind one of the security guard's masks.

"What? This plant is mine. My mother gave it to me when it was just this long," he insisted, holding his fingers apart by about three centimeters.

"That plant consumed light and water from Nanogate. By inference, it must belong to the corporation—Portland Statute eleven-fourteen-baker."

Tony thought seriously about raising a fit about the plant, the only link to his parents, dead nearly a year now. But his mind still functioned. He remembered the derision heaped on him by Anson for being a good and trustworthy employee. His shoulders, set strongly up to this point, drooped in defeat. His eyes dimmed as his head slumped forward just the tiniest amount. He carefully set down the plant after visions of Anson playing the part of a vengeful and self-righteous god darkened his mood even further.

Tony knew that fighting anything Nanogate or Anson decided to do to him was a useless waste of time and resources. If Anson gave him the truth about the charges, no court in the world would entertain any case he put forward. Even if he did get it before a judge, the corporate lawyers would crush any representation he could possibly afford.

He was finished in this world. The best he could hope for now was menial labor or migration, if any of the colonies would consider him. His past employment didn't exactly push him into any critical need category.

The briefcase seemed very empty compared to the number of hours he had labored here. He took nothing from the office except memories of an already extinct corporate career. With a sigh he closed the lid.

"I guess that's all. Go ahead and do it." As an act of finality, Tony lifted his wrist. The scanner sniffed the DNA from the loose cells at his wrist and crosslinked with the Nanogate mainframe. In picoseconds, every door, every machine, and every positive record within the corporation would now deny Tony's very existence, irrevocably.

Silence filled the cubicle farm. The word passed quickly as the people with whom Tony had laughed, cried, supported, torpedoed, drunk beer, played softball, and competed against for the golden nuggets of corporate politics lined the hall. There stretched a human gauntlet of his life. A variety of reactions played on the faces of his former peers, subordinates, and everyone else who somehow had learned of his demise. Some wore faces that did little to hide their joy, sadness, or outright fear. Above everything else, the silence stung Tony. He half expected to hear the muffled sobs of a grieving widow. The analogy seemed fitting. Instead, he got nothing.

Tony maintained his composure through the procession, saying not a single word. He would go out as a man wronged with his head held high, not catching the eye of any of the silent witnesses. It was the longest two minutes of his life, putting one foot in front of the other, staring at a faded, four-year-old dental seminar poster on the far wall.

As he reached the exit, someone in the gathered crowd actually mustered the audacity to cheer, but only for a brief second and without great enthusiasm. Tony stiffened and stopped in the portal. He wanted to shout that they were next, to scream and plead for respite. Instead he looked to the group, now clustered in the entry under the monstrosity they called a sculpture. With as much sarcasm as he could muster, he quietly said, "Good luck to you all."

Turning at once, he stepped out under the awning of the building. He bitterly rejected the protection of the corporation's roof and he took several more steps. His dignity held until the light Portland rain chilled his cheeks. Finally he afforded a weakness that wouldn't show. Tears rolled down his cheeks, invisibly mingled in the wet, hiding his shame.

Very briefly he considered just jumping off the ledge and plunging countless meters to an ignoble demise, but he needed to prove they hadn't beaten him. Instead, he stood with a ramrod-straight back, mixing salt from his tears with the drizzle's pollution as he waited for the lift-bus and a new, if unknown, life.

"I'll make this right."

* * *

Night herself held too obvious a danger. It caused decent and semi-decent people to guard themselves carefully. It gave hunters a place to lurk. It also gave camouflage and life to the hunters of the hunters.

The night gave rise to a backward kind of danger. With the predators that stalked the night dropping off to sleep and the daylight denizens not yet stirring, the afternoon provided, as it had for centuries, the perfect cover for the trade of thief, mugger, or in this case, terrorist.

Direct sunlight never soiled the shadow of the lower barrio. The weak sun fought its way through the gray smog and ubiquitous mist, just barely chasing away the darkness of the night. Sonya left her apartment wearing a black, white, and neutral pattern-disruptive cloak. She'd made the cloak herself four years ago, weaving cat hair and energy together for a simple efficacy. While not quite as good as light-bending clothing used by the military, it served its purpose—to make the wearer unnoticed and anonymous. As an added bonus, cloaks held the distinction of being nearly the universal slum outer attire, keeping occupant and cargo reasonably warm and dry. A large sombrero bundled up her long, brown hair. The hat's excessive brim and a green surgical mask covered a good portion of her face.

Fortunately, Sonya preferred walking. By losing good people, the GAM learned years ago that lift-buses and taxis used automatic sensing equipment. They detected most high-order explosives, firearms of any caliber, and most edged or thrusting hand weapons. As a result Sonya had a four-hour walk west into the Pearl District, across the nearly rusted-through Steel Bridge—an ancient relic valued only as a tourist attraction to show people what life was like before lift vehicles. All this because the Metros objected to her cargo—fifteen kilos of high-explosive devices.

A thick cloud of some noxious chemical hugged the ground like an early morning fog. Sonya's presence parted the worst of the mist for a meter in either direction, repelled by the energy-laden fibers of her outerwear. The few people who milled around the ground level streets in the afternoon light in Lower Portland were as dangerous as working with explosives in an oven. As a rule, they all had the capability to either deal with troublemakers or to be troublemakers themselves. The vast majority bore outward signs of heavy artificial body augmentation with metallic arms, ablative armor, or even artificial eyes.

While many would be frightened if the Greenies succeeded, Sonya's mind instead drifted to what she hoped to remake of this world—one where green plants thrived, instead of withering sickly. A world where animals roamed freely, living as they should. A world her great, great grandmother would recognize, not this burnt-out, overpopulated place without hope. A place where justice came not from the credits in one's purse but from men equally to all other men. A world where not being registered in a computer wasn't a death sentence.

Any movement in any of those directions would be welcome. Her jaws clenched tightly and her fists formed and released.

Every single day the megacorps committed new atrocities. Governments couldn't stop them as they learned to bend to the will of the highest bidder, either in the form of cash or threat. The last holdout to this corruption, England, finally knuckled under to Advanced Biometrics when they promised to poison three major cities, including London, if the Genetics Freedom Law passed. Since then it had become business as usual. Examples included China's sale of absolute mineral rights of the Province of India to Materials Matrix Corporation for an undisclosed sum, or the Russian Coalition's transfer of one third of all their nuclear devices to Priory Unlimited to prevent a war with the Czech Republic.

Corrupt police, city services, and government poisoned every corner of this world and all those it had colonized. Those with the money could buy anything they wanted. Only those innocent people who could afford to purchase justice could actually obtain it. The list went on and on.

Sonya's dark musings kept her busy until she completed the first leg of her journey. Three of her fellow terrorists waited at ground level of their current target, the Colonization Unlimited Building. They milled around, chatting and blending into the rest of the scenery, dressed in dirty and heavily worn clothes with only a couple of the boxed internees in the vicinity.

The boxed—another abomination of this world, Sonya thought. A tiny minority of fearful Nils listened to the megacorp and government propaganda. They volunteered to have their brains placed into robotic equipment to do menial tasks just for the hope of someday earning the right to be returned to cloned bodies and legally registered. Just the sight of the two automatons trying to shore up the footing of a crumbling building left her sickened by the way one man enslaved another.

Turning her mind away, Sonya perceived her fellow comrades and wondered if they weren't enslaved even more strongly than those inhabiting metal and plastic bodies. But by the same token, they carried hatreds that forged each into a weapon or a tool that might just change the world—but one that also condemned them, even as it might one day save others.

Arthur Lewton, a tiny man at 1.3 meters and only 60 kilos, ran an accounting department for OldsTransport until a lift-bus dropped on his wife as she installed a new undercarriage. OldsTransport faulted Linda with improper alignment of the grav impellers and refused to pay any benefits. Arthur's private investigation revealed OT used out-of-specification impeller casings that showed a tendency to burn through and fail to lift.

Instead of admitting their mistake, the VPs of manufacturing at OT fired Arthur and discredited his findings by replacing all the faulty casings before he could prove anything. Despite his diminutive size, Arthur's rage couldn't be underestimated. Once, caught red-handed without a weapon, he rammed his finger up one corpie's eye socket deep enough to perform an impromptu lobotomy.

Slightly chunky but nonetheless quite attractive, Beth Watkins wore the figure of a woman who'd birthed one too many children, yet she'd never been a mother. Beth's grievance with the megacorps started when she received a temporary contraceptive which permanently damaged not only her uterus but also her abdominal wall. The contraceptive damaged thirty percent of the test subjects before being released to the market by Caring Health Systems anyway. A former runway model, Beth lost her looks, her job, her fertility, and her husband.

Martin Fox's sympathies most nearly matched Sonya's own. A Nil of average height, average weight, brown hair, brown eyes, and no distinguishing marks, he used these physically nondescript features to his advantage—basically, they made him a complete nonentity. Sonya had on more than one occasion watched him vape a corpie, drop the weapon and melt into a crowd. He could then stand a scant two meters away as the Metros arrived, with none the wiser.

Martin wanted to make nature a dominant force in the world again. His heartfelt dreams were even more radical than even Sonya's, however. Given his choice, Earth would be cordoned off as a "no-human zone."

Loyalty and passion embodied the most important traits of each member of her core group. All had been on more than one mission. She knew the color of their emotions.

"You all know what this mission's parameters are," she said in a voice barely above a whisper as she entered their circle. "Seven bombs planted at this corp's primary entrances and set off at end of shift will remove a great number of their key people," she reviewed, removing the deadly metal tubes from within her cloak. None of the other three offered a word in reply. They knew their tasks. Grim determination showed on their faces as they accepted their weapons.

"Each of you will carry two. I will carry only one but will be planting it in the most dangerous location. All of these devices are already armed and timed, so place them and get out. Just like last time." The dirty, worn appearance of their clothing concealed their true nature as the bombs disappeared within specially designed pockets.

"One last thing. Remember, they must be placed outside the building, or they'll be detected. You have your assignments."

"For Nature," Martin mumbled as he shuffled off into the mist. The others said nothing.

Each of them had to make their way up between one-hundred and one-hundred-fifty levels—or four times that number of meters—using long-forgotten elevator shafts and disused, prelift emergency stairs. Once in place, they'd attach the homemade explosives to walls, stonework, or any handy outcropping using a small chunk of adhesive putty. Success would be determined by a grisly count of dead and maimed.

Shaking her head, Sonya steadied herself for her own task. Each team member carried their own weight. She couldn't do anyone else's job for them, or she wouldn't be able to perform her own.

Sonya mentally rehearsed her own assignment, blanking out worries about dangers to her team, human losses, or the chaos that accompanied her successes. Human and electronic security on a building as bare as a billiard ball made her target by far the riskiest. While the most difficult, it also promised greater satisfaction, for the structure she'd chosen served as the corporation's executive landing pad.

Her green mask hid the smile of a predatory animal. Sonya liked most challenges and the rewards they brought.

* * *

Tony ripped off the filmy stuck to his door. He read it as he let the door sniff his wrist for epithelials.

From: Council Crest Tenant Association

To: Tony Sammis, Owner of 115-16d

Pursuant to clause 17 subsections j through n of the Organization Code (section IV of your Conditions, Covenants and Restrictions) your property will be placed under forced sale at the next available auction.

Proceeds of the sale will pay, in order: auction fees, Council Crest Tenant Association penalties and expenses, and lienholder fees and loan balance. Any additional funds or balance due will be forwarded to your electronic address and/or account.

In order to expedite this sale, please remove your belongings no later than this Saturday or CCTA will have to resort to employing a professional eviction service as an expense incurred within the sale of the property.

We regret having to take this action but your lack of character and willful flaunting of civil, criminal and moral codes makes our community a lesser place to live.

Sincerely,

Association President,
Rosa Cleveland

cc: Portland Metro Police

"I wonder who else can spit on me." Tony would've laughed if it weren't so tragic. The equity in his home would easily be eaten up in the vastly inflated fees and charges. There'd be nothing left for him, and as a cherry on top they'd probably present him with a balance due bill.

"Music, classical." Tchaikovsky filled the room. As Tony let Cin out of the bathroom, tears welled up in his eyes again, but this time didn't quite escape. Cin brushed against his legs. Tony picked up his new friend and held her tight.

"At least I have one friend. And maybe Carmine. Maybe she just needs to get to know you so she won't think of you as sausage." Purrs and a rough tongue across his nose made him smile weakly.

"My job and home both taken," he said to Cin. "I'm surprised they didn't kill me outright. It would've been faster. I didn't even get to tell my side of the story." The ramrod Tony received involved only standard operating procedure for those his society deemed misfits or criminals. He'd seen and approved of it in others. Now they turned it upon him. All of a sudden its injustice rankled.

"I guess that makes me a hypocrite," he muttered. "Well, girl, I can fight this. I think it'd probably cost me somewhere around forty thousand credits to get my case heard in front of a judge. Then another quarter million to get any kind of impartial judgment.

"Now with all this severance pay Nanogate's throwing at me, I probably could scrape that much together by begging and borrowing from friends, maybe a loan from the labor union and another from the Justice Department." He watched as Cin toyed with a thread from an antique wool throw rug. "But what am I going to do in the five years it'll take to get to trial? What would I live on? Where would I live?"

Tony picked up Cin when she managed to pull the thread into a runner. He looked her right in the face. "Worse, my case isn't all that powerful. Oh, possession of a personal vehicle and resisting arrest would be easy to beat, but practicing medicine without a license—that's a horse of a different color. I've got several hundred people, not to mention the TriMet sensors, willing to testify that I helped save the old woman, but that's about it."

The kitten licked his nose and gave him a nondescript meow. He put the kitten down. She wobbled off to find more fun, the runner forgotten.

"Even if the court rules in my favor, nothing would happen. Nanogate and Council Crest Tenant Association would be bound to do nothing. My only compensation would be an almost clean record—almost, because there'd still be those who think I bought the verdict.

"I guess then I could try and find another position with another corp, but it's very unlikely anyone would take a chance on me. Knowing Mitch Anson, he took out a full page ad in the *Post*, the *Times*, and every third-hit banner on the net about my morals. So the odds of getting a new job rank right up there with getting a nice warm wind on Pluto."

A crash issued from the kitchen. Tony went in to find an open cabinet, and Cinnamon sitting in amongst pots and pans scattered on the floor.

"Hmm. Seems like you're having an interesting adventure, Miss Cin." He began picking up the cookery.

"I guess I could just accept what's happening. My money and status will be sucked away. All I can do now is go dig in a mine or something equally pleasant. And that's assuming I could find something at all. I'd have to live on welfare in a commune—or worse, a relocation camp. No health care, recycled food to eat." Tony continued to confide in the cat and shuddered as he put away the last pot.

"Another choice, if you can call any of these choices, is to chuck everything and out-migrate. But, most colonies require specific skills or a huge quantity of money—more than I'll ever see in my lifetime. The only other choice I've got is to settle on one of those colonies where you need genetic and prosthetic manipulation just to survive.

"And then there's being boxed, probably the worst of the choices…"

Getting on the floor with Cin and dragging a sock around as bait for her fun, Tony considered his other options. "If I cashed out, I could disappear as a Nil—with no identity and no status. I could do that before they sold my home. But as a Nil, I'll have no rights. Anyone could take my property or my life away, just because they felt like it."

The rest of the day drifted by. While listening to the soothing vocals of the legendary Italian opera singer Enrico Caruso, he slapped some mayonnaise on bread, following it with salami, turkey, and some accidental horseradish. He ate it silently, eyes glazed over, not even tasting his mistake. Cin sat patiently on the table next to him and nibbled at the tidbits he fed her.

"I could look at this as a unique opportunity, if you want to call it that, of deciding the course of my life. How often do we get to choose our future? Rarely. Then again, what would I choose if I could?" Tony grew silent for a moment as Cin pounced on one of his dirty socks.

"Let's be honest. I want a penthouse home, above the pollution level, a wife, a mistress, and enough clout to own my own limousine. I want to be able to control everything and everyone around me." Tony realized the truth about himself when he heard it. Until yesterday morning his mind had brimmed with that exact future, just like any other good corpie. "And if I could, I'd put everything back the way it was.

"But that was yesterday," he rationalized. "I'm not one of them any more."

To the recorded sounds of a Martian sandstorm he did two loads of laundry, in typical male fashion—throwing everything in until he had a full load, totally ignoring the color and fabric. Cin rummaged in clothes Tony piled and perched on top of the warm dryer between attacks. Tony didn't notice. He turned on one of the ever-popular daytime dramas, but not a single scene registered.

"So many people really don't know what they'll live and die for, Cin," Tony said sometime around ten P.M., a serious look on his face. His mind held the clarity of the air after a summer thunderstorm. "I certainly didn't know what I stood for until just today. I stand for life, else I wouldn't have even tried saving the old woman. I stand for justice, else I would've taken you, you escaped miniature rug, and flushed you down with the rest of the dinner leftovers. I may be hypocritical, but I think that's about it.

"What I don't know is what to do about it."

Tony lay down on the couch. Cin climbed up to his chest and settled down for a nap. He stroked her softly and scratched her under the chin and around the ear. The problem, as Tony lay there getting more and more resolute, was that he hadn't the foggiest clue how to accomplish any of his budding lofty ideals. Cin purred loud enough to finally drown out the solidoset.

* * *

Sonya clung precariously to the wall of the Colonization Unlimited Building, some seven hundred meters from the slums below. Luck had followed her thus far. By climbing the wall itself, using a plant extract cum adhesive created in her own container garden, she managed to avoid all notice. Windows she avoided as much as blank stone, and iron was her friend. Her cloak, plus a few muttered words learned from her proctor, altered the perception of those random few who saw her. To them, she became nothing more than a window washer, or a pigeon, or maybe even a stone gargoyle—anything but a strange woman climbing the side of a building, bent on who knows what kind of mischief.

The drain on her body and her mind, in keeping up her mental guise during the three-hour climb, showed in her labored breath, aching muscles and a migraine starting just behind the right temple. Her trek wore on her much more than expected. She needed time to rest and recover. Sonya glanced through a nearby frosted window into a bathroom where dark shapes moved within. Highly unlikely there'd be continuous DNA or explosive detectors inside. She promised herself just two minutes.

Her research hadn't included whether this corp had unisex bathrooms like most companies. Sonya timed the actions of a glass worker's tool with the flow of dark shapes within. When nothing moved, the tools reached behind the molding and released the pane as if she'd been doing it her entire life. A fugitive's upbringing provided one with all manner of useful skills. With exaggerated care, she pulled the window out on its slides. This made just enough room for her to slip inside, every muscle in her body poised for fight or flight.

She dropped silently to the floor in a crouch as she scanned the peach-colored room with overstuffed lounging chairs. By the mock chandeliers and an abundance of well-lighted mirrors, Sonya obviously found herself in a ladies' powder room. With no other movement or sound nearby, she relaxed a little. She pulled the window back into place using a suction cup on the inner pane. With the window set in place but not fastened, it could've been blown out by a strong gust, so as a bit of insurance, she set a tiny bit of putty in one corner.

She slipped into a stall and sat. As her body relaxed, her mind continued to work. Her target occupied this same height level so when she returned to scuttling like a spider on the outer wall, she merely needed to crawl around the corner to place her present. With that thought in mind she closed her eyes and opened her mind. She let mnemonics roll quietly off her tongue as her mind surged outward.

Near her objective she sensed four guards and one executive limousine with driver. As usual, they each carried repeating weapons, though she couldn't make out the type. Sonya rarely worried about such things. If they discovered her, four months of work on this setup would be for naught, even if she escaped. That would hurt more than anything they might do to her body or mind.

The sounds of two women entering the bathroom broke her from her mental journey. Their high heels echoed in the tiled bathroom. "Did you see Rhonda with George?"

"Yeah, she was all over him like a ground-level girl."

"As if you can't tell, that little bitch is sleeping with him for the promotion."

"She's sleeping with him?"

"From what I heard she's moved in with him."

"Weeble it all! If she's really sleeping with him, I guess that means I'll never get that job. I've been working for three years for that spot and now some bed dancer is going to get it! What is that, her third manager this year?"

"Fourth, not counting the two she's been seen with from Masterson Controls."

"Gads, I hope she goes over there. It'll get the slut out from under our heels, and I can't imagine working for her. I'd probably just claw her eyes out."

"You won't attack her, but you won't like working for her either. At least she'll be gone soon. All she has to do is find a bigger boss to sleep with and she'll be out of your hair."

"Personally that wouldn't be so bad, but I don't know if I'll be able to stand another year in this position. Marvin is such a beastly manager…"

The conversation faded as the bathroom door opened and closed once more. Sonya might've listened, but something got lost in translation. The conversation went beyond her comprehension. Oh, she understood the words and the meanings, but couldn't understand how people subjected themselves to such things. She couldn't understand the lure to maintain that mockery of a lifestyle.

Her strength returned enough to finish. Before anyone else invaded her temporary sanctum, Sonya worked her way back out the window, replacing it as skillfully as she'd opened it. It wouldn't do for anyone to even suspect that she'd paused there.

A breeze whistled in from the east, insistently plucking at her clothes as she eased around the corner of the building. While always careful, she slowed even further because of the wind. She pulled flat against the surface to prevent the air getting between her and the wall, where it might increase its grip upon her.

Corporate guards were paid to be alert, and generally succeeded. Her approach needed to be exceedingly careful in order to maintain the effectiveness of her protections. She needed a painstaking hour of creep-and-stop to cover the last hundred meters. The two guards exchanged banter but took no notice of the shadow, or the sign, or the stonemasonry that barely moved along the wall.

Anticlimactically, Sonya's act of sticking the pipe bomb above the executive entrance compared to playing with clay in kindergarten. Just pressing the device into place caused no problems, entailed no additional risks. She sweated with tiny but continuous efforts as she eased her way back around the corner.

The danger passed quickly with the corner between her and the only real threats. Her fatigue also flew as she could now move much more openly. She used her tools once again to open the window of a vacant office. Now it didn't matter if anyone caught her, as the most they'd do is kick her out of the building. Once safely inside, she mumbled a few words, rubbed a red powder across her lips, dripped yellow paint into her hair, put a pea into each cup of her bra and wrapped a length of ivy vine around her waist, cloak and all.

Unlike her cautious entrance or the long, slow sojourn around the building's perimeter, not one single person failed to note Sonya illusionary façade as she left. Men drooled and women narrowed their eyes jealously at the overly buxom blonde with full, cherry-red lips and the kind of hourglass figure men have lusted after and women have coveted for millennia. Sonya appropriately swayed her hips and gave cold stares to the few men who dared approach her. Once out the primary exit and onto the lift-bus, she became even more untouchable.

Now, waiting was all. Sometimes that was the hardest part.

* * *

Tony dreamed of a night with Carmine, sealed inside a luxury hotel room surrounded by hot and cold running delicacies of both the flesh and palate. The two of them spent a fortune on a bacchanalia where they indulged in every way possible—women, men, and some who were in between.

"Open up under Civil Code Fourteen-eighteen, paragraph J! Metro officers identifying themselves and their right to enter."

But every time Tony got close to Carmine herself, she giggled and slipped away, leaving someone else in her place.

"If you do not open the door, we have been authorized to override the command sequence."

Tony bolted upright. He had thought the melodramatic voice an annoying, if simple, part of his dream. Intending to step down from his bed, he instead tripped getting up off the couch. Disoriented though he was, he knew the Metros couldn't be allowed to find Cin! Where was she…?

"I'm on my way! Keep your helmet on!" Tony shouted as he scrambled about, looking everywhere he could see. "I'm in the back room and getting dressed. I'll be there in a second."

The kitten didn't want to be found, so Tony hoped she'd remain that way. Sweat crept over his scalp as he opened the door. Two Metros towered over him in full black riot gear, faces fully obscured. "Out of the way," came the voice sonically enhanced with seven hertz anxiety infrasound. One of the pair slammed Tony aside with one power-assisted arm, briefly pinning him against the entryway. Even without being able to see his back, Tony could feel the bruises forming. "We have a right to search and seize chattels upon your premises."

Tony panicked to do something to deflect an all-out search for whatever they were looking for. With sudden purpose, he spun to face the fair protectors of Portland. "Your authorization?" he barked.

While the blank face-mask gave no emotion, Tony got the distinct impression he both amused and annoyed the man. Massive ebon fingers held out a recording crystal the size of Cin's paw and dropped it to the carpet. Tony picked it up as the armored policemen went into the bedroom.

"You can't be too sure these days," Tony offered feebly. "You never know. Fake cops and all."

The solido crystal went into his player and a solido image sprang forth in the middle of the room. Carmine's image, life size, spoke to him from behind the faux wood desk he'd given her as a present on her last birthday.

"Mr. Sammis, or whatever your real name is, I had no idea you were such a deviant. I don't know how you could've deceived me for so long, but I must've been seven kinds of fool for having trusted you with any part of my life." Crashing sounds issued from the bedroom. Carmine leaned forward over the desk and shook her finger at him, like scolding a naughty schoolboy. Some part of him, despite her reaction to his news about Cin, still had hoped she would be the anchor in his life, just as she'd been with every other disaster. Instead she chose to inflict even more abuse.

"It's obvious I can have no more to do with you, so I've sent the police to retrieve my things. Don't interfere with them, for I've paid them well to make it unpleasant if you resist." The image carried a feral smile.

"Do not attempt to see me. Do not attempt to contact me. Do not attempt to contact anyone we know. If you do, I'll have the Metros return and show you real justice.

"My skin crawls to think I ever let you touch me. You must've been quite pleased to get a nice real girl like me into your clutches, you pathetic Nil. Have you no shame? But then your kind rarely does.

"May your skin burn from acid fog at ground level." The solido image gave him a universally understood and despised gesture before winking out. One of the Metros chose that moment to return to the room. Seemingly at random he picked up a lead crystal lamp and smashed it to the floor.

"What the hell are you looking for?" demanded Tony.

"We have everything but one item—necklace, Black Hills Gold, with double grape cluster and differing colored leaves." Tony had worn it since his time with Carmine in college. It had been reciprocation for him giving her a friendship ring. Without a thought, he snapped its tiny chain from his neck and held it out to the cop.

"There is your fucking item. Now get the hell out!"

"Sergeant, I've got it. Let's make jet-tracks."

"Rog-O."

Tony watched as the two walked out the door with an armload of booty, some obviously Tony's own property. They didn't even bother to close the door after they left. Tony heard a muted hiss from under the couch. Cin only now gave her opinion of their unwanted guests.

"I agree."

* * *

Sonya violated her own prohibition on technology in her home with one item, an old-fashioned FM radio. If she played with the dial just right, she picked up one hundred eighty-five stations in the metro-Portland area.

She sat at her dinner table with a ball of gray fur in her lap and listened to the seven o'clock news report. As usual, the news depressed her, but she must know if everything went according to plan before she took credit for the action. Her favorite, Plutonia, purred and kept her company while the headlines were read. The tiny, still unnamed Chihuahua sat shivering on the tabletop side by side with her Pomeranian, Maxine. Sonya smiled at it and placed a kiss on its tiny nose. She made only the fourth headline story.

"In sadder news, four bombs detonated on the Colonization Unlimited Building in downtown today. Seventy-three confirmed dead and one hundred eighty-six others injured.

"Police refuse to speculate if this bombing had anything to do with recent GAM actions. Chief Adams, is this related to the other bombings?"

"How can I tell? We haven't had any time to run tests, talk to informants, or even get their call to confirm it—"

Absently Sonya wondered if four actually went off. Were they censoring the total number, or that a corporate exec met his maker? Sonya imagined the cruel way she'd just killed seventy-three (or more) people, and the destruction wreaked by her bombs. She had reconciled herself to this course long ago. Wars like this weren't clean and neat—lawyers had claimed the cleaner kind of warfare centuries ago. Her deeds of death and destruction didn't warrant a smile, but as hard and demanding work, they did. She grinned and set Plutonia on the floor.

Sonya switched off the radio and walked out her apartment door once more. Her next task wouldn't work up any sweat.

* * *

Tony found himself awakening much later than his norm, once again on the couch. His body crawled and itched like his poor days back in college—sleeping in his clothes, no shower, stubble on his face, too much stress. He walked back into his bedroom.

His bedding was filled with glass fragments from the antique mirror which once had hung on the nearby wall. Smashed splinters of the chest of drawers lay sprawled about the floor, the jewelry box and what had been its contents spread all over the room.

"Bloody Metros," muttered Tony. "I'll bet they just enjoyed the hell out of this."

Cin padded behind him, sniffing only at the odd bit of fluff strewn about the floor. Tony trundled into the bathroom to find, placed neatly on a clear spot on the bathroom vanity, the friendship ring he'd given Carmine. The once meaningful trinket now sat just slightly pushed into a small pile of human excrement. Obviously the Metros made deliveries as well as pickups. Carmine's message didn't need a solido sign.

"It figures she'd think up something so tasteless," Tony said, using some toilet paper to brush the entire mass, ring and all, into the toilet. That part of his life disappeared with a simple flush.

He needed nearly three hours to make some semblance of order out of the chaos of his home, all the while bantering back and forth with himself and the kitten, as the mood suited him.

"I don't know why I bother. They're still going to take my home away.

"But then I guess I still need to have somewhere to stay.

"How could they be so callous?

"The solido of mother, ruined…

"Cin, don't play with the glass!

"What could they possibly have been looking for in there?"

Each broken item he swept into the garbage set the muscles in his jaw dancing to a dark tune. With everything he placed back into its proper place his fists clenched tighter.

"Radio, news."

"…dder news, four bombs detonated on the Colonization Unlimited Building in downtown today. Seventy-three confirmed dead and one hundred eighty-six others injured.

"Police refuse to speculate if this bombing had anything to do with recent GAM actions. Chief Adams, is this related to the other bombings?"

"How can I tell? We haven't had any time to run tests, talk to informants, or even get their call to confirm it."

"So you have no ideas?"

"Sure we have ideas, you moron. But we aren't stupid enough to give them out where anyone can hear—"

Action crystallized within Tony as he stalked out of his home, leaving Cin loose inside.

For the first time in a dozen months, the clouds above parted and allowed in the silvery light of the moon. This omen lightened Tony's mood slightly but didn't stop his flight. He jumped onto the first lift-bus that showed up at his condo's platform. By chance it happened to be the same one he usually took down to the Rose Quarter. Out of sheer habit he exited the bus near the Wilted Rose. But this time the scenery took on a whole new meaning.

In the past he unconsciously lorded over everyone in this slum. Now he clung just a precarious rung above the people here. A male prostitute flipped his long hair back and batted his brightly painted eyes. A street performer played his antique guitar to the tune of "Stairway to Heaven" and nodded to each person passing. Three beggars sat patiently holding signs proclaiming their inability to find work and starving families. Three hucksters tried to sell him imitation Rolex watches, guaranteed-not-to-break condoms, and bed-space in a local abandoned warehouse. Two recycled food vendors competed with one another for the few credits which could be made on that end of the street just outside the zone patrolled strongly by the Metros.

The people and class changed as he got closer to the Rose. The hookers were cleaner and prettier, the merchandise a bit more upscale—or at least better disguised knock-offs. And Jock stood as the usual intimidating doorman for the Wilted Rose.

"Howdy, Jock," Tony said, as he saw that one friendly face. A massive alloy arm came out and barred his way into the club.

"Sir, I'm afraid I have special orders dealing with you. You are not allowed to enter. The staff has reports of you bothering Miss Carmine."

"Excuse me, Jock? How long have I been a patron here?"

"I have my orders, sir."

"Has everyone gone mad? I'm not a criminal! I'm an ordinary guy." A tiny hesitation crossed Jock's face with the barest humanity flickering to life, and Tony pounced on the opening. "Why are they doing this, Jock?"

Jock waved a few other patrons into the club, and then looked around surreptitiously before lowering his voice by at least half.

"Sir, had it been anyone else, I wouldn't have given it another thought. But you've been good to me with a kind word and a smile. It didn't seem to matter to you that I was a Nil."

"Why should it?"

"It shouldn't, but stop sidetracking me. I don't know all the details, but what I see happening to you has all the earmarks of a top level megacorp hose job.

"Miss Carmine showed up at the club yesterday and talked to the boss. She passed him a stack of bills that even I couldn't tear in half." Jock lifted a velvet rope and passed another high class couple into the loud venue. "About ten minutes later I got my orders to keep you out. You add it up, sir."

"Where would Carmine get that kind of money?"

"That's what I mean, sir. Someone's paying to put you down and that usually means the resources of a corp. I shouldn't say any more. I've probably said too much already."

"OK, Jock, I've got just one more question for you, please. Do you know how to get in touch with the GAM?"

"Sir?!"

"Sorry, I just thought you might know."

"They're violent. I don't want any part of that." Tony had seen Jock tear off the arm of one man for not responding to a less than subtle hint to leave a lady alone, and shoot another through the neck when the welf pulled a stun grenade. Violent or no, Jock didn't know. Unfortunately.

"Jock, you've been a true friend. And for that I'll always be grateful. I may look you up after I get myself settled."

"I'd like that, sir."

"You can knock off that 'sir.' I'm just plain Tony now."

"OK, Tony."

Tony didn't offer him any money. What Jock had done was for friendship, and paying him would've convinced Jock that Tony was just another one of the masses—out for himself only. Tony knew it and Jock knew it. They parted honorable men, as only honorable men know how.

* * *

She knew the disposable percomm call would be traced. The Green Action Militia had learned from an ex-Metro, one of their own now, that it took one minute, fourteen seconds to trace such a call under the best of circumstances. Thus the GAM kept all calls under forty seconds and delivered their message crystal to a different person every time.

"This is the GAM," she stated succinctly. "If you want to hear our statement, you will retrieve the recording crystal from the women's restroom, fourth stall from the end, on your third floor. You have until someone flushes."

Sometimes to mix things up they called anonymous tip hotlines, and once a media lawyer. The delivery location changed as well. Sometimes it arrived in place of the morning paper, and other times it might steer a person through seven levels of scavenger hunt.

They used only standard Fuji commercial recording crystals from a different supplier each time, picking a random device from each lot. Sonya purposely left her right pinky fingerprint on each crystal so they knew exactly whom they were dealing with. As no one had a name to match to that print or her epithelial DNA—except on other crystals— she stayed as safe as any other Nil.

Sonya dropped the ring comm to the ground and crushed it with her heel. To make certain, she stomped it three more times. She moved immediately to the edge of the not-yet-complete level 144 TriMet platform in downtown Corvallis. For security's sake she needed to be at least a full 600 meters from this place in under a minute, the top response time of even Interpol.

The average Metro response time fell into the dismal category of days, but she had to assume they'd set a trap this one time and somehow knew exactly when she would transmit. With her survival—and that of the whole organization—at stake, Sonya played to win.

She took the easy way to get away quickly from the platform—she jumped. Her stomach once again reminded her that this wasn't her favorite of tricks. The nausea never quite elicited regurgitation, but it always came close. Her mind silently counted to nine full seconds before her fingers wove a pattern in the air.

As she landed, at almost ninety meters per second, her body lit up like a miniature sun. The brightness receded rapidly, though she still glowed as she walked away. Waves of heat distortion also wreathed her as the kinetic impact energy flowed away. The few people at ground level who observed the flash or her new thermal aura chose wisely to mind their own business. People with that kind of power at their disposal didn't make good victims.

* * *

The opulence of this meeting room matched, if not exceeded, the previous. Despite imports from Mars costing nearly ten thousand credits per kilogram in shipping alone, a Martian lacquered-sandstone table, weighing close to a metric ton, dominated a room of orange, rust and umber. The ten matching hand-carved chairs sat arranged for the powerful individuals in attendance. Vivaldi played in the background as they entered to take their seats.

"I want to thank you all for the change in venue," said one. "I hope you will be comfortable here. If there's anything my staff can provide, you have but to ask." If sacrificing a live virgin would've been the whim of even one member, the staff would merely have asked what sex and hair color, and the blood would be spilled before the request went cold on the guest's lips.

"Thank you. The first order of business is the GAM Initiative," announced Nanogate as they all took their seats. "Phase two has moved quite according to plan, with another unexpected bonus. The girlfriend not only was bought to stay out of the way but to actively participate in our plan. This reduces operational security risks considerably. The motivation was first order greed."

"Have there been any contraindications?"

"Only one. A single employee of the subject's normal bar told him that he believes it's a corporate plot. As this is intrinsically obvious, it doesn't warrant further action."

"And that employee?"

"Nothing. We don't want to alarm the subject—he's already skittish enough. The employee, a bar tough, is a Nil, so I propose no action against him.

"I call for a vote. Opposed?" Silence was his answer. "Then there is nothing further to report. Oh, one minor item to note. Once the subject has contacted the GAM, we'll almost certainly be unable to monitor his actions as we are now."

"Then how are we going to be able to gauge his effectiveness to plan?"

"Only by observing the results. Clearly this falls into the 'results oriented management' category defined in the late twentieth century. It's not nearly as effective as our current invasive management techniques, but it's the only course open to us with this scheme."

"Agreed. I suggest we move on to the next topic."

"I'd like to bring to your attention New Zealand's proposed execution of one of Taste Dynamics's midlevel managers for the industrial accident of May third. It's a message of sorts that I suggest we respond to vigorously…"

* * *

Her breath wheezed as her chest went up and down steadily in deep sleep. A tribute to his fast thinking, Tony thought. His visit held no rationale, not even the merest whisper of a reason. It took quite a good deal of time and effort to find her, not to mention the three-hundred credit bribe to have a nurse let him in.

No different than any other hospital room for the last three centuries, the stuffy room smelled of alcohol and bleach. The cramped space held only a single horribly uncomfortable bed and two equally uncomfortable straight back chairs in sickly green. Odd instruments clung to the off-white walls like lichen adorning an undersea rock. Her standard hospital issue blue gown could've been on any patient all the way back to antiquity. It split down the back and barely covered the hip nearest him. A small plastic tube from the wall dumped oxygen right into her nostrils.

She held all the changes of his life together like a keystone. Save a life, lose your own. Some dark, twisted force seemed to have manipulated that equity around to apply to his life. While probability played a cruel role, he felt more at work than mere fate.

He sat quietly, barely moving. His own breathing matched in rhythm to that of the old woman in the bed. A nurse came in to take blood pressure and temperature readings as if she didn't trust their remote monitors. Tony slipped the nurse another hundred for good measure. A dull ache behind his eyes pulled at his thoughts, but none coalesced.

Some time later, before the sun lightened the sky enough to call it morning, the patient's eyes flickered open. Groggily, the woman looked over at Tony as the sleep fled from her eyes. "Do I know you?" Even as she said it, her expression started in realization. The volume of her voice matched the early morning hour. "You're from the bus! They said you saved my life."

"I just did what my grandfather taught me."

"I could sue you for malpractice, you know. I've had five lawyers a day in here trying to get me to do just that."

Tony sat silently. He had nothing to offer.

Her eyes softened. "I have absolutely no intention of doing so. I just want to know why you risked yourself. No one else would have."

"Maybe that's why. There are too many 'no ones' in this world and not enough 'some ones.' I wanted to make mine count."

"You are a very odd man."

"I've never considered myself all that odd."

"Well, perhaps unusual would be a better descriptive."

Tony looked into her wizened face. It held only honesty. Wrinkles and age-spotted hands showed her veins beneath the thinned skin. He realized he'd never really seen an old person. Oh, they were around, but he'd never really looked. They just blended into the background.

"I guess you could call me unusual," he admitted. "Is this bad?"

"No, not at all. The world needs unusual people." She sighed for a moment before continuing. "Please don't take this the wrong way, but did you know I'm going to die anyway?"

Tony instantly saw the futility of his sacrifice in a blinding flash.

"Of course you didn't know. How could you? I have a rare disease in my liver and I'll be dead within the week. I can feel it pulling at me now, deep inside."

This interview had played itself out in Tony's head much differently on his way here. He must regain control. He needed to look into her eyes as he asked his question. Tony felt that he'd know if she were telling the truth. On this one thing he must be positive.

"Do you know why they're doing this to me?"

"Doing what?" Nothing but surprise wrinkled her face. "I don't understand."

"You don't know. It's all coincidence." Tony's shoulders slumped and he turned away.

"I don't understand."

Tony decided to spare the woman the grief he held like a poison within him. "It's nothing," he said, turning back with a smile on his face. They sat quietly looking at one another for a few moments.

"I am happy to have met you, sir. It is rare to find someone so...sure of himself."

"I'm not all that sure."

"You are. You just don't see it from the outside. You see only your own insecurities, your own problems, your own 'if onlys.' The face you project to the world is much stronger."

"I wish I could see that sometimes."

"You will in time. Take it from someone who's been there and back." The woman could see the doubt on his face. "Trust. I see the world hasn't yet beaten it from you. I will trust you so that you can trust me. Did you pick up my parcel?"

Tony suddenly stretched higher in his chair. He'd almost forgotten that the kitten had been hers.

"I see that you did. I give it to you as a gift of the love you showed me. Just care for it as much as you did me."

A tear formed in the corner of Tony's eye. "But I'm going to lose it all. I'll have no way to care for myself, much less..." Tony trailed off because of the monitors that surely recorded all that went on in the room.

So like his own mother, this old woman drew him out and soon Tony told his entire story. She listened, without surprise, as the tale unfolded. With remarkable strength and speed, she grabbed one of his hands and pulled it beneath the covers. Her skin felt rough against his. Something pressed across the palm of his hand as she began speaking in loud, agitated tones.

"You're a criminal! Get out of here! How could I have been talking to such a louse? No, lower than a louse. NURSE! Get this vermin out of here!" She released his hand gently and with her eyes, much softer than the tone in her voice, she gestured for him to the door. She smiled brightly at him for all of two seconds until the orderly entered.

Tony's mind whirled with all the incongruities. It took several milliseconds for realization to dawn.

"Get this filth out of here!" she screamed, coughing heavily. "He's a cat lover and probably grows his own vegetables!"

"Sir, if you'll please step this way," the bribed nurse said, softly. "We can't have our patients disturbed."

"I understand. I don't want anyone upset. I'll leave. My apologies, ma'am." She turned away from him as he left.

He waited until he fully exited the hospital before looking at his hand. Written there, in ink, he found, "GAM, Sonya, ground level, Arcade Aerobics."

Realization dawned at its own pace. He glanced up in the direction of his benefactress's room and shook his head slowly back and forth. She had offered no name and asked him no name in return.

* * *

A servant, dressed in traditional coat and tails, rang a tiny silver bell and entered the Mars room. Conversation ceased as he silently marched the length of the room to the heart-stirring beat of "Ride of the Valkyries." There he delivered a tiny slip of handmade paper to his master and exited in the same manner as he had entered. Nanogate very deliberately opened and read the note.

"A tiny interruption if you please. I believe we have a break. In the GAM project, our subject has made contact.

"Unfortunately, the primary contact, an old woman in the hospital, has died before we could question her. The subject disappeared from his usual haunts shortly after his interview with her."

Cautious smiles accompanied his next statement. "Phase two appears to be complete."

Implement — Phase Three

The remains of asphalt streets, obsolete with the advent of lift vehicles, now only served as potholed walkways. The usual overcrowded throngs that populated them during the day had retreated long ago to the relative safety of their homes or hovels. A myriad of colorful characters took their place. An undocumented body mechanic glanced hopefully in Tony's direction, but just as quickly looked back to his portable lab, working on something that looked vaguely like a human leg in vermilion. A not-so-proficient pickpocket accosted Tony. "Lay off, weeble," Tony said, backhanding the young boy who grabbed him in the crotch to distract him. The youth staggered briefly before fleeing the scene, his middle finger extended above his head in a universal gesture.

Half a dozen burns gathered together in a doorway halfway down the street, laughing quietly at nothing much. A ubiquitous ground-level drunk heaved his lunch into the alley, prompting half a dozen rats to scurry out and partake of the unexpected bounty.

"What am I doing here?" Tony asked himself outside an establishment whose ancient neon lights declared it "-rcade Aerobics," the first "A" conspicuously dark. Further down the street, two junkies pummeled a normal-looking citizen with a meter and a half length of corroded pipe and size fourteen boots.

"Good place to be chewed up and spit out." Tony took a deep breath and marched across the street. Without hesitation he opened the door that might alter his wrecked life even further.

A low-resolution recording of surf sounds and beach birds matched the dust-covered plastic palm trees which nominally shaded the foyer. Fake coconuts littered a heap of sand against a grainy solido of a stylized

Pacific Ocean. Broken scan lines in the bad representation added electronic gibberish horizontally. In a merchant stand ostensibly made of grass and bamboo, a fit young woman bearing a Star of David tattooed on her bald head didn't quite ignore him.

"May I help you?"

"I'm looking for Sonya."

"Reeeeally, corpie," she said, drawing it out almost in an insult.

"Ex-corpie, actually."

"Suit yourself. You wanna sign up for Advanced Pilates?"

"Uh, sure."

The young woman laughed without smiling. "You couldn't even do the elephant," she added, smirking at him.

"I guess I'll show my ignorance about the topic, because I have to assume you aren't talking about having sexual relations with extinct African beasts."

Once again she offered a mirthless laugh. "No. So I've now ruled out that you want Pilates. What do you really want, corpie?"

"I told you, I'm looking for Sonya. Someone said I could find her here."

"Look, I don't have time for anyone that doesn't want to enroll in classes or become a member of the gym. There ain't no Sonya working here."

"What if I were to give you a hundred greens." Mentally he hoped he had the money on him. He didn't think she'd take a credit chip. His worry dissipated almost instantly.

"Get nilled, Metro."

"I'm not a cop, *pizda*."

"Sure you ain't. Even if you were, I don't nark out anyone. Besides, I don't know no Sonya." The young woman's eyes lost focus in the age-old look of someone concentrating on her neural interface rather than the here and now. A square-jawed face strutted in to the reception area clad only in a thong, bristling with more muscle than a prize fighter. The bulky man nodded as he strode behind the shack and through a door that magically buzzed just before he touched it.

Without missing a beat, Tony reached for his wallet. "I'd like to join the gym. Can I have a tour?" Her eyes lost the glazed-over look and got hungry. "I'll even put down a deposit."

"Nonrefundable."

"Of course. Will sixty do it?"

"One hundred." The five plastic bills Tony found in his pocket evaporated like a teaspoon full of water on the sunny side of Mercury. Tony turned and pushed the door the young woman absently pointed toward, just as it buzzed to let him in.

In marked contrast to the facility's scummy lobby and ground-level location, a surprising panoply of shining, high-tech bio-mechanical exercise equipment greeted Tony in the basketball-court-sized floor space. After his bold move to get into the gym, Tony looked around, drawing a blank as only four people occupied the exercise area and none of them really fit his mental picture of a Sonya.

The square-jawed face stood in front of a free weight stand, buckling a wide Kevlar belt around his middle. As Tony entered, the square jaw smiled enough to show a mouthful of sharp, pointed teeth that belonged in the maw of a shark rather than a human.

Three dissimilar individuals clustered around a juice-steroid bar chatting among themselves. An exotic young woman, who looked like something out of a combination mercenary/porn rag, would draw anyone's eyes. Her legs bulged thirty centimeters thick of gem-like green polymer. In place of her arms waved a pair of tentacles of the same material, flexing in multiple directions. Twisted emerald tiles overlapped on her buxom torso, giving her a sensual, reptilian look. Only her head seemed human, sporting short red and orange hair like overlapping waves of fire.

Next to her a dwarf, genetically engineered for subterranean mining operations, squatted on a stool, his copper-colored skin contrasting with the verdant young woman beside him. The bartender, outwardly unmodified, wore an apron stained in purple and crimson. He leaned against the semicircular countertop and absently wiped in an oval pattern.

Tony drifted over to square jaw. "I'm curious, do you know a Sonya?"

"*No hablo ingles. ¿Hablas espanol?*"

Tony dug into his high-school Spanish to communicate. "*¿Conoces a Sonya?*"

"No."

"*Gracias.*" Having gone well beyond his Spanish language capabilities already, Tony passed on further conversation with the large man and moved over to the juice bar.

"Drinks and drugs are listed above," offered the man behind the bar as Tony sat on the stool. "We don't have a medical license, so all drugs are oral."

"Do you know Sonya?"

"Don' know no Sonya," offered the green woman in a high-pitched voice with a smooth lisp. In spite of its sharpness, her voice caressed a deep spot within his loins. She never looked in Tony's direction, but this didn't stop him from wondering. When he regained a modicum of control, he went on.

"Thank you, miss. Do either of you other two know her?"

"Nope. Don't know any Sonya," offered the short, leathery-skinned man. "What about you, Linc?" he directed to the server. Linc just shook his mostly bald head from side to side.

Tony looked up and read the menu. "I'll have a raspberry and lemongrass smoothie. Might as well have something to tide me over while I wait."

"Wha' you wai'n for?" yelled the green woman over the sound of the blender. Even at this volume, and despite its desperately high pitch, her voice once again brushed a longing within him. He coughed.

"Someone sent me to see Sonya, here at this gym. I've been given to believe she's a regular. I'll have to hang around until I find her."

"Good luck, friend," came the deep voice of the dwarf as he hopped from his stool. "I'm outta here, Linc." The green woman stood with him.

"Don't dig up any bones, Carl. Suet, keep those tentacles to yourself," the bartender said, putting a pink drink down. Tony dropped a bill on the counter. "No charge for members."

"Oh, yeah," Tony mumbled as he picked up the drink. "That's just a tip."

"Well, thank you, sir!"

Tony's eyes swayed in time with the hips of the green-skinned woman. Absently, the drink went to his lips. Grimacing, he tore his eyes to look down at the grainy pink drink. "Blech."

Over the next six hours Tony sipped as many different drinks between asking his question to everyone who entered. Tony found no success as the night wore on, either in finding the woman Sonya or a palatable liquid. In fact, one concoction of orange, shitake and ginkgo with the dubious moniker "Remember Rise" specifically drew his ire.

Hours dragged by. He entertained himself watching some of the fittest of the female members as they came and went. He even went so far as to try some of the equipment, only to discover how ill-suited he was to the surroundings. Apparently he'd experienced plenty of muscle atrophy since his football days. By four in the morning he finally threw in the towel.

"I guess this was a snipe hunt, then," Tony muttered to himself.

"A what?" the bartender named Linc asked from across the bar.

"A snipe hunt," he repeated. "A snipe was a mythical bird that people in the twentieth century would send others to find."

"If they were mythical, how did you find them?"

"That's the point of the exercise—to make people look foolish."

"Well, it worked. You look pretty flarking foolish, all right."

A tiny suspicion rose in Tony's mind. "I guess it is time for some sleep." In the mirror on the opposite side of the room, Tony watched carefully as he turned to walk out the door. The bartender's cosmetically enhanced blue eyes followed his movements, confirming his hunch. This place held his answer. Linc knew Sonya. Tony knew he must return. He needed to think of something to get either Linc's or Sonya's attention.

Tony stepped out of the gym into Portland's perpetual drizzle. He stopped to let his eyes readjust to the night's darkness. A gang of girls, each bearing multiple militant body enhancements of one form or another, sauntered down the middle of the pockmarked street like they owned it. As things stood on street level, they probably did own this patch of ground.

Tony decided he'd come back tomorrow and formally join the gym. If he didn't stir anything up that way, he could always trail that Linc fellow. The decision made, he relaxed—a little too much. The largest mistake anyone could make in any world, especially ground level, involved not paying attention. Usually the payment involved a painful death.

"I hope Cin made it through the day," he mumbled to himself. "I didn't mean to be gone so—"

The world suddenly painted itself a parody of even Salvador Dali as a solid wall melted into a twisted pretzel, two of the girls melded into one distorted figure with two heads and six limbs, and the earth beneath him rolled like an ocean wave. Even his body joined the insanity as it wavered and slumped upon the wet pavement like a jellyfish taken from the ocean and dropped upon a rock.

Another shape grew out of the pavement, a giant green octopus with the head of a woman. Sometimes it waved two tentacles and other times eight. Tony couldn't seem to care one way or the other. Drool rolled out of the corner of his mouth. "P'eas feed m'cat."

* * *

Tony struggled to consciousness to the gritty strains of a classic oldie, "Persian Slide" by the Violent Slugs. A conversation took place just outside his understanding. Tony's scrambled thoughts sorted out three distinct voices but couldn't yet drag coherence of the words, or even a desire to interpret. No part of his body responded to his commands. His arms, legs, and other pieces he hadn't yet identified as his own tingled like a thousand ants gnawing on each exposed surface. By forcing dominion over his rebellious body he managed the Herculean task of opening his eyes.

Even though only a single low wattage bulb brightened the room, the ants stabbed daggers into his eyes. Squinting, Tony found himself stacked behind boxes proclaimed Smirnov Vodka, Seagram's Gin and Jack Daniels, mixed with kegs of miscellaneous beer. One portion of his mind wondered at the immense value if the boxes contained what they advertised. The illegal alcohol in those containers could allow anyone to retire with lifetime full medical in their choice of luxury resorts.

A new sharp pain, announcing itself in his wrists, brought the tenuous thing he called attention back to his predicament. Twisting his head around, he found golden tanglewire wrapped around his arms and legs. A certain trivial part of his brain shouted that amateurs tied his bonds. Everyone knew from solido that you either did two opposite figure eights, or you went around and around with a cinch wire between the limbs.

"Who's he?" said a familiar high, velvety feminine voice.

"Who gives a rat's testicle, Suet? He's a corpie and wants Sonya. Vape him," offered a male voice.

"Ya hear' him ask abou' his ca'? Maybe he's 'ooking for her 'o fix his purry?"

"Probably a Metro trick. Maybe they figured out that she fixes pets."

Quietly, Tony commanded his mutinous body to squirm to a point where he could view his captors. The balding juice mixer still wore his stained apron.

"It's 'veterinarian,' Carl," offered the bartender.

"Veteran or fixer, don't make no difference to me. This feek needs to be buried," offered the dark-colored dwarf.

"He don't seem like a bad Joe, even if he is a corpie. He don't cause no trouble. He even talk to the Nils."

"We cou' crash his f'at n'see if he's go' a furry," said the green woman.

"Not a bad suggestion, Suet. When we're done here, I want you to check it."

"We ain't gonna let him speak to Sonya?"

"You know how she is," the green woman identified as Suet said without a single lisp for a change.

"Yeah, you don't screen her and she'll turn you into a lizard instead," Carl mentioned, pulling a monofilament blade from his proportionally small pocket. "Linc, I say we screen her and let her give me the order to whack him and shove him into the sewer."

"Already did. Instead of killing him, she wants to meet him in person."

"What?!"

"Wacky biach. Why ya no' make her screen him?"

"Do I look stupid? I mentioned that possibility, but she insisted. I told her she was crazy. You know Sonya."

"Only thing I know about her hollowed-out head is she slug-thinks sometimes."

"How soon before the drug wears off?"

"No' sure. I jus' gave him everything. No' know his me'abolism."

"Ain't no matter."

"True. Let's strip and scan him," Linc the bartender commanded.

"If'n he go' even a finger nail file you may jus' haffa 'ell Sonya he go' an acci'en'."

Tony let his body slump back to the floor, a much more natural state considering the tingling across most of his muscles. The rasping of Suet's monochromic tentacles against his skin a few moments later nearly broke his façade. The mechanical arms made short work of his clothing without the niceties of unfastening them. Despite the rush of air against his bare skin, Tony remained still.

"Scan's 'one. He's got an ancien' min' jack and a mech han' with a three go gauss gun with very shor' range. A self 'efense gun, but 'ook the ammo. He wasn' aim'n for Sonya with tha'."

"He coulda if he got her close enough to use it. I still say vape him."

"We see," said the female voice as Tony felt the tentacles around his throat. Certainly those green monstrosities could snap his neck as easily as a pretzel. Instead he felt another tentacle around his waist. They lifted him and almost as quickly dropped him a meter or so to collapse in the bottom of some container. Even through his closed eyes he could see the frail light being stolen away. Opening his eyes didn't change his visual information input—darkness. A cursory touch examination defined his cage well enough—a cylindrical plastisteel shipping container, usually used for carrying liquids. Muffled, the conversation continued on outside. He caught the meaning even if he missed every fifth word or so.

"Suet and I will take this one with us. You check his apartment and then call us. I'll drive us around for two hours. That should give you enough time. If there's no cat then this one will fall out of the air truck. Sonya can punish me if she wants, but we're going to keep her safe."

"Agreed."

After a rough loading onto a vehicle, Tony searched with his bound hands, rubbing over the entirety of the interior. He felt nothing but smooth surface with no purchase, no weak point, no opening, and nothing to use as a tool or weapon. He leaned back and sensed the truck's motion, but the ride flowed so smoothly he often couldn't tell if they moved or not, much less the direction.

With his options exactly zero, he followed the advice his grandfather once gave him. "Tony, if you ever find yourself in a position that you can't do anything...sleep."

* * *

"Wake up in there. There's no way the drug we slipped you lasted five hours." Tony recognized the juice-tender's voice—Linc.

"I'm awake," Tony muttered groggily. "Why do you want me awake if you aren't going to let me out?"

"There's someone here that..."

A low and pleasantly feminine voice interrupted. "Let him out."

"But you're too important—"

"Let him out," she said in a calm but firm voice. Quickly the barrel upended, dumping him none too gently onto a carpeted floor that smelled of urine. "But that other one. He's a bounty hunter. We are well shut of him."

"Hey, I'm not a bounty hunter," Tony heard muffled from another barrel identical to his own. "You can trust me. I can prove—"

The bark of some high-tech weapon sounded, followed by silence. Tony tried not to think what that meant, but his mind fantasized a suitably terrifying outcome in spite of itself. At that moment Tony decided his nakedness would be fine until they decided he should have something to wear.

"Thank you, I think," Tony said finally. He put his feet beneath him, but decided that sitting on the floor he posed a lesser threat. While others stood closely behind him, Tony only had eyes for an extremely tall, gaunt woman who decided on only half a hairstyle, the other side of her head bare of anything but undecipherable glyphs. She wore a simple, white linen dress that didn't disguise the tattoos covering the majority of her body. He wouldn't have given her a second look if he'd bumped into her on the TriMet, but here she unconsciously demanded attention.

Tony found his body and mind reacting in unexpected ways.

"Welcome, Tony. I'll be blunt and hope you will be as well. I so dislike wasting time." Each Hispanic-accented word rolled off her tongue as if precisely cut by a laser. Tony managed to close his mouth and nod. "Good. I'd offer you some clothes, but no matter the outcome, you won't be here long enough to offend anyone's dignity."

"Why am I here?"

The woman with skin the color of well-polished oak looked at him with the contempt one reserved for someone who'd passed gas in the confines of the TriMet. "Why don't you tell me that?"

"I was told I could find Sonya at the Arcade Aerobics. As they talked about you while I was trussed up and nominally asleep, I'll assume that you're Sonya."

"One must guess and guess correctly in life to survive," she said cryptically. "You have exactly one minute to tell me why you wanted to speak to Sonya. If I'm not convinced, you'll not only not be allowed to speak to her, you can join that bad rubbish over there—or worse, we might just bury you alive."

"I have to say that normally I'd be afraid of such talk. I probably would've even been offended by such outright threats, but this hasn't been an ordinary few days. To be honest, that seems like the sweetest thing anyone's said to me. OK. You said be blunt, so I will. In brief, I want to join the Green Action Militia."

He ignored the chuckles. Every instinct screamed that he must convince the woman in front of him, not the clowns behind him.

"Why should we trust you? What reason do we have to trust you?"

Honesty before deceit, Tony thought. "You shouldn't, and you have none. I could give you a song and dance about the crap thrown at me over the last two days, but it could just be another corpie setup to try and trap—"

"We have to move," said a voice behind him. "If he's bugged, your time is up. They'll be onto the Faraday cage gimmick if they're quick."

"I must say you haven't given me much, corpie. I won't lie. My inclination is to have you disappear."

"Don' be quick," came the dangerously silky voice of the green-gemmed girl. "He has a furry." Sitting on her left tentacle rode Cin bearing all the dignity of the Egyptian cat goddess, Bast.

"Cin!" Tony exclaimed. The brightly colored cat jumped down and marched properly over to her person. She brushed up against Tony with an air of ownership before examining the rest of the room's occupants.

The tattooed woman bent down to offered her finger to Cin. The calico sniffed it daintily and gave it a gentle lick before returning to grooming her reddish coat. "A very handsome creature."

"Thank you."

"You can leave us now," she off-handedly commanded the other three, not taking her eyes off the tiny bather.

"But Sonya, if he or the cat is bugged…"

"We'll move shortly. The cage should buy us at least a few minutes. Leave us!"

"Yes, Sonya," Linc offered meekly, gathering Carl and Suet by eye before drifting out through a door. Tony caught tiny noises just outside the door, placing her three compatriots with the accuracy of a life detector. Sonya flowed as if boneless down into a lotus position on the floor next to the tiny kitten. Her fingers played over the cat's spine, eliciting closed eyes and deep rumblings.

"I don't think we've been properly introduced. My name is Sonya."

"Uh, Tony. Tony Sammis."

"What can I do for you?" Sonya asked with a voice that combined the innocence of a child and the world weariness of a veteran of several wars. She gently stroked Cinnamon.

"Funny, now that I'm here, I'm not sure." Tony looked at Sonya for some sign. She never took her eyes off his cat. "I guess I'd say my life is over and I'm looking for a new one. An acquaintance gave me this." Tony held up his hand to show the writing across his hand by a dying woman. This drew Sonya's eyes.

"Jasmine's handwriting. She has the sight of people. I've never known her to be hasty or wrong in her judgment."

"I can't speak to that. You knew she was dying?"

"Dead, now. She died six hours ago. And yes, I knew. Her liver burned under the weight of a corporate poison. As an employee, they used her as an experimental animal without her consent. Once she learned of this, she used the fire and death in her belly against the corporate machine."

"Sounds like what happened to me. I'm not exactly waiting to die, but they've taken everything from me. My chance of fighting what they've done is effectively zero. I have no job prospects above garbage sorter. I haven't the skills nor enough cash to out-migrate. I might have to live on welfare and live in a commune or worse, a relocation camp, or even worse on ground level. No health care and recycled food to eat." Tony shuddered.

Sonya gently shook her head. "Superficial reasons to join us terrorists, or as we style ourselves, freedom fighters. You should out-migrate or get another job."

Tony sighed. "It's not just that. I'll be honest. I used to be everything you despised. I followed all the lines. 'Get it while the getting is good.' 'Do unto others before they do unto you.' 'He did what everyone else did, he just got caught.' 'If I'm quiet, maybe they won't notice what I'm doing.' All the signs of the times. They were my watchwords. They aren't what I believe in anymore."

Sitting up, Tony pressed home his point. "I don't like any of my choices if for no other reason than I don't want my old life back. For quite a long time now I've believed that something was wrong with my life, or maybe the lives of everyone everywhere. Someone once said, 'Might for right!' For some reason it lit a fire in my heart that's only just now starting to burn with a fury."

"King Arthur, I believe, Mr. Sammis."

"Uh, yeah."

"Any start is a good start, but tell me, how would you use the fire in your heart? Don't answer, just think.

"Come back now, Linc," she said with no increase in volume. The threesome appeared quickly enough to assure Tony they'd been listening. "We must process him quickly. Also, send an emergency communiqué through the cells that the health club is compromised.

"Until I see you again, Mr. Sammis," she concluded, taking his hand in hers. Despite her warmth of personality, her hands felt like unpowered prosthetics. She shook his hand firmly and turned to leave at an unhurried speed.

Linc directed Tony through another door that led to a loading dock, shrouded to the outside by curtains of stained plastic sheets. The back of a closed truck stood open and as one they hustled inside. Tony almost backed out, as the rear section held a hanging cage of metal straps in the shape of a human body, plus a rack full of cattle-prods and other less savory devices with sharp edges. The trio closed off his one escape route by pulling the door down. Without a beat the truck pulled away from the loading dock.

"In here," Linc said, motioning him toward the cage.

"Uh, why?" Tony balked.

"Noobs. Did you ever think your implants might just do more than they tell you? We have to neutralize them before you give all of us away."

"Uhhh…" Tony continued to hesitate.

"Freaking corpie, either get in or we boot your ass out the back of the truck, and you can find out what happens when you fall two hundred meters to ground level. I don't know what'll get you first, the Nils or the bugs."

Tony eyed a cage that curved just where a person curves and wore a wig of wires dangling from strategic points. The wire-hair twisted down into a single braid that disappeared into the back of a moderate computer array.

"Will it hurt?"

"Depends on what they got inside you," Linc said, "but don't worry, we'll patch you up better than new. Now get in the bleeding cage!" He motioned with a gun for emphasis.

By wedging his arms down to his side, Tony could just squeeze into the contraption. Linc brought the cage door around, closing him in tight. The latch didn't have a lock, but was situated well away from Tony's hands.

As the cage faced the wrong way, he couldn't see anything except a wall with dubious stains and markings.

"Everyone clear. Fire one!" Linc cried out. A very mild electric shock wandered across Tony's body, feeling more like a tickle than anything painful. "I have three implants. Start with the scalp." Some metal device poked into his hair, scratching his scalp above his right ear. "Seven centimeters back and two down." The probe moved accordingly. "Right there. Clear! Fire two!"

Expecting the tickle once again, Tony remained calm. Instead, his brain revolted at a sensation like acid filling his skull. His body convulsed uncontrollably within the constraining chamber. He must've blacked out because next thing he knew he only felt something wet and viscous slowly dripping down both of his cheeks. One of the wet trails fell into his mouth and he tasted the salt of his own tears. He felt nothing else at all. No sensation of limb or self.

"Help," he barely managed to croak out.

"Shut up," Linc snapped.

"Next. Right shoulder, front." This time he saw the probe as Suet positioned a 2 meter-long pike with a blunted metal tip against his flesh, bracing it on the floor. "Six centimeters down. Perfect. Clear! Fire three!" The shoulder he couldn't feel now flew into a rage of hot, stabbing pains. With force he didn't know he had, his arm tried to break free of the cage. Tony experienced, not quite heard, the sound of his humerus breaking beneath his bicep. The agony muted the other pains spread through his body. The cry he let out wasn't conscious.

"Left wrist." Tears rolled freely as he watched the sharp pole move down to the other side. Tony could barely feel it press against the flesh. "Good enough. Clear! Fire four!" Unlike the pain from the previous two attempts, his hand went completely numb from mid-forearm down. "No reaction. Increasing charge. Fire five!" Again, Tony thankfully felt nothing.

"OK, it's gotta come off. All of it."

Tony took one look at the saws-all in Carl's thick hands and fainted.

* * *

With only one door and no windows in the cell, Tony paced around the eight-by-eight cell in boredom. He once again touched his new hand just to reassure himself it still existed. He never missed the old one, and the new one seemed identical in every way. He'd lost consciousness before its removal and awoke after its replacement. No discomfort from either shoulder or head lingered. Linc had been as good as his word.

"Hey! I didn't agree to go through all this just to be locked up," he shouted at the door. When no one offered him even a word he plopped onto the only piece of furniture in the room, a fabric-covered metal bunk bolted to the floor. "How long are you going to keep me in here?" he questioned the silent walls for the eightieth time. He would've done more than yell, but he found banging on the plastisteel brought only a bruised palm. "I want my cat back!"

He'd awakened in this room some unknown amount of time after his trucking ordeal. Since then, eight institutional-style meals had appeared through a slot in the door. At least they'd given him some clothes, even if he did look like a deliveryman in a utilitarian green jumpsuit. "I guess we didn't have a meeting of the minds after all," Tony muttered. For about the four hundredth time he went over it again. "OK. Reasons they might keep me: security, my intentions, a show of faith."

"Not a bad deduction," said a muffled voice from the other side of the door. Old fashioned keys rattled in the lock. "Actually, we waited only to include you in the mission we have planned." Linc's bald head popped through the door. From the look of the stains on his orange smock, he looked like he'd just left work, but obviously not at the same health club if the embroidery "Sunrise Athletics" were any indication.

"OK. What are we going to do?"

"Not we, Mr. Sammis, you."

"Me? Why me?"

"Look, if I had my way, corpie, you'd already be ground up and sluicing your way down a recycle chute." Tony decided not to react, visibly anyway. "But Sonya has her own mind about these things. She wants to see how dedicated you are. If you succeed, then she may trust you further. If not, well let's just say the police don't take kindly to Greenies."

"I'll ignore the implied threat. With that in mind, what's my mission?"

"You'll find that out shortly. Follow me close, but don't say nothing." Linc's massive paw, fingers stubby but thick, handed him a small penlight.

Linc lead Tony from his dry cell down two flights of stairs and into a twisting maze of mold-covered, masonry passages that oozed moisture. Linc's broad shoulders marked his way through halls covered ankle deep in putrid liquid the consistency of custard. The Greenies clothing proved competent, as the work boots held the fluid at bay. The smells, on the other hand, ranged from bad to worse including at the base of them all the bitter tang of excrement, urine, and *eau de* rotting garbage.

Conduits, steam pipes, and random corroded and broken wiring wove in and about their path. Even had he stooged for the police, he couldn't have found his way back through the spider webs and rusted equipment without an inertial locator. Only his light on Linc's broad back kept him from losing the rest of his way.

Thinking about it, he knew little of the GAM that he could possibly use against them, even if he wanted to. He didn't know whether to feel heartened by this or depressed. Instead, he decided he should just do the job they asked.

He dearly wanted to ask questions, but the first time he heard voices above his head through the ceramcrete ceiling, it muted his desire. He shut off that train of thought and quietly picked his way through the muck, avoiding the worst of the sewage and smells.

For over an hour Linc never slowed. Tony began to wonder if they were lost together when Linc pointed to a nearly rusted-out metal door. "Go in there and you find your instructions," Linc whispered.

"How do I get back?" he softly murmured into Linc's ear.

"All your information is in there. Don't mess up. We'll be watching." Linc turned and sloshed off back through the drains.

Tony watched until he disappeared from sight and then even longer until the light of Linc's torch faded around a distant corner. With a shrug Tony went up to the door and pushed it. Instead of opening, the door fell inward to land with a combined cacophony of metal on stone and a loud splash. Tony froze.

A brief flurry of sound above him startled him, but settled down as quickly as it began.

His torch lit up a small room with a white plastic table high and dry atop a rust-stained ceramic landing. Perched on the table sat the incongruous sight of dozen brightly-colored, floating balloons bearing the proclamation "Get Well Soon" tied to a gaily wrapped package and a vase full of flowers. Next to this absurd group sat a solido tablet and an archaic ring comm, still used as a disposable method for making nearly untraceable calls.

The solido tablet read, "Take the package, flowers and balloons to Mercy Hospital. They are a delivery for Janice Gordon. There is a map through the underground to Mercy in the memory [press here].

"The chemical components of the bomb are inert and thus undetectable until activated by water. You have until the flowers are watered to get away. From a safe place call 555-1215 after it is reported on the net."

"A hospital?" Tony said aloud. Without hesitating he picked up the ring comm. "Five, five, five, one, two, one, five."

In the background of the standard bone conduction he heard a very faint countdown. "One minute to detection. Fifty-seven. Fifty-six…"

"You can't have even gotten there yet."

"It's a hospital with sick people—"

"Don't be a *pizda*! It's an executive hospital for those with full medical," came a harsh male voice. The line went dead to the sound of "Forty-two. Forty-three."

"Can I really do this?" His own words mocked him as they echoed in the underground. "It's a big stretch from thinking things are wrong to killing people." Three times he reached out to collect the deadly delivery and three times he pulled back. He walked deliberately around the table. "At least now the clothes make sense." Tony wiped the sweat from his hands on his pants before picking up the flowers in one hand and the balloon-adorned package in the other.

* * *

"Listen, candy-striper, I've been delivering here for two years and nobody's ever scanned my packages before," Tony barked with as much vinegar as he could muster. The young redhead's pale skin blanched even whiter. Tony wondered if she could possibly be more nervous than the TriMet air-show racing through his stomach.

"I'm sorry, but that's what they told me I was supposed to do."

Tony could only wonder if the GAM used this to get rid of him. He imagined Linc over his shoulder with a remote detonator going for a twofer, getting rid of an interloper and another strike against the megacorps. "Whatever," he replied after a moment, rolling his eyes. "Don't worry about it, sweetie. I just don't wanna be late for my next delivery."

"Thanks. I'm really sorry," she said putting the packages into a huge door in the wall and pushing a large red button.

"So does that hair come with a fire extinguisher?" Tony flirted to cover the shakes in his hands.

"Blarney."

"No, really, you don't see many true redheads these days. Want to get some dinner?"

"No. Sorry, my husband wouldn't approve. I've already got one boyfriend. He wouldn't stand for two."

Tony sighed in relief when the indicator behind her showed green. "Well, can't blame a guy for trying," he covered up. "Maybe next time."

Leaving his package for delivery within the hospital, Tony turned and tried hard not to sprint for the front door. He breathed rapidly, sweat trickling down and soaking into his shirt, but not yet showing through. He got in line for the TriMet. He kept himself from fidgeting only by making false notations on his solido pad. He pushed his way on the first TriMet that showed up to the platform, not caring where it went. The TriMet bus clock above his head counted off the seconds between success and failure. He knew if the bomb went off before he got off the bus, he would be caught. The bus would instantly home to a police holding space.

"Those Spiders sure are coming back," said a man in the seat next to him, gazing off into space where his paper was displayed on his retinas for him alone.

"Huh?"

"The Aussie Spiders?"

"Sorry, I don't follow sports."

"If you say so."

Tony visibly cringed when the TriMet pulled up in front of Portland Metro Police department, only three blocks from the hospital. "Can my luck get any worse," he muttered. Swearing under his breath, he climbed out of the car, one of two people brave enough to do so.

"Audit?" asked the other courageous traveler.

"Naw. I'm here to pick up a delivery," he dissembled uncomfortably.

His eyes darted over the imposing black monolith and the one place he didn't want to be any closer to.

"Oh. Metros say I made a seven figure bonus last year. It wasn't even high six and I have the receipts to prove it."

"Good luck to you. Those police auditors can be vicious."

"Yeah, I know. I've been losing sleep for the last two weeks."

Tony shortened his stride. The lie he offered provided him with the best option. If he turned around and caught another bus, he'd be advertising his guilt. No one changed TriMets at Metro—no one. Whipping out his solido pad, he programmed frantically, finishing just as the audit victim passed through the door, waving in irritation. Tony didn't understand, but had to act as if he'd been everywhere as a courier, as though being here meant nothing in particular. He fearlessly pushed through the whispery nano-curtain, barely feeling the full body scan it performed.

Inside the foyer stood a smiling twenty-meter propaganda solido of a Metro in familiar blue body armor without his helmet. Gentle music, spiked with subliminal messages of respect, floated down. "We keep you and yours safe!" The imposing solido bent down and gave a young girl back her purple teddy bear. The adrenaline running through Tony's system shed the subliminals like rain off a Burberry.

Turning to the right he found a brutally ugly Metro sergeant sitting atop a five-meter-high obsidian desk obviously designed to intimidate anyone who hadn't already been cowed by the display in the immense foyer.

"I'm here for an a-a-audit," the man stammered.

"Show me your chit," the sergeant barked.

"Chit? The m-mail said to show up today or be forfeit."

"You have to have a chit to get back to the auditors."

"You didn't send me a chit!"

"Read the law, civ. It clearly reads that you're required to show up one week before your audit to get a chit. Without it we can't do a background check on you."

"So what do I do now?"

"Not much, civ. Pay the tax and the fine."

"But it's wrong!" he said turning purple with rage.

"Civ, I'm going to give you just one chance to turn around and walk out. If you don't you'll be doing five months harvesting yeast in the Antarctic Sea, and that's after I break all your teeth."

The man blanched and backed away slowly. Tony caught a foul whiff as the man turned and ran out the front door.

"Stupid ghit," Tony said in fake derision, handing his solido pad to the desk sergeant. "I'm here for a pickup from Officer Nguyen."

"Pickups are in the service entrance on the level ten pad."

"Yes, Officer, I understand that's normal, but I was told to report here to pick up something personal, as you can see on the pad." He put as much respect in his tone as he would for the CEO of a major corporation.

"Yeah, I can see. Lee Nguyen is on vacation right now and he didn't leave anything here. You have your databases crossed."

This didn't surprise Tony, as he'd accessed the publicly available Metro files for just such an absentee. "Well, I don't want to anger you, Officer. If you ain't got nothing, you ain't got nothing. I get paid either way. I better check with my office, though." He stepped away from the desk and spoke into his ring. "Triple Five, Eight Thousand."

"Stanford Courier Dispatch."

"Hey, I'm here at Metro…" Tony's luck finally played out. The air in the foyer compressed, stealing his breath. He didn't even hear the explosion.

"What was that?" Sergeant demanded. Tony's heart stuttered in his chest. Three full seconds silently passed before sirens within Metro began to wail.

"This is Dispatch. What do you want?" Tony's ring comm demanded.

"Oh, they say they have no pickup from Nguyen."

"One second…I show no pick-up at Metro or from Nguyen. You must have a damaged pad or downloaded the wrong DB. Please return to base." This also didn't surprise Tony.

"Affirmative." He cut the connection. "I'm sorry, Officer. I seem to have a damaged pad. Can I get that back so I can get it fixed?"

"Here." Frantically coordinating some other action from his net link, the sergeant barely offered him a glance. Tony scooted out the door with a heavy sigh. The audit victim stood quivering at the landing platform.

"Did you hear that?" Tony asked as the TriMet number 6784 pulled up. His fellow traveler didn't say anything, but he had a blank stare and his skin bore a mottled paleness, not to mention the foul whiff coming from his pants. Tony felt he'd be just as happy to get away from this place.

Tony dared a look in the general direction of the Mercy Hospital to see a malignant gray cloud slowly billowing around the skyscrapers of downtown. The thick smoke didn't lose opacity as it expanded out and down. A silence that never existed in any city now cloaked Portland like the sheet pulled over the recently deceased.

Implement — Phase Four

Back in his underground cell, Tony sat with a hangman's noose twisting his guts and Vise Grips on his vocal cords.

"…bomb went off at a particularly bad time as the shift change in an operating room caught nearly twice as many heroic medical workers at their post," said a computer tablet sitting on an old-fashioned maglev table between him and Linc.

"The CEO of Colonization Unlimited, the parent company of Mercy Hospital, insists the perpetrators will be caught and punished." Linc leaned back in his disposable chair with half a grin.

The picture on the solido tablet panned across the blackened chairs, walls torn in half, and a melted desktop. A woman cradled her bloody arm to her chest, ignoring the fact that it no longer connected to the rest of her body. Two small children of indeterminate sex, wrapped tightly in one another's arms, shuffled along through the gray rubble with blank stares on their face.

"This kind of barbarism isn't a form of warfare, but rather large-scale murder. None of these victims carried a gun. None of them threatened anyone." The scene switched to show a morgue, where a row of corpses lay in body bags, and then flipped back to a hospital emergency room, every surface covered in gray dust where people paced or sprawled on the floor, weeping and crying.

A vile taste crept into Tony's mouth. From never having even struck someone, to a multiple murderer in a single stroke. He regretted eating the soup before Linc picked him up. He regretted it even more when he doubled over and the contents of his stomach ejected from his mouth and nose onto the floor.

"In the end, however, it's only a matter of time and resources. We've increased our private security by seventy-five percent." The picture snapped to thousands of Pinkertons in shiny-gray riot gear receiving special weapons and instructions. "We will find them. We will try them. We will execute them."

"To wrap up here, the Green Action Militia has claimed responsibility for a bomb that killed seven and seriously injured twenty-seven in a midmorning bombing of Mercy Hospital. Updates as they arise. This is Cindy Bindle reporting for CNI."

"Thank you, Cindy. We return you to your regular programming currently in progress…"

Tony wiped his mouth on his sleeve as Linc stopped the solido playback.

"Congratulations. One of the best kill counts we've had from such a small device."

* * *

Brown plastic boxes piled at random acted as impromptu chairs and tables for a loudly debating quorum. Linc, Suet, and eleven others, none bearing any resemblance to the next, sprawled amongst the crates in a loose circle. Sonya sat on the floor in a perfect lotus, her simple white cotton dress loose around her.

"So he lai' one farging bomb. Anyone can 'o. I say he's a prob'em."

"He questioned the orders."

"He doesn't know anything about security procedures. Just let him go."

"Yeah, he's a corpie. Corpies can't be trusted."

"Vape him and let's get on with our work."

"How could he possibly have gotten away from the Metros?"

"Yeah, none get away from the peelers unless they are one…"

"Like I said, vape the…"

Sonya's slowly raised hand stopped all of the discussion cold. In a voice barely above a whisper, she said, "Andrea, did you not go to the police when we first met?" The redhead sitting behind Sonya blushed pink all the way down the v in her blouse. Sonya didn't even bother to look up at the people in question but rather stared blankly ahead, letting her comments do all her work for her. "And Linc, didn't you try to blackmail Suet? Jonah, weren't you a Metro when they framed you for murder?"

"That was—"

"And Beth, didn't you try for a corporate bounty on Jackson's head over there? My point is that very few of us started with trust in this organization. Trust must be earned in our business. Mr. Sammis earned his first piece today. And if that isn't enough, he's wanted by the Metros. Even if they didn't post his picture, you know as well as I do that they have him on one of the seventy thousand cameras in that building alone."

"But he can't handle the work. He left his tucker in the cell."

"And Andrew, how long did you retch after you shot Black Charlie?" Andrew squirmed under the full attentions. "How many nights of sleep have each of us lost for some of the horrible things we're forced to do?"

"What do you possibly see in him, Sonya?" Arthur asked.

Sonya looked at a matronly woman with eyes looking like solid silver balls.

"My run on the nets show skills in first aid, explosives, and a stint with corporate security," the elderly woman said, not looking at anyone in particular. "His physical prowess alone likely can be honed. He demonstrated leadership, individuality, and creative abilities in solving problems in his work."

"And, if you haven't forgotten already, he did save Jasmine before any of this happened to him," Beth said with empathy dripping from her voice. "He cares."

"I still say it's too big a risk."

"He has a furry."

"Enough," Sonya interjected before the discussion fed on itself. "How often have I been wrong? How often has a spy crept within our midst? Why do you think we don't use the formality of a straitjacketed cell system? You've all seen that I know about people. Enough of this," Sonya said softly. "It serves no purpose. I've made my decision as our leader. Unless you wish to proceed to a vote of no confidence, let Tony in. He has a right to be heard and give his voice to this council." Sonya looked around confidently. Two of the ten looked like they had more to say but chopped it off, in one case with the look of an obstinate child and the other in resignation.

Tony stumbled over the doorsill and staggered against a box that clattered loudly. Several members snickered.

"Sorry," Tony said pushing the boxes back into place. Sonya stood with a silkiness of movement that belied the bones in her body.

"Welcome, Tony," Sonya offered warmly, extending her hand. "I'm sorry we couldn't have started on a friendlier note. I hope you understand."

Tony's mind whirled as too many changes hit him one after another. "I do," he replied, gently taking her hand. Her palm, callused in an unusual way, still felt exactly like a delicate ice sculpture. Impulse took him and he lifted her hand and gently kissed its back.

"Very cavalier of you, sir," Sonya said only loud enough for Tony to hear. Then, louder, she added, "Let me give you some background.

"I lead our group in something similar to a parliamentary style. Everyone attending has an equal voice in decisions and a simple majority carries. As leader, I can change the decision by executive veto. If I do, the team can bring a vote of no confidence where a two-thirds majority would remove me from leadership."

"How long have you been leader?"

"Since we began action, twelve years ago," she understated.

"Oh." A dramatic pause followed.

"Let me introduce you to the rest of our present team. You know Linc, but you may not know he was a private detective until he made the mistake of taking a domestic abuse case for the wife of a senior Metro officer. He's had a price on Linc's head ever since.

"To his right is Suet, who you also know. At the tender age of seven, a couple of corpie teens on a lark took their limousine through the ground neighborhood, shooting anything that moved with flechette guns, including her Nil parents. She learned quickly how to live on the streets. I'll let her discuss her enhancements when you get a chance to talk to her on your own time."

Tony waved tentatively at the emerald woman, who didn't respond or even glance in his direction.

Turning to her right, Sonya pointed to a slight, swarthy man. "As head ranger of Big Basin National Park, Andrew tried to stop the expansion of the San Francisco development. He put together a team to sabotage the lumber clearing effort. Unfortunately, his number two man was a police mole. Andrew got away only by luck.

"Arthur is the small man to your left. His wife died from a lift car accident because of cost-cutting by megacorp executives. Beth, sitting next to him, was a model until some corporate alchemy went awry."

Tony looked closely, suddenly realizing why she seemed so familiar. Yes! You used to be the Bingo Condom Girl!"

"That was a long time ago," she all but purred.

"Ahem."

"Sorry."

"Now, Jonah, Frances, and Colin were all Metros."

Tony looked at the trio in surprise. He hadn't expected to find ex-Metros in this company.

Sonya smiled briefly and continued. "Jonah, the redhead with the six gazillion freckles, had his partner frame him for murder. Frances and Colin, partners, both tried to be honest cops. You know what happens to those."

"Tolly," Sonya went on, offering a hulking blonde Adonis for his consideration, "came to us as a liaison from another social engineering group down under. Things are no better there, but his group disbanded because of internal dissension.

"Martin wishes us to return as much of Earth back to nature as possible. Some would say he has the purest motives. Many of the rest of us are vengeance motivated.

"Christine, to your left, is one of the unusual ones amongst us." The pretty, unaugmented teen stood less than 150 centimeters tall and massed less than 40 kilos. "Christine is what psychologists call a biological sociopath." Tony scanned Cristine's deadpan face and shuddered. "She enjoys killing and has a talent for assassinations. Her loyalty for the group has been tested and is solid, but don't have sex with her.

"Across from you is Augustine. Tina is our resident icebreaker." Tony saw a woman who, if you removed the wetwire jack from her temple, looked like someone's great grandmother with silver orbs for eyes. "She's on the run from the time she almost got caught breaking into the NaBiCo executive database."

"I only wanted the Oreo recipe," she offered, smiling vacantly.

"Andrea," Sonya went on, pointing at what appeared to be a twelve-year-old girl with the natural flaming-red hair that women would kill to have, "was an exceptional professional thief—"

"I still am."

"My apologies. She *is* a gifted thief, until she accidentally left some DNA behind when she lifted a Norman Rockwell from a corpie bigwig.

"Jackson had the misfortune of being the valet for Goldstein of Goldstein, Hammons, Hammons & Funk fame." Jackson, an older, bookish black man, nodded. "He overheard something he shouldn't have and reported it to the wrong cop. He escaped only by the skin of his teeth.

"Carl can't attend tonight but you've already met him briefly. Carl had the misfortune of being the victim of a he-said-she-said rape case involving the daughter of a very high-level corpie. That's bad enough even if you're a regular slob, worse if you're a genetically engineered dwarf.

"I guess that sums up our action committee. There are many other members, but they aren't part of this executive staff. The less you know about those right now, the better."

"Hello all," Tony said cheerfully. Silence greeted his wave. "May I ask a question?"

"Yes. Now that you've asked it…" Sonya said with a sly grin.

It took Tony just a few moments to realize he was being teased. He smiled back. "If there are support personnel, why did you put me with the action group rather than support?"

"We dug up your background. You know explosives. You know first aid. Both are skills vital to us here on the action side of things."

"Oh, OK." Tony leaned up against a nearby post, trying to look comfortable, but his stiffness betrayed him.

"Shall we get down to business?" asked Sonya, taking her eyes off Tony and glancing around the group. "Before we get to the agenda, let me just say the hospital bombing succeeded beyond our wildest dreams. Our hacks uncovered high level corporate communications on how aggrieved they are at their perceived vulnerability. We need to strike again soon to widen that even further.

"Now, we have two items on the agenda: a new safe house and our next target. Linc."

"Safe house Zulu-Bravo has been set up in the sub-basement of Green's Supermarket. To enter, go into the produce department and through the service doors. Announce that you're from Petri Trucking and go down the stairs to the left. The combination to the door is seventeen left, fourteen right, eighty-eight left, and sixty-nine right. Everyone got that?"

"Seventeen, fourteen, eighty-eight, sixty-nine," Tony muttered.

"And I know you'll all forget it ten minutes from now, so I've created another nano implant. Zulu Bravo." Linc held up his wrist and it glowed with the combination. "It'll only trigger on the safe house name, just like the others. I'll pass around this lick pad. Suet, as usual, yours will show up on your right breast."

"Thanks, Linc. Anyone found a target in their reconnaissance?" Suet handed a notepad to Sonya.

"Sonya says that the Wintel corporate office building is too well guarded and has a state of the art air displacement scanning facility we haven't been able to penetrate yet." Suet nodded.

"We turned up what we thought was a weakness in the OldsTransport sensor net, but it only led to a loading dock. Beyond that, security increased beyond acceptable levels."

"I have a possible," Augustine put in. "My team and I stormed an ice list site. In it I found reference to an upper level management training facility in Ohio."

"That sounds promising," Sonya said.

"I thought it might. We raided their database last night. Tough security. Two of my people got injured, but nothing serious.

"The good news: The site houses anywhere from fifty to one hundred ten high-level managers training to be executives for any number of corporations." A collective gasp went round the room. "The bad news is that it's heavily fortified. The guard force payroll is over a thousand, and we found records for some heavy duty firepower, including monoflyers, SCAP turrets, and much more." Another more dejected sound went through the group. "It's going to take all of us to make this one work, and probably not without a huge cost."

"Could it be a trap?" Colin asked.

"Doubtful. We hacked some serious ice. I've had easier runs into dedicated corp mainframes."

Sonya looked about the room. "This is almost too good to pass up. Any objections?" The room fell silent. "Let's move on that, then. Colin, you're chief of this op. My only requirement is that you include Tony. He must be part of our team."

"As you will, Sonya." Colin's brunette curls bounced lightly as he turned to look at Tony. The steel gray eyes gave no indication of what went on behind them.

"Is there any new business? Yes, Andrew."

"We're low on explosives. Frances and I have been working out a plan for a raid on the Hillsboro Metro sub-depot—it has the least security. But that having been said, no plan has shown even a moderate chance of success."

Tony stuck his hand up.

"Yes, Tony. This isn't school—you may speak without raising your hand."

Tony smiled. "Why raid a building when we can have them FedExed to us?"

Everyone exploded almost simultaneously.

"Wha' ya chomping at?"

"Nonsense. No one ships explosives, it's too hazardous!"

"Should we just call them up and request them?"

"Why don't we just invite the Metros to our executive meetings?"

"HOLD!" Sonya's voice cut through the mass of hubbub with the power of a chainsaw. "Let him speak."

"I wasn't kidding. It's actually shipped in special protective containers. When I worked for Down Put, we used to order our demolition explosives—up to a quarter kilo—and have it shipped overnight, sometimes even couriered."

"So how in the farg we gonna ge' them to ship 'o us?"

"We have an ice jockey, don't we? It shouldn't be hard at all. We just ship to fictitious demolition companies we inject into their own databases. We use random addresses and make sure we're there for the pickups. Tenth kilo here, quarter kilo there, fifth kilo elsewhere, and pretty soon you have enough to blow this city off the map."

Sonya smiled at him.

* * *

"I'm making this report to keep you apprised of the development of phase four," Nanogate reported quietly to a recording device in his private office, this one decorated in wood and warm earth tones. A real polar bear rug lay at the hearth of a slate fireplace that crackled merrily. The fire was real, but the wood wasn't.

"The subject was positively identified as the perpetrator of the Mercy Hospital bombing, and an audacious bit of improvisation at the Portland Metro Precinct. The simulations show a near unity chance he's now ensconced within the ranks of the Green Action Militia. The odds that the GAM killed him, or he committed these acts on his own, are each on the order of one part in ten thousand.

"As a result, we should anticipate an increased tempo of GAM operations with increasing effectiveness. Projections now indicate a fifteen percent increase in losses, plus or minus three percent, before the weapon begins culling the membership.

"This is a full five percent higher than the original projections. However, we didn't anticipate just how effective this perfect weapon would be."

Nanogate paused the recording and pressed one of his call buttons. A meticulously dressed butler entered the office space. "You sent for me, sir?"

"Yes, Williams. In five minutes I'd like you to send in the natural redhead I purchased in Cairo."

"Very good, sir. Should she be attired as usual?"

"No. I don't feel like being bothered tonight. Nude will be fine."

"Yes, sir. Will there be anything else?"

"No. Please make the arrangements." Nanogate waited until his servant closed the door behind him before resuming the recording.

"In spite of the higher than anticipated losses, the project is proceeding down the most likely course to fulfill our desired end result.

"Signed, CEO Nanogate."

As he shut off the recorder, the door opened almost as if on cue. A young girl edged in, just old enough to have spouted pubic hair and the barest roundness of breast, shaking and as unsteady as a newborn fawn, and wearing less.

"Come over here to the fire, dear. You should be comfortable."

* * *

A sound like sheet metal being ripped in two reverberated through the abandoned basement. Mold and other less savory materials clung to all but one of the graffiti-covered walls.

"At least aim in the general direction of the target!" Jonah barked through Tony's ear protectors. "How can you possibly be able to take down muggers with your finger and not even touch a target twice the size of a man at 20 meters with a gauss gun?" Jonah pointed off toward the wall with the big red target. A trio of 30 centimeter circles of scoured clean ceramcrete, 3 meters to the left of the target and not a single one within a meter of the other two, marked Tony's shots.

"I think it's because they were always within a meter and I never had to aim," Tony said sheepishly. At least none of the other GAM members witnessed his lackluster marksmanship. "Just get my finger in the general direction and it blew a hole large enough to never have to worry about aiming."

"Holy…" Tony watched Jonah's freckled face go nearly as red as his hair. "I thought you'd be proficient with the gauss. I've had raw recruits that never held a gun before do better than that."

"Sorry, but I wasn't even good with first-person shooter hologames."

The redness in Jonah's face actually increased to a dark maroon. Jonah opened his mouth to say something but closed it unsaid. In fact, he didn't say a word, but wandered around in circles ignoring Tony for the better part of five minutes.

"OK. We don't have time to train you from scratch here." He checked his watch. "The blue bellies could be here as quickly as ten more minutes.

We'll have to put you in the simulator for the basics. And we don't have the time for even much of that before the op.

"Just for the record, what are you good at?"

* * *

Lightning backlit the floating fortress like a photo negative. Sonya realized they'd picked an exceptional night for their work. Rain poured down from the Ohio sky like some angry water god revisiting a flood upon the earth. The torrents of October rain, barely above freezing itself, scoured through the light dusting of snow, making the earth dark. Floating 10 meters above the ground, the fortress protected a 60 meter triangle of white crystals from the deluge.

Another bright flash in the sky preceded four almost simultaneous crashes that sounded at least a little like nearby thunder, if one wasn't aware of their more sinister origin.

Sonya activated her wrist countdown timer, marking the best case response from Dayton Metro.

"Sniper Team reports guard towers neutralized. Explosives Team, you're up," came Colin's crisp, businesslike voice over the sub-dermal links. "Assassin Team, prepare."

Sonya motioned to Tony to take the lead. She wouldn't let him out of her sight on his first joint mission. She knew his mind and heart were in the right place, but she couldn't read his abilities the same way. Some things relied on the old fashioned methods—observation and analysis.

Sonya eschewed the multi-spectral night mission contact lenses the rest of the team wore. A few simple mnemonics, and her vision nearly equaled theirs without the technology. She watched as he moved well against the dark, wet ground, even at a dead run. She couldn't tell if he consciously moved around the noisiest of the puddles or whether it came naturally. Even in a pounding run, Tony's breath barely showed, even to the enhanced. His feet never slipped underneath him, even in places Sonya found herself taking tiny skids. Through the downpour's sound, which swallowed up their noise and that of any passing herd of buffalo, Sonya watched Tony's skills and up-ticked his value.

Sonya followed as Tony dodged to the left of a runoff waterfall twice the width of a bus and into the shadow of the building. In spite of being a hardened guerilla, Sonya sighed in relief from the continuous sheet of rain.

Sonya watched as Tony put a little bit of separation between them, leaving more of their muddy brown footprints in the white façade covering the earth. With 30 meters between them, Tony slapped at the grav belt activation switch and missed. Sonya read the curse that fell from his lips. He didn't miss the second time, but overcompensated and leapt much too fast into the sky. Before she could radio anything, he modified his ascent to something more reasonable.

Sonya chanted a mnemonic to herself as she traced a single tattoo line down over each shoulder beneath her poncho. Spreading her arms she indulged in a spiral lift-off. For a brief uncharacteristic moment her mission awareness faded. Wind tickled her long lashes and caressed her cheeks. She never lost her joy for flight. She spent nearly a week in the air when her mentor finally beat this skill into her thick skull. She then spent nearly a month recovering.

As Sonya caught up to Tony's height, her mind reengaged with the deadly mission. They both approached the underside of the floating citadel on either side of the faint golden aura that marked the boundary of two large grav fields impinging on one another and the characteristic ozone smell of the grav drive. She pulled explosives from beneath her poncho as she fought the urge to rub away the tickle in her nose.

Sonya could just make out Tony's form pressed up against the roof on the other side of the distortion. Immediately, she realized that Murphy had bollixed up their mission. Instead of ballistic steel reinforced ceramcrete, a mesh of interlaced monofilament held the entire fortress like a giant net. Their explosives couldn't possibly penetrate the monofilament that distributed everything done to it over its entire length.

Sonya tongued for her mic to abort the mission when Tony crawled upside-down in her direction, waving at her. She paused long enough for him to get close.

"Don't abort. I can still bring this down."

"How long do you need?"

"Ten to twenty minutes."

"Too long. The blue suits could be here in twenty-three."

"Then I'd better make it in ten. Let me get to work."

Sonya just gave him an odd look. She realized moments later that no one in her team had ever brushed her aside so completely before.

Tonguing her mic she said, "Mission hold. Hold positions." She watched as Tony, with the proper handling gloves, took three small filaments of the same material as the mesh from his pack and tied them each in a bow, one right atop the other. He then placed a very small bit of explosive on each of the exposed ends and loops.

"Monofilaments distribute all forms of energy at a remarkable speed throughout its entire length and width," he explained. "I have to create a surge through each of these extra filaments that hits the same point at the same time. If I'm successful, there'll be too much energy for it to dissipate quickly enough.

"I've done it twice before, but never without calculations and computer control," he said, attaching the last of his bits of explosive. "Move back about 3 meters."

Backing up himself about a meter, Tony flattened against the building and triggered a remote. A small crack and flash about the same magnitude as a pistol shot resulted. As she crawled up with Tony, Sonya saw he'd severed the junction of two of the monofilaments, their ends straining downward. Between the severed ends stood a 1 centimeter-deep hole in the ceramcrete.

Sonya couldn't say she saw exactly what happened until Tony described it later one step at a time because now his hands were a blur as he spoke. "We don't have time to rupture the entire net," he explained, whipping out his own primed explosives and pulling them apart, a task Sonya would've done only with the greatest of care. Tony seemingly cared only about speed.

"So we're going to have to destroy the grav generator in place," Tony concluded. He tore open the nearly sealed end of the explosive, throwing the lid away into the dark before ripping the entire assembly out of the case. He squeezed the detonator out of its gelatin capsule, and the capsule from the plastique itself. Packing the box again with the moldable explosive, he hollowed out one corner.

Sonya started to object, because more was always better, but he interrupted her.

"Here, hold this." He held out the excess explosive putty, wiping it into her open hands. Then he stuck the completed device into the gap in the monofilament web, keeping the open face against the bottom of the citadel with the hollow corner just touching the tiny divot.

"Give me your explosives." While juggling, upside down, the putty in her hand, Sonya handed the two 25 centimeter cubes over to him.

"I'm building a quartet of shaped charges I hope will be powerful enough to blow directly through to the generator and turn it to slag."

Sonya watched his hands fly through a repetition of the same motions. Each time the clump of explosives in Sonya's hand grew larger and each time he stuck the completed box with the hollowed corner at the tiny dimple until, with the final one in place, he ended up with a two-by-two grid of boxes. If they had been one unit the boxes would have a hollow cone-shaped depression in the center.

"Give me back that extra plastique. Now for the hard part." Tony broke the explosive into four blobs, rolling them into rough spheres. Each one he jammed onto the four farthest corners from one another on the underside of the boxes.

"I hope this works," Tony said. "Time to make like a drum and beat it."

Sonya spread her arms and swooped straight down. She beat Tony to the ground by about two seconds as she pulled up hard at her landing. Sonya counted out loud. Out from underneath the building they sprinted, once again covered by the cloudburst. On the count of thirty they both threw themselves into the muck.

She tongued her mic. "Fire in the hole." Tony looked up enough to toggle his detonator. A flash preceded two sharp gusts of wind and a gout of expanding flame from a half-meter hole. Like a three-legged table with one leg suddenly yanked away, the entire mammoth complex began to tilt downward.

"You did it, Tony." Sonya checked her timer. Five minutes remained. Not enough time, she thought, but they had to try. "Assassin teams, execute."

The ponderous structure hadn't even struck the ground when an even dozen dark-clad figures, in two loose groups, erupted from the mud and muck sprinting toward the falling corner.

Sirens began to wail and klaxons to bellow. "Yell and complain all you want, beast. You took one in the belly and you're going down," Tony said as the mass slammed into the ground with enough force to make every one of the assault force bounce almost 5 centimeters off the ground.

Sonya herself rolled during the impact, clogging her nose with mud. She spit and snorted as she watched a 10 meter corner of the platform actually snap off. This alone caused the closest tower to break free of its remaining moorings and continue the fall.

After she cleared her nostrils of the silt, she called out, "Good sim, Augustine. Fell within 3 degrees of your prediction." Because of this, both the Assassin teams closed safely on either side of its deadly swath.

The platform, now canted at almost fifteen degrees, showed only sporadic areas still with lighting. Electrical shorts of blue-white flared out in random locations. Alarms continued to make useless noise. Loose material still slid around on the unnatural tilt. Sonya could pick up no deliberate movement by any of the internal response teams.

"Sniper Team, switch to covering fire mode."

The first of the Assassin Team grav jumped up to the top of the first line of wreckage.

"Team lead, we have Dayton response team inbound," Augustine called over the link. "ETA six minutes. Response team is heavy. Repeat—response team is heavy in Sierra, India, X-ray minutes."

"Roger, Overlook. Assassin teams, abort. We can't hold off a heavy weapons squad. All teams fall back to rendezvous point Bravo. Explosives Team will supply retreating cover and extract at Charlie."

"Overlook en route. Extraction Bravo forty-five. Extraction Charlie ninety."

"We didn't get the prize, Tony, but you did well."

* * *

"The Greenies once again perpetrated an outrage in a cowardly attack on a low-level computer training facility just outside the Ohio town of Fairborn." The action committee of the GAM sat huddled around the tiny solido projector. From the large "LIVE" at the bottom, the feed presumably showed the listing and broken platform as it appeared right now. It looked different in the daylight. Firefighters helped injured people out of the wreckage as others shored up the rubble to make sure there were no other accidents. A line of ambulances waited off to one side. "The outlaw group butchered sixty-three, and wounded seventeen others."

"What the fark?"

"Shhh," several said in unison.

The picture switched to one man wearing the blue coveralls of a computer tech. His face bore red splatters of blood and wept even more from a bandage covering his left eye. "They didn't even give us a chance. First there was this horrific bang and the world tilted. Next thing we knew, they charged in with flechette rounds flying. I saw one of those bastards fire into my buddy Ron after he put up his hands to surrender."

"What is he blathering on about?"

"Shhh!"

"If it weren't for the private security force SecWest," the announcer continued as the view switched to show the tan and red uniformed gunmen keeping watch over the rescue operations, "the death toll would've skyrocketed."

The screen changed to an overly beautiful reporter questioning one of the SecWest officers, who wore a bandage around his shoulder. Without prompting, he said, "We were only able to apprehend two of the suspects and we were forced to kill four more as they open fired on us even when we had them surrounded."

"What a load of—"

"Shhh!"

"Captured? Are they barking mad?"

"Will you shut up, too?"

"…of our force lost their lives: Benjamin Anderson, twenty-five, and Celia Pauls, thirty. There will be a memorial in their honor Sunday at noon. At least their devotion to the sanctity of life and their ultimate sacrifice wasn't in vain." The view panned briefly to a grav litter, where the sheet pulled back to show what had once been a beautiful woman, now horrifically mutilated and torn apart across the throat. The image flashed back to the officer's wounded shoulder.

"And what about your injuries?" inquired the reporter.

"Oh, this is nothing but a scratch. Not even worth worrying about. Honor Ben and Celia."

Someone in the room let out a Bronx cheer.

"…is the security spokesman for WalMaCo, the parent company of the training facility, with a prepared statement."

"'This is another case of patience leading to victory. While the Corporate Protection Act of '24 allows us to try these two villains ourselves, we believe it's in the better interest of the public to remand them to the custody of the neutral agency of the Dayton Metro Police. In this way everyone can understand just what monsters these terrorists are through due process of law.'"

"I'll give him terrorists…"

"Will you shut up!"

"…Director Atwell went on to say that the perpetrators were humanely questioned, revealing significant tactical data that may lead to further arrests. In other news…"

The solidoset snapped off with a mental command from Augustine's implants.

"Well they didn't cage or vape any of our people, so this cast is make-believe," Linc said, jumping in again.

"So what? We move on. And keep going. This doesn't mean anything to us."

"No way. I go' peeps insis'ing we're hur'ing peeps."

"Who cares," Andrew said, standing on a crate and waving his hands vehemently. "Let them go to hell in their own way."

"I have to disagree," Tony said as he gently stroked the recently reunited Cin as she slept in the crook of his left arm. "This is concentrated propaganda intended to drive the people away from us; make us into enemies of the people instead of their savior."

"What makes you so special, corpie?"

"Shut up there, Andrea."

"Tony, you did a right smashing job on that training center."

"Yup, he sure did. He took just long enough for us not to finish them. Maybe he had friends inside," Andrea objected.

"Now, Colin, they have the right to whatever opinions of me they want," Tony offered as nonchalantly as possible.

Sonya finally intervened by standing from her customary lotus. The room fell silent. "I'd like to make two things clear," she began. "One: as leader of the explosives team I take responsibility for failing that action. Tony worked faster than I thought possible and accomplished more than I've ever expected. Had it not been for Tony's quick thinking and expertise with explosives, we wouldn't have even brought the training center down."

Sonya turned and walked away, passing almost through the doorway before Linc spoke up.

"Wait a minute. That's just one. Second?"

"I'd work with Tony any time against any odds. Any of the rest of you who won't are idiots."

* * *

The two static bursts Tony heard in his earpiece meant only one thing, "Patrol." Nothing could be worse in the middle of a transition move. With no choice he hung by one arm from a ceramcrete cornice one hundred meters high on the outer façade of the NikInc Building while cursing to himself. No longer strapped to his chest, the 2 kilo explosive charge dangled from his left hand.

"I tell you, that girl from the Beaverton mailroom is shooting eyes at you," came a voice below him. "I say go for it!"

Tony couldn't move for fear of drawing attention to himself, pattern-mimicking clothing notwithstanding. His mission brief told him the guards carried gauss guns capable of flaying the entire building face to dust with millions of steel slivers. That thought alone gave him a healthy dose of respect.

"Chrissy would castrate me," the other guard complained.

"She's been leading you on for months now. She'll never sign a cohab contract."

"Why not?"

"Didn't I tell you what she told Cher?"

Tony's right arm began to throb. Shotgun bursts of air batted against him like a kitten at a ball of fluff at the end of a string. He listened intently as the pair slowly moved around the perimeter of the football-field-sized landing platform.

"Yeah, yeah. That don't mean nothin'."

"I tell ya, it ain't gonna happen. You got a smoke?"

"Sure, but don't let O'Donnell catch you. You already have two reprimands. One more and you could get sacked."

"O'Donnell doesn't worry me. I got the dirt on him. He can make all the noise he wants but he can't get rough with me."

Tony could feel every crenellation of the cement digging into his skin. Fatigue rolled through his arm as his body rocked back and forth in the wind. Gritting his teeth gave limited relief.

"I can't believe that little dance with Candy has made her that gun-shy."

"I think it had something to do with the fact that you were both dancing on your clothes instead of in them."

Tony couldn't wait any longer. He passed back the emergency signal, four quick bursts with his tongue to the mic in the roof of his mouth.

He expected nothing more than Colin to run for his life while Tony tried something equally stupid to escape before betraying his presence. Instead, Colin walked out onto the platform in plain view.

"But it isn't like we we're doing—Hey! Who the hell are you?"

Tony didn't hesitate at this break, quickly sliding the plastiques back to their carrier. Almost in the same motion, he slapped his nanite-coated climbing gloves and shoes against the wall. As designed, the nanites penetrated into impurities and pores in any surface they touched, giving him nearly perfect grip.

"*Soy perdido*," came Colin's perfect Spanish.

"Buddy, I don't care if you're lost or not. You stop right now or we'll cut you in half," the first guard demanded, training their guns smartly on the intruder.

"*¡Arrepentido!*"

"You'll be sorry, all right. Kneel and put your hands behind your head."

"*Si.*" A few grunts on the platform later, Tony risked a look back to see one of the security guards using a low-tech fiber-graphite binder on Colin's wrists as he lay face down on the ground. The second guard stood professionally, 4 meters away, with his weapon trained on the prisoner. Another binder went tightly around each of Colin's legs, with one loosely between the pair. The best he could hope for was a night of crude physical torture, and Tony couldn't imagine the worst.

"Up on your feet."

"*Si, jeffe.*"

"Walk straight through that door."

Colin complied, never once attempting to resist. Tony watched in amazement as they walked directly beneath him and disappeared from sight. Nothing in his life had prepared him for someone willing to sacrifice for someone else. Nothing. Every fiber in his body screamed for him to plant the bomb and run. He hesitated, unable to move, his mind adjusting to something completely new.

His tongue flicked the mic on his right molar. "Augustine, I need you to break the security on the electrical hatch to my right. I need it in the next forty seconds."

"Not asking for much, are you?" the old woman chided from over forty kilometers away.

"Are you going to work or are we going to jaw?"

"Door alarm disabled," she offered almost immediately over his earpiece. "Paralysis gas and electroshock ice disabled."

Sweat rolled off Tony's brow because at Nanogate they wired two manual deterrent systems above those attached to the computer systems—a little tidbit he learned during his brief stint in the Physical Security Division.

Opening the door, Tony crawled into an oval orifice, barely larger than a sleeping capsule, pushing aside bundles of wires and fluid tubes. His eyes and mind focused on looking for traps. The temperature dropped as he belly-walked in. Again, his career broadening assignment paid off. Cooling the tube improved infrared sensor capability, but infrared sensors generated more false alarms than all other parts of a security system combined.

As Tony's breath clouded the air, he spotted the sensor, right where he'd seen similar devices at Nanogate. Balancing on his elbows, he snapped off three silent shots from his automatic at the sensor three meters away before a tiny arc of electricity announced its demise. Holstering his weapon, he chose to assume security would be similar to what he remembered. In that case, the only boundary yet to deal with would be a nanite stream, a simple group of mindless microscopic robots continuously sampling for foreign DNA. Invisible, but not invincible.

Tony unhooked his Kevlar canteen and began running a thin bead of water on the floor. As he crept slowly forward he watched the water. The stream suddenly took a left turn as if a knife-thick wind blew it. Looking at his watch, Tony sloshed a larger amount of water, pushing the stream forward, breaking it briefly. Three minutes and four seconds later, the stream again interrupted itself for just a moment, letting him know the exact cycle time. Definitely not invincible, he thought.

He poured the entire canteen empty, breaking the stream significantly. Tony also blew on the water, scattering it even further. Precisely 183 seconds later, he scrambled forward as fast as he could. If his legs still lay in the stream, it would only be acknowledged when security of one type or another tied his own wrists with graphite bands. Just ahead another access hatch opened down onto an empty hall.

The 5 meter ceiling height caused an indecorous landing, but with no damage except to his pride. "I'm in," he sub-vocalized. "Do you know where they're holding him?"

"I've isolated a single room that has no net access, no room monitors, no halon fire suppression and no fire alarm. I'm assuming that's it. Fifty meters and turn left. Third door on the left."

The sterile white hallway demanded speed, not stealth, for his special clothing would be of no help here. Tony sprinted down the hall.

"Yup," he agreed. Spitting out only a few syllables at a time, he managed, "Can't imagine anything except a closet would be designed that way."

"It isn't a closet. Those are clearly marked on the plans. This is called a 'utility room.'"

"Keep an eye on the alarms."

"As if I wouldn't. You pay attention to your job, son. I just disabled the tangle field you were about to run through."

Tony didn't have any more breath for chitchat, or to even choke out a thank-you. His breath came in hot, ragged gasps.

"What is your plan, anyway?"

As an answer Tony put the muzzle of his assault weapon against the lock and fired just as he slammed the door with his full body weight.

The door exploded inward. Colin struggled, chained to a chair. Two guards wore surprised faces.

During his brief training, Tony's marksmanship had improved from abysmal to merely awful. His first three shots stitched almost at random across the room, one creasing Colin's hip and the last flattening against the chest armor of one guard, staggering him backward where he fell flat onto the floor. Colin screamed, falling backward in the chair, lowering his profile.

Tony's momentum, barely slowed by the door, carried him right over the chest of the downed guard. Tony's boots elicited crackling noises as he trod over the man's head. In a classic mistake, Tony fanned his automatic like a death beam, spinning up and to the left with the recoil of the old-fashioned weapon. None of the bullets even came close to his target. The remaining guard, responding quicker than most would to the mayhem, drew his gauss gun and fired a burst, but he misjudged Tony's headlong speed. Instead of ripping Tony's head off, the guard's shot tore a gaping hole in the wall behind his target's maniacal charge. The guard's second burst chewed a dinner plate-sized hole in the plaster ahead of Tony as he slammed into the wall with a loud grunt of pain.

One of Tony's second bursts, wobbly and hurried from his impact, remarkably caught the second guard in the lower thigh between the armor plates and the knee. A second scream reverberated through the room as the he went down. A third cry followed as Colin rolled his chair over on the guard's injured leg. Tony placed the red laser pointer dot on the man's forehead and squeezed off the final projectiles of the battle.

Breathing hard, Tony checked the man he'd stumbled over, finding a boot-sized impression rapidly pooling with blood in the corpse's head.

"You all right, Colin?"

"Good enough to get out of here. Find the cutters."

With a certain amount of distaste, Tony scavenged through the deceased guards' pockets before finding a pair of wire cutters.

"You have three alarms going off," came Augustine's voice. "Vital function monitors from each of the guards, and environmental alarms on the nanite stream."

"We're already on our way out."

"Don't tarry. You have less than a minute to clear the building before they lock it down, and you have less than thirty-four seconds before guards erupt all around you."

"Not a problem."

"Don't have to tell me twice."

"By the way, what's the third alarm," Tony asked as he ran.

"Explosives detectors. You still have the package."

It wasn't conscious thought that grabbed the explosives from his chest, flicked the timer down to as short as it would go and stuck it in the first doorframe he ran past.

Tony thought Colin, even injured, probably set a new unassisted record for speed—less than fifteen seconds later the pair sprinted off the landing platform in a 300 meter base jump.

"Yeehaw!" Colin yelled over the abyss. Behind them a bass roar and gout of flame announced their mission accomplished, if in an unorthodox way.

Their chutes opened barely high enough over the ground to allow them a rough but survivable landing. Other than the quizzical looks of three nearby Nils, nobody noticed or cared. Tony and Colin cut off their chutes and quickly dove down a manhole. The remainder of the escape proved only silent professionalism.

* * *

After two weeks of walking nearly everywhere, Tony missed the comfort of the TriMet. Suet led him off the TriMet at Vancouver Tower. While no civilians moved away from the green warrioress, none actively crowded her either. Her body modification demanded respect.

"Where are we going, now?" Tony asked for about the third time.

"You run your mouth more than anyone I know," Suet said in mocking tones about an octave above comfortable.

"Talking is one of life's great—"

A jade-colored tentacle placed itself gently over his lips. "P'ease be quie'."

Tony contained himself for the better part of the two elevator rides down from the platform by leering at his companion. Unlike the majority of men, Tony never carried a bias against girls who went for permanent body modification, not matter how far it went. Only the end result mattered. Suet's form curved in and out at just the right places and the right amount. He didn't care that it had been sculpted rather than grown. Her green emerald shape undulated and swayed just like real living flesh. Who cared that a diamond bit couldn't drill through it? The tentacles in place of arms cooled his ardor just a bit, but not enough to matter.

Getting off at the thirtieth floor, Suet's broad hips and natural rhythm forced Tony's eyes into a pendulum motion as she sashayed along in front of him. Tony nearly walked into her as she stopped abruptly at a door marked 30117. "We're here," she announced without fanfare.

"We are? Where is here?"

"Home," Suet said, using an electronic keycard to gain admittance.

Realizing his sudden lack of attention to anything but his female companion, Tony looked around and did a mental double-take. By United States codes, the thirtieth through fortieth floors were reserved for commercial and retail enterprises. Across the narrow hall from him, a door announced "Hentai Carpet Cleaning," and the one adjacent to that read "Falcon Pewter Service."

He shuffled through the door into an open warehouse brightly lit by hanging fluorescent illumination. The lighting didn't do the room justice. Only the darkness of a morgue would help this place.

The space rose fully two stories high, filthy with dust, mis-sprayed paint, and bare ceramcrete floors bearing the mark of untold equipment dragged and dropped repeatedly. The only walls that marred the boxy space belonged to a tiny bathroom in the far corner.

"Whose home?" His voice echoed in the mostly empty space.

"Yours."

Tony couldn't help seeing the cherry on the top of a pile of dung— a nicely appointed full-sized bed occupied the corner near the bathroom, leaving twenty meters of emptiness between. He had been bunking in a comfortable bed in his old cell in one of their quiet underground safe houses. He didn't see this as a step up.

"You are kidding, right?"

"No. We make some green for you to re'ecora'e," Suet said, closing the door behind her. She ambled over toward the bathroom and peered in. Tony didn't need to enter the bathroom to know there'd be decade-long stains ground into all of the fixtures.

"Does the cast of *Makeover Thunder* come with it?"

"No, but I'm sure others give assis'ance if you ask." She plopped down on the bed. Tony heard the springs squeak even from the entry. His back gave a sympathy twinge at the thought. "We have a warehouse with sofas and other junk. You can pick and choose and we bring them here."

Gawking his head in all directions, Tony shambled in. "Are you sure my fairy godmother isn't a part of this deal?"

Suet ignored the impertinent question. "OK. I have more for you. 'ime for you to become someone e'se."

"New identity?" he responded absently. "Maybe if I put in a false ceiling below the lighting, do some painting, toss in a few lamps and put up a few walls, I could make this place look a bit less institutional."

"Your new nom of guerre is An'onio Kars'. Having same firs' name makes it har'er to mess up."

"Not a bad idea," Tony said, still gawking about and visualizing changes.

"Here's your chip, papers to this p'ace, and some convincing papers of your his'ory; break up papers, union receip's, passing away papers for your mother, gym membership, and even a no clothes solido of your non-gir'friend. The usua'.

"Augus' and her peeps scrub' the memory p'aces an' threw this junk back in. She's thorough. No worry abou' using them."

Tony came over to the bed and sat down next to the mass of paper and plastic that suddenly redefined his life. "No, I don't imagine that I do." Suddenly he felt kinship to the echoing emptiness of the home the GAM gifted him with—everything emptied and ready for a new owner. He just needed to make it a home.

Suet grabbed him with one tentacle and pushed him to his back on the bed. Her lips locked with his almost at the same moment as he hit. Her other tentacle tore open the crotch to his pants.

"What?" he sputtered.

"Park your mouth. Jus' enjoy," she whispered into his ear as one of her appendages found its way around his genitals.

Remarkable, one part of his brain thought, it feels soft and silky, not rough like sandpaper.

"You think with all this biowear tha' I no fee' your sex?"

"But…"

"Hush up for once, will you?"

Tony hushed.

* * *

Nanogate nibbled on a Stilton cheese puff, dreamily considering how the GAM action, once successfully completed, might boost his own standing in this council. No longer the new man, his voice would carry weight.

"Taste Dynamics is recognized," said the chairman.

"I'd like to make this council aware of an action I unilaterally started which may, possibly, have some effect on our efforts against the GAM." Startled, Nanogate raised his head slowly so as not to show his inner turmoil.

"Please go on. You have the floor."

"Before our agreement to action, I put together a team of experts to investigate guerilla tactics and strategies to see if we could find a method to mitigate the GAM. Unfortunately, or fortunately as the case may be, I put a very sharp operator in charge of this project. I honestly forgot about the think-tank until I received notice of an intentional reduction in our firewall from the inside. Oddly, it pointed only at data that, upon quick correlation, was false.

"It didn't take long to find the perpetrator—the long-forgotten leader of my think-tank. In an effort to advance himself, in the face of my extremely loose reins, he chose to take unilateral action without reporting to me.

"Before I could do anything to stop the activity, a net hack blew down the wall and scooped up the Trojan Horse."

Nanogate couldn't read her body language well enough to know if she lied or not. Before or after Nanogate's initiative? Before or after she discovered it? Key questions to how it specifically impacted him. But how to inquire without sounding aggressive or threatening?

"And this action can jeopardize our current solution?" Nanogate asked tentatively.

"Very doubtful. This gambit strikes at the most vulnerable aspect of a terrorist organization, not its manpower. In fact, it could heterodyne with our current efforts or," she said looking directly at Nanogate, "in the face of the very small possibility of failure of our current efforts, this alone might end the GAM."

He felt a cold chill run down his spine. He needed to find out what plan was in the wind and, if necessary, sabotage it.

"Very well then," the moderator concluded. "I don't think this calls for any action on our part.

"Next order of business?"

* * *

Tony opened the door to 30117 wearing thick latex gloves and smelling of chlorine. Ignoring both, Sonya grabbed onto one of his arms and dragged him bodily through the barely opened door of his still-unfinished apartment.

"Hey! I was cleaning."

"Time for fun instead," she said as she waved to the rest of the GAM action committee that stood in the hall. Even the colorblind would've objected at the badly mismatched patterned shirts they each wore.

"Huh?" Tony asked with startling brilliance. She motioned for Beth to take up the attack.

"We're in a very stressful line of work. We have to blow off steam when we can, or we go, in technical terms, crackers."

"Give me a second." He stripped off his gloves and tossed them inside the apartment, locking the door behind him. "OK. So now where are we going? I hope my old sweats aren't going to be out of place."

Christine pulled out a Hawaiian shirt that just didn't quite match everyone else and handed it to Tony. He shrugged and swapped his chemical smelling top for one that assaulted the eyes instead.

"Just wait and watch. Learn to trust," Sonya said, stroking his other arm. Together with some bulky parcels, the group occupied an entire lift car. She felt rather than sensed Tony's nervousness. "Trust," she said again.

"I can't imagine what kind of fun you'd all enjoy. Couple that with those heavy bags and we have…what? Blowing up sushi bars? Feeding corpies to the lions?"

She laughed. Christine came over and sat on Tony's other side. Sonya managed to not quite frown.

"No, nothing so 'ame," Suet said from the other side of the car. "Use these bags 'o carry the hea's of our assassina'ions." Sonya smiled to herself.

"Yeah, we put them on pikes around the bush telly and dance around them," Tolly embellished.

"Haha. Very funny." Christine tugged his shirt. When she had his attention she swung her arm like a pendulum at the side of her body.

"We're all going to turn into clocks?"

"No, but we're almost there, so curb your curiosity just a little longer," Colin said, kneading his thigh where one of Sonya's poultices caused his jeans to bulge—the unfortunate results of Tony's poor aim.

The bus dropped the group on the fiftieth floor landing of a nondescript building in the Rose District. Suet moved to the side of Tony opposite Christine. Tony's confusion showed on his face.

Sonya heard the crash of pins before they could see the door. She mentally cringed when she heard country & western music twanging over the top of it all. Not her favorite music to bowl to.

"Bowling!" Tony exclaimed as the sign proclaiming "Dance and Bowl" jumped around the corner. "We're going bowling? I don't have any idea how to bowl."

"We'll teach you," Sonya insisted, pushing him in the small of the back as he began to balk.

"I'll look like an idiot. I don't even know how to throw the ball."

"Relax. None of us knew how when we started, except the Metro trio up there."

"Smile when you say that," Colin said, opening the door and holding it for the rest. "Really, we will teach you and you'll be bowling like a pro in no time."

"I don't know…"

"Besi'es. Everyone 'ooks juveni'e the firs' 'ime."

"Well, I'll be stuffed. I never figured you for being shy."

"I'm not, I just don't like doing things until I figure them out."

"Don't worry. This is just an excuse to have a coldie or two."

"Don't listen to the aborigine," Colin said. "This is a game of skill and finesse."

"Well…"

"Skill and finesse? Lob a rock down at some sticks standing up? Lotta skill and finesse there, donger."

"Don't listen to those two," Sonya said over his shoulder. "They'll go at each other for hours. Now come with me and we'll get you initiated. I'm assuming since you know very little, we'll start you with a standard ball." The rest of their crowd broke to various tasks of their own.

"As opposed to an advanced ball?"

"No. As opposed to a fingertip ball. You're a big guy with thick muscular fingers. Let's try you out on a sixteen pounder. You know, I don't see how you could've ever been a dentist. You couldn't hope to get your fingers in a patient's mouth."

"I was never a dentist. I was just in the dental design department. I actually was very talented in ergonomics of dentistry. I designed a new dental dam and increased the efficiency of ablative picks by seventeen percent."

"I'm sure. How about this one. Slip your ring and bird finger in. Nope, too big. This one? That should do it for your first day," she proclaimed, giving him back his hand.

He looked at the bowling ball like she'd just gifted him with nothing more than a big black stone. "By the way, what's a 'pounder?'"

"Hah. Old terminology. Bowling ball weights were determined by how heavy or how many pounds they were. And before you ask me, a pound is around two kilos...or was it the other way around?"

Sonya led Tony to the four lanes they rented. Frances and Jonah immediately hooked Tony in and started discussing five- versus three-step approaches, with Beth chiding them about running before Tony even crawled. Sonya left him in the capable hands of the other more proficient bowlers. While others may have time for fun, this offered another way to observe her charges interacting. She felt a deep obligation to each and every one of them to make certain the team flowed smoothly.

She admired Tony's offhanded way of deflecting Christine's silent advances without being cruel. He sat close but not touching. He paid her no more attention than anyone else. Sonya couldn't tell if he was oblivious or he took an easy care for her feelings. In either case, Christine's smile said more than anything else. Tony's life expectancy went up considerably, knowing what Christine did to her lovers.

Tony brought down four pitchers of beer, two each of light and dark, plus one pitcher of soda. No one says "no" to beer. It provided an excellent lubricant for the team to help shuck off the worlds' woes for the night.

"My turn to get the pizza," Andrew offered.

"You haven't bought pizza in three years, you cheap bastard."

"Fair dinkum, Andrew. Get on the bounce."

The more Sonya watched, the more she decided that Tony wore about him a subtle charm. She couldn't immediately decide if it came sincerely or whether he projected it with forethought. She didn't like witching her way into her comrades' motivations unless necessary. Instead, she used her own instincts as she followed him even more closely.

He deferred naturally to Frances on bowling and learned enough to at least keep the ball on the lane. He exchanged sarcastic comments with Linc. Sonya watched as he calmed down the irascible Suet after her ball, with far too much spin, leapt into the adjacent lane. He even spent some time honestly listening to Beth's tedious and redundant ramblings about her modeling days.

Sonya watched as her people took to him as one of their own after so little time. As one, the group jumped up and down as Tony scored his first strike. Hugs were shared all around.

One fly swam in the ointment. Andrea failed to hide her dislike of the newcomer. He seemed confused by the antipathy, but tried hard to work around it with very limited success.

When Tony finally worked his way through the team to herself, he asked her about her low tech lifestyle. To her surprise he honestly listened to her answers and could debate the benefits and costs. Within a few minutes Sonya realized his natural charisma even worked on her. "What more could one leader ask for?" she chided herself mentally. Despite her best judgment, Sonya found herself warming to him as more than just another member of the team, but as a friend as well.

* * *

"Is the operational tempo always this high?" Tony asked from the back of a brightly painted panel truck dubiously labeled "The Party Bus— Birthdays, Bar Mitzvahs, Weddings, and All Other Occasions." He crouched next to a huge bomb that all but filled the 9 meter cargo bay. "This is the third attack this week."

"Sometimes we don't do anything for weeks or even months," Jackson explained from the passenger seat. "But sometimes we have only one chance at a target, like today. This one's like a sign painted by God. No one turns off their surveillance grid without a backup."

"So where are we going again?" Something nagged at Tony's subconscious about anything being this open.

"Will you shut up back there," Andrea barked from the driver's seat.

Tony didn't understand the continuing animosity from the diminutive, red-haired thief. He'd been friendly with all the team members and gotten cautious approval even from Sonya. Andrea didn't make any effort even for common courtesy. Tony felt her eyes following him more often than not in the few quiet moments the team shared since his acceptance.

"That's enough," Jackson said. "I know you don't like Tony, but that's no reason to be rude. He did save Colin's ass."

"Old man, I'm not going to get into this with you."

"That's right. We have a job to do right now. Park your high horse so we can do it professionally."

"Yes, SIR."

"Sarcasm doesn't become you, either, young woman."

"Seventy seconds for grid deactivation," Tony offered.

"We *can* tell time! Hell, I don't even know why you're along. The explosives in the back of this thing are powerful enough to bring down the whole building. All we have to do is park and walk away."

"I suggest we merge into the Yelser Airway for three blocks before cutting back," Jackson offered in a feeble attempt to change the subject. "We don't want to get there too early and be seen driving around the block."

"Gotcha."

"Now a left onto the Em-El-Kay." Tony's senses perked up as they rounded the corner. Memory flooded back in an instant.

"What was that address?"

"Fucking shut up about it. We know where to go."

"Goddamnit, tell me the fucking address!"

"101 North Martin Luther King, eighty-fourth level," came the snappy reply.

Tony's mind went into overdrive. "Fuck. We can't do this. It's a trap."

"What do you mean, corpie? Augustine dug this out. No one gave it to us. How much better can you get than to knock off a g'damned data center for Unified Petroleum?"

"I tell you, it's a trap. Even Augustine said it'd been the easiest hack she'd had in years."

"Talk fast," Jackson insisted.

"It's a trap. UP is under the Nanogate umbrella. When I worked security, I signed off on a number of construction changes. This was one of them. The power was inadequate. Just by accident I noticed later that the space was to be converted into a day care and nursery school."

"Bullshit," Andrea countered.

"No, it's true."

"That's nothing but a load of crap!" Andrea hissed. "We have a bomb to deliver and I, for one, am *not* going to let Sonya down again."

Tony could just make out the determination on her face. He realized nothing he could say would change her mind. He changed tactics abruptly.

"Jackson, we can't let this bomb kill children."

"Even if you're right, corpie," Andrea said again, spitting out the epithet, "they're just corpie kids. It's another blow against the corporations."

Jackson said nothing but Tony could hear him breathing heavily.

"Here comes the building," Andrea announced as she pulled up into the loading zone. "Get ready to scoot."

Tony didn't know where he found the courage. He knew it would probably end his association with the GAM, but he couldn't abandon his own principles and allow the Greenies to commit suicide. He pointed his gauss finger right at Andrea's head. "None of us are getting out. We're going to fly this bomb right back where we started."

"And if I get out anyway?" Andrea said, slowing to park.

"Then I'll put a hole in your head the size of the Philadelphia Crater."

* * *

"That corpie threatened to kill me. I want his head!" Andrea demanded, standing as far away from Tony as the small storeroom allowed. Several of the team held their weapons ready, but didn't know where to direct them. It pleased Sonya that the guns pointed only at the floor.

"I'm telling you, it was a trap. If killing me will make you feel better about not blowing up a school full of little kids, then go ahead."

"Fuck you, corpie."

"Knock it off!" Sonya yelled. Everyone turned to her in amazement. She forced her emotions down three notches and continued more sedately. "Jackson, please tell me what happened."

"In short, Tony blew the op claiming it was a trap. He claimed inside knowledge that our target was a day care, not a data center."

"It doesn't matter," Andrea went on. "We had—"

"Andrea," Sonya interrupted making her voice as cold as a breeze on Io, "I'm trying to understand. Until I do I can't make any decisions. So shut the fuck up!" In an attempt to break up the disaster this promised to be, she had broken two of her own rules—no yelling and no profanity. It bought at least a modicum of stability to the chaos in shock value. Silence held as Sonya closed her eyes and took four deep cleansing breaths.

She opened her eyes to see Andrea with her arms crossed over her chest and her mouth pursed up with the look of a four-year-old saving up more spit. Tony's visage wore a look of resignation.

"Now, Tony, why would killing children be a trap? I mean, I don't like the idea any more than anyone else, but it doesn't seem to be a risk to us."

"That's where you're wrong. I tried to mention this to you before but no one really listened."

Andrea opened her mouth, but closed it as Tony gave her a glare.

"Well you definitely have our attention now," Sonya said, her voice back to her normal imperturbable levels.

"OK. Look at it from a guerilla warfare perspective. We gain strength from the common folk—money, protection and recruits. They are trodden and spit on by the corps. They look to us as their heroes. We're

Robin Hood and her Merry Men. What would happen if those same people looked at us as a threat?"

"…their hear's and their min's," Suet muttered.

"What was that?"

"I think she said, '…their hearts and their minds,'" Linc said.

"Yes. Something I remember from some 'raining as a mercenary in Africa. We foun' ways 'o win the hear's and min's of the peeps. This jam covere' shi' may be yanking the peeps from us. They're yanking the foo', clothes an' roofs away. Peeps run from us, no' with us. Maybe even Nils."

"That's right," Tony took up again. "I mentioned that killing people might be a danger to us. Look at the corps' propaganda from our last few actions—they're already exploiting this, painting us as the bad guys. You've seen it already. Augustine, what are the net polls on us running?"

"About three percent less favorable across the board."

"See? They're already making an impact with pure fabrication. What would happen if they really had gotten us to kill a bunch of kids? They wouldn't even need their talking heads to say anything. The blogs, the hack parlors, and tweets would be full of it. We'd be the Manson family. The very people we count on would turn against us. We wouldn't last a month."

"I don't give a damn," Andrea said, breaking her silence. "No one threatens me. We're a team!"

"Hold on, Andrea," Tony said quietly. "I'll concede your point. We are a team, and I acted badly, but I didn't see any other way to get your attention. If you want to beat the crap out of me, go ahead. If you all think I should be expelled, go ahead. At least I saved the cause."

"We only have your word for that, you f—"

"Not exactly," Augustine interrupted. "When I heard Tony's thesis I went back and did some additional net work. He may have a point. I didn't even need to hack and I've found any number of references to that location being "Bumble Bee Day Care." Worse, it's for low to no income families.

"I don't like to admit I'm wrong any more than anyone else, sister, but if anyone's to blame, it's probably me. I didn't cross reference the address I got in the hack. I just assumed it was correct."

Sonya almost sighed in relief as Andrea's shoulders dropped a bit. The ochre didn't drain from their leader's face, however. She wasn't home free yet.

"I'm going to have to agree with Tony's observation," Sonya said calmly. "We're a guerrilla fighting force. If you aren't in tune with your people, you'll soon find yourself in the hands of the Metros. I also have to agree that Augustine probably dropped the ball." Before Andrea could muster up an interruption, Sonya put up her finger. "That does not, however, deal with Andrea's grievance. Should some kind of sanction be placed against Tony?"

"What the fuck?" Colin spurted. "You're all agreeing he saved our collective asses—AGAIN, I might add—and you want to kick him out or worse?" Colin moved over to stand protectively in front of Tony. "I for one will go with him if he leaves. He risked his own ass to get me out of a jam. You all can suck Nil juice if you think I'm going to put up with that."

"I don't think anyone was suggesting anything quite that drastic," Frances offered diplomatically.

"Like hell I wasn't," growled Andrea. "He's a fucking menace."

"Folks, we need to calm down," Andrew said, moving over in front of Andrea, but facing everyone else. Sonya imagined she was watching some schoolyard game where the two captains chose sides.

Sonya looked into the face of each of her team members. Because of her anger, Andrea hadn't realized she'd already lost. Sonya felt her only hope lay in dictating a solution to give everyone enough time to cool down. She hated the role of disciplinarian.

"Enough. And I do mean enough from all of you. Tony, I have to say that I appreciate your abilities. At the same time, I've never seen this kind of polarization within our action committee. We've always been united. This gives me serious reservations about us as a team."

Sonya didn't give Andrea enough time to make an ass out of herself by preening. "Andrea, I've never seen such childish, intransigent behavior. I can't even begin to wonder why you're so unfairly prejudiced against Tony. Oh, I can understand being angry about having someone threaten you, but knock his block off. I know you can do it. You don't talk about pushing him out where we lose his abilities and let the Metros murder him." She paced back and forth, looking at the floor.

"If you were children, I'd make you shake hands. You aren't. Andrea, I can't make you like Tony. Tony, I can't make you less of a natural force.

"This is my final word—"

Tony interrupted by thrusting his hand high.

Sonya closed her mouth on her next words. "I thought I already told you this isn't a classroom. You don't need to put up your hand to speak."

"Sonya, I think I need to get this in before you finish. I'm afraid I need to ask everyone some probing questions for my own peace of mind—otherwise your pronouncement may be moot. I don't know that this is the right time, but I don't think I can wait any longer."

"Go ahead."

"What are we trying to accomplish with our actions?"

Sonya felt stunned with the question. She wasn't the only one. Several seconds passed before anyone spoke and then they all spoke at once in a cacophony.

"Bringing power back to the people…"

"Returning the balance of nature…"

"Makin' the bloody corps listen to the law."

The simple answers dissolved the room into even more chaos. Tony held up a hand to quiet the babble as everyone tried to get everyone else to agree with their viewpoint. While he didn't get the respect that Sonya normally received, he did get eventually get their attention in the end.

"You can't even agree why you're getting together and killing people." He received nothing but puzzled looks. "Why should I stay committed to you as a group, other than my personal loyalties, when you commit the murder on a wholesale scale but can't even decide why you're doing it? Oh, sure, the megacorps do it daily, but you've held yourselves up to be better than they are."

Sonya barely noticed the silence as her own mind whirled around his challenge. She spoke first. "Why do you fight, Tony? It's been almost two weeks now. Do you know why you kill?"

"I'll be honest. At first I killed to stay alive. I can't quite claim self-defense, but that's as close as any. I then realized this is almost the only true comradeship I've ever known in my life. In this short time, you've all touched me.

"But I've changed my mind. I've decided I have some morals. Now I'll only kill to bring about positive change. I don't see things moving toward any change at the moment. That probably means you're going to feel you have to murder me to keep me from talking, but that's the way my heart and soul is pulling."

Somehow Tony made Sonya feel dirty, just with a few well-chosen words about something she'd spent most of her life building.

"You only bring up more things nee'ing answers," Suet said pointing a green tentacle at him. "How 'o we make tha' change? We though' we were."

"This world is run by the corps. That isn't right. There are no checks and balances. The rich run everything and there's no way to get rich because they rig the game against it, unless you want to become just like them.

"I'll be honest. If I go forward, I do so to remove the current people from power. I don't know what needs to be righted, other than that."

"How?" Frances said seriously. "We've been fighting the megacorps for years. Talking doesn't work. All they recognize is violence."

"Nothing wrong with violence," Tony said quietly. "Just stop killing people."

Seven people all opened their mouths to interject, but Sonya's hand stopped them. "Tony, I think for all our sakes, except maybe our loving lady, Christine, we'd stop killing in an instant if we had another way." Nods went around the room. At this moment Sonya realized how the tenor of the room shifted from confrontation to expectation.

"It's simple, actually. Let me ask some rhetorical questions. What does killing corpies do for us?" Before anyone could answer he went on. "Frankly, nothing good. There are always thousands who are willing to not only climb over the corpses but to perform sex acts with them to fill their now-vacant positions.

"Killing hurts the corps not at all. They've learned a lesson. You see in the nets. Killing now helps them and works against us. They make us into the evil ones.

"Now ask yourselves, what drives the corporations?"

"Profits," Andrea offered, her anger seemingly gone from even her posture.

"Power," Collin offered.

"So how do we hurt the corps and not hurt ourselves? Step right up. Three tries for a quarter," Tony said in all seriousness.

Once again Sonya broke the tableau Tony had created. She began to see light through the fog over her brain. "Target and destroy visible corp assets while reducing the kill count to as close to zero as possible."

Murmurs of assent floated through the room. Sonya felt an energy unlike any since the GAM's birth.

"You just won a kewpie doll. Better than that, the targets we'll be picking will have little to no protection. Who protects a warehouse except from thieves? Who protects a manufacturing plant? What about a mine?"

"Yeah."

"I like that!"

"And now that I know you're paying attention, I have a few more ideas. Right now you pick your targets by those who present an opportunity. I think that by a better selection process we could make each target work for us double, or maybe even triple."

Sonya just raised an eyebrow at him. Everyone else now politely or respectfully hung on Tony's every word.

"Look here. By attacking across all corps we're draining only twenty ccs of blood out of each of them. We're down in the dirt as far as their bottom line goes. Now, what if we were to focus our attacks on just a single corp?"

"Crashing marke'."

"Their board of directors would have a fit."

"Take the tucker out of the bag!"

Augustine pointed out the practical in Tony's idea stream. "We could also make a fortune. Place 'puts' on the companies we target, and when the price plummets, we sell our puts and finance even better actions."

"Yes, now you see it. This would add even more pressure on the corporations. With a little luck it could cause some of the weaker ones to declare bankruptcy, removing them from the scene entirely."

The room stood silent for several full minutes. Sonya's own heart leaped. "I never thought I'd live to see it happen," Sonya said finally. "Do we even need to vote on this?"

* * *

Nanogate's nine-month-old grandson, Michael, giggled as he bounced up and down on his grandfather's knee. Drool flew most everywhere as the infant simultaneously decided to eat his fist. Everywhere included Nanogate's antique Armani lounging gown. Nanogate smiled. His eldest son married an intelligent as well as beautiful young biochemist. They gave him a grandson to carry on the family name. What wasn't to be pleased about?

"That's a good little boy. Ride the pony. When you get old enough I'll buy you a real pony." Nanogate gave the giggling child an extra bounce and wiggled him side to side.

"So that b… that gentlewoman from Taste Dynamics told the truth about starting her little experiment before I proposed our Greenie solution?"

"That's correct, sir," Mr. Marks said, standing at ease in the center of Nanogate's home library. Scores of actual bound books lined the walls of a room ornate with real leather furniture, hardwood floors, and an authentic wool rug, dyed maroon red. Mark's neon yellow tights clashed badly with the ancient décor. "Want to play airplane instead?" Nanogate swooped the boy up and down without leaving his wingback chair. "But she lied about authorizing action."

"That is correct, sir. I liberated a copy of her personal notes. You will find it appended to my report. In short, it appears your action jogged her memory. Three days later she authorized one Michael Upton to proceed with an action he proposed three months earlier."

"I guess that isn't a big surprise. I probably would've done the same thing." The baby suddenly got rather quiet even though still flying about. "And what results have they seen?"

"The answer to that didn't come easily, but good research always wins out. Apparently Mr. Upton has a fascination with trains. I managed to come into possession of a vintage B&O locomotive and flatcar in T-scale he needed for his collection. I swapped him for the information.

"The action was in two parts. The first involved intense propaganda, most of it fabricated, pointing to the evil ways of the GAM. The goal of the propaganda was simply to drive a wedge between them and their support base.

"The second action involved disguising a daycare for the underprivileged as a prime target in several nearly open files on our network. The Green Action Militia did, in fact, read out the data as projected. The perpetrators of the hack are conjectured, of course, but the GAM rarely misses data of that nature in the open even if they didn't themselves do the raid. It approaches a near unity probability that they ended up with the data, one way or another. However, nothing happened."

"She was going to let them blow up a bunch of children?"

"Yes, sir. She deliberately set them up as bait. If I might be allowed an opinion, I believe it's as if she would've murdered them herself."

The baby let out a noise, somewhat approaching a grunt before starting to coo and giggle again. Nanogate wrinkled his nose at his grandson's latest offering. "Susan," he said, "would you please come get your son?"

As always, his servants, listening in to hear his slightest whim, got the message passed. Within a minute the mahogany doors opened and a beautiful blonde, not quite back to her perfect size six, sauntered in, heels clicking staccato on the floor.

"Certainly, Father," she said, picking up her baby. "Did little Mikey make a doo-doo?"

"I wish you wouldn't call him Mikey. It's Michael."

"Yes, Father." She turned and left, cooing to the baby. The doors closed behind them.

"Have we come to that, Mr. Marks? Killing children? Never mind, don't answer that. I guess it's a case of the pot calling the kettle black. Who knows how many I'll be killing in the next few days."

Nanogate stood up and walked to a stack of books on his desk. He picked one up and pointed it absently at his bodyguard. "So it sounds like her primary action is dead in the water before it even gets started. And the other is a pipe dream. Good news. I can use that against her."

"Anything else pertinent to report?"

"Not that I can think of, sir. The details are in my report."

"OK. Thank you for your efficiency, Mr. Marks. Oh, and make sure the cost of those trains gets into your expense report. I know from experience just how expensive those models can be. My son's a railroader."

* * *

Mark Linderheim, sixteen and a student working his way through Oregon State University, busied himself restocking Doritos when the first customer of the day, that being a relative term as they were open twenty-four hours, entered the store. An attractive woman in her thirties moved directly to the counter and stood there waiting for him. Probably just wanted a pack of narcosticks or some lottery tickets, Mark thought. He tucked the last of the bags on the shelf and took the empty delivery crate with him back behind the counter.

"May I help you?" he asked affably.

"I'd like to place one hundred puts of twenty-three credits per share on Nanogate," replied the lovely customer.

"No problem, ma'am," Mark said, punching the numbers into the computer. Just another version of the lottery, he thought to himself. Some people thought it gave them airs to play such risky ventures in business rather than take the equivalent risk in the lottery. Didn't matter. Odds didn't change. Either way provided ample ways for idiots to throw away their money. "That'll be ninety-four credits," he announced flatly, keeping his feelings to himself.

The woman opened her Coach bag and drew out a hundred-credit note. Per company policy, Mark waved a forgery detector over the bill until the green light and the oh-so-annoying female voice sensuously offered, "Valid." Mark made change without another word and meaninglessly offered the woman a nice day.

Working as a convenience store clerk offered millions of ways to numb his brain. Mark moved on to cleaning the trays of the Fozone machine. As he removed the drawers from the massive freezers, another customer came in, a man with his little girl. In the time it took the four-year-old—with considerable help from her father—to make up her mind and pick a candy from the rack, Mark managed to empty, scrub, and return the tray to its place. He made it back to the counter in time for the pair to walk up.

"Good morning," Mark offered.

"Good morning. We'll have this, and I'd also like to get some puts, please. Can I get sixty-five at twenty-four credits a share?"

Mark nodded and entered the codes into the machine, wondering about the coincidence. Two puts in a row were unusual, but not earth-shattering.

"I'm getting candy," the little girl announced firmly.

"Yes you are, dear," agreed Mark. "That's a pretty dress. What stock, sir?"

"My momma desneged it on the 'puter fer me," the girl added smugly.

"Oh, I'm sorry," said the man, smiling. "Nanogate, please."

OK, Mark had seen unusual coincidences before, but this seemed extreme. As he currently took statistics as one of his math courses at OSU, he immediately began to run numbers in his head on how unlikely this combination was. He kept losing decimal points in his head before giving up. Statistics did say one thing that very few people remember, though—no matter how unlikely something might be, it still happens sometimes.

"She did a wonderful job, honey," the customer said to his little girl, paying Mark's confused look no heed.

"With the candy, that'll be sixty-three nineteen."

The man and child left without another word. Mark managed to earn sixteen more credits in the hour it took him to restock the walk-in cooler with beer and energy drinks before two separate people rang the entrance chime at the same time. Both went for the coffee. One, a regular, always spiked his double-shot espresso with energy creamer. Sometimes Mark wondered how the man didn't have his hands fall off with the jitters.

"Morning, sir," Mark offered the newcomer, who absently carried a fruit pie and a cup of normal black coffee. The man seemed somehow nervous.

"Morning. Can I get these, and can I short sell from here?"

"ConVenEE is a recognized broker. If you are properly registered you can sell short here."

"Excellent. I'd like to sell short one hundred fourteen shares of Nanogate."

Mark's ears buzzed. "Can I get a saliva sample for identification?" he asked reflexively, numbers dancing in his head.

The man opened up automatically, allowing a simple swab of the inner mouth. The swab went into the machine, which immediately identified the man as someone named Michael Henderson.

"Mr. Henderson, the put will more than cover the cost of your purchases. The remaining four thousand nine hundred fourteen point twelve credits will be retained on your account until the return of your short sale. Is there anything else I can do for you?"

"No, thank you."

Mark's brain worked overtime. His teacher could surely give him the odds against something this outrageous, assuming the number of zeroes wouldn't overflow the archaic campus computer.

The regular stepped up to take his turn. "Morning, Mark."

"Howdy, Jimmy. Just your coffee this morning?"

"Well, no, I'm going to also take a hedge against Nanogate tanking. Say eight hundred shares at thirty credits."

Mark's eyes bugged right out of his head.

It took four hours and three more anti-Nanogate stock sales before Mark's relief showed up to give him his mandated break. He wasted no time calling his girl, Julia, who worked at the Red Salmon Creek casino just north of town. "Julia. I want to pass something by you. I've had a rash of people betting against Nanogate."

"Did you say 'Nanogate'?"

"Yes, why?"

"I've had like fifteen short sales and puts this morning, all on Nanogate."

"Someone knows something. I think we should get in on this. Should we call our folks?"

* * *

"One hundred three meters, but I can't see a freaking thing," Tony said between chattering teeth. He floated in a concentration of green and gray moving flecks, only barely pierced by the powerful light on his forehead and that of his teammate, Tolly, tethered two meters to his left. Tolly looked like a cross between Batman and the Creature from the Black Lagoon in his formfitting scuba outfit. After an hour, the water's coolness started to penetrate even Tony's dry suit.

"Good," Linc offered over his long-range audio link. That storm really stirred up the ocean currents. You're getting silt and algae storms. Makes it nearly impossible to see."

"It's also making it freaking cold." Tony could almost envision his companion's disapproving expression through the audio connection, even without Linc saying a word. "OK. That's great, but where now?"

"Target is 216 meters to the northwest."

"Northwest?"

"Turn to your right, mate," Tolly offered, consulting his wrist compass. "A little more. There. Dead set."

"Switch to stealth mode for approach."

"Turning off jet packs and lights," Tony said, plunging himself into absolute blackness as Tolly followed suit. The pair, still tethered together, kicked gently in their target's direction.

"Why am I doing this?" Tony remarked absently as the cold continued to seep in and the lack of other stimulus started playing games with his mind.

"Cause you and Tolly are the only two with the deep scuba experience necessary. Oh, you're bearing just a little west. That's got it. You should be seeing something soon."

At first he saw nothing but blackness, and then the water started glowing in one direction. The fish started becoming more plentiful, attracted to the food attracted by the light.

"After dark to your left, Tony," Tolly said cryptically.

"Huh?"

"After dark, shark. Look left."

Tony made a mental curse at rhyming slang as he twisted around. He caught the signature silhouette of a hammerhead shark, about four meters long, snapping up a 40 centimeter squid. Two other smaller sharks drifted into view, but all gave the humans a wide berth. In front of him, a dome started to take shape through the murk.

"OK, first placement location identified," Tolly said, pointing toward a light mounted on top of the nearly transparent dome. It wasn't until the huge light gave perspective to the size that the immensity of the structure made itself felt. 86 hectares stood dry beneath the Loihi Bubble, growing wheat, rye, oats and dozens of other grains. At sixteen billion credits, the farm, dome, and precious metals mine—which they couldn't see below—represented a significant investment to the NaBiCo Corporation, a subsidiary of Nanogate. The loss of Loihi would dent even that deep pocket.

Together Tony and Tolly swam over closer, pulling items out of their pouches as they approached. Tony stuck a suction cup to the dome to hold himself in place as he lengthened the tether between himself and Tolly. The pair of saboteurs slowly rotated at six meters from the suction cup, affixing devices to the dome. Tolly gave him a thumbs-up and showed three fingers. Tony showed him back three of his own.

Tony's experience and math showed that three shaped charges, placed six meters apart, would splinter the entire dome, creating a hole between them large enough to overcome any possible emergency repair. Doubling the number of charges provided assurance of destruction. The same procedure at two different sites ensured that if, by some miracle, a grouping was found or the holes somehow plugged, the second would be sufficient. All timers were set to detonate seventy-eight hours later. This gave the divers more than enough time to exit the area and decompress.

Tolly and Tony repeated their hex placement 75 meters away.

"Site two complete. En route to submersible."

Despite chattering through his teeth, Tony couldn't help but smile at another successful mission.

"Watch your depth. I don't want you bending," Linc offered.

"Go bite your bum. I can watch my own depth. And make sure you have some hot coffee ready. I'm freezing."

* * *

"Erecting itself in front of you is the Nanogate Spire, a marvel of modern engineering and construction," claimed a propaganda board in front of the construction site with a pleasant female voice. "When completed, it will be the tallest free-standing structure on Earth, at a lofty 1.83 kilometers tall, stretching over 200 meters taller than the Tovarich Tower of Moscow."

"How fitting," Tony remarked, leaning up against the brick façade of the building next to the construction. "Nanogate, the corp that kicked me out, is taking the brunt of our attacks…our first of many victims." With the GAM's change in targeting, he didn't even worry about security or Metros. This site's sole guard slept most of the time, and its single obsolete surveillance drone scoured the wrong areas three times while leaving the rest of the site open.

The spire's framework curled up into the air like the gruesome skeleton of a unicorn's horn. The metal shimmered, not in its own light but rather like it crawled with millions of tiny insects. No pests infested this site, but instead trillions of nanites carried materials up to the top, where they fused them into the growing crystalline structure before returning for more. The spiral grew in height as Tony and Sonya watched.

"The opening of Portland's Nanogate Spire is planned for February fifteenth," said the sign.

Sonya looked at Tony and then wistfully up at the seemingly self-growing building. "My grandfather once told me that people used to build skyscrapers by hand. Men would actually climb on those metal arms hundreds of meters above the ground with no gravity belts or safety harnesses. A huge machine would lift massive beams into place, and they'd heat bits and pieces of metal together so they stayed put. Each building often measured its cost in the number of lives lost."

"Sounds like we shared some similar relatives."

"Yes," Sonya sighed. "By the way, don't think of what happened as anything but a one-night stand. She isn't romantically involved."

"Huh?" Tony asked, confused by the sudden subject change.

"She was gone when you woke up, right?"

"How—"

"Suet's environment taught her only one way to show gratitude. She's protective of us as her family. You saved Colin, someone she's come to think of as a brother. She showed you the appropriate gratitude. She'll come to love you like a brother as well, but don't equate her sexual outbursts as anything but friendly fornication."

Tony mulled this over. "Thank you, Sonya. I honestly didn't know what to think. Don't get me wrong, I enjoyed myself, but it was so sudden and so unexpected." His eyes stared off into nothing and his mouth hung slack.

Sonya gave a soft, girlish giggle. "She has that effect on many men and women both."

"Whew! I just…"

"You're among good company, Tony. Also, you're best off not remarking on it in any way. She gets testy if you do, thinking she hasn't pleased you."

He nodded. "So why are we taking this out?" Tony asked, pointing to the spire, trying desperately to change the subject. He didn't like talking sex with others, especially other women. It made him feel somehow dirty.

"Well, Augustine said that Nanogate's already behind on construction and every day in delay is costing them hundreds of thousands because of extending leases."

"So add the cost of rebuilding to the cost in delays, and it's going to make them sting."

"That it will."

"Actually, I'd give a pretty penny to watch the faces of some of my coworkers when this comes down. All the stock options lost, the bonuses evaporating…"

"The layoffs," Sonya offered.

"True, which can work for us even more. We should be able to recruit from their losses. We'll have to be careful, of course, but maybe form a second cell that isn't tied to ours. Only one of us needs to be exposed."

"Have you ever been a guerilla before?" Sonya asked quizzically.

"No, why?"

"I've been running this group for years. You've made more progress in a few weeks than I have in my entire tenure."

"My grandfather fought in the resistance in the Australian revolution. When I was very young, he used to tell me stories. They were never pretty, but they were romantic. I dreamed about his adventures. But even more than those stories, I've been reading from the local library since I've been with your group—Che Guevara, Mao Tse-tung, and even Girish Taqueur of the Martian revolt. While this isn't directly the same kind of war I've been reading about, it has enough similarities that I can pick my way through basic strategies."

"Reading?"

"Yes."

"Unbelievable." Sonya shook her head.

"Shall we get on with our fun?"

"Yes."

"After you, ma'am." Tony followed Sonya over to the ceramcrete walls hiding the underground vats of raw material. "Rare or well done?"

Tony asked, pulling out a plasma cutter. He traced his arm in a broad circle just like a fairy godmother waves her wand. The 3 meter circumference he outlined fell out of the wall with only a minor cacophony that no one noticed at ground level.

"Either of two minor changes should bring this building down. First the mixture." Sonya poured the contents of her handbag into one of the two vats. "The compounds in this should oxidize this material, making the material bond the nanites achieve much weaker."

"My turn," Tony said, waving an electronic probe over a 2 meter section of the microscopic workers. "If Augustine's correct we've reprogrammed these nanites to build sections of the frame with a different crystalline lattice. This will make a 2 meter weak point out of every 40 meters or so."

Sonya looked up at the visibly growing spire and smiled. "It's poetic justice that we're using their technology against them. I approve wholeheartedly."

"I agree. I don't know when it'll come down, but it'll be a long time before completion. Even better will be the exceedingly spectacular show it provides."

* * *

Using low-light contact lenses, Squib crawled along above a false ceiling using a grav-belt fine-tuned to just barely carry his weight. Too many years had passed since someone in the army gave him his nickname—he couldn't even remember its origin.

His employer put a rather attractive price on this clut's head. Tracking this target caused him some problems until he called in a favor from a wirehead. That worthy individual offered that he'd captured a sideband transfer worming his target's identity into the database as owner of this flat. One in a trillion shot, but he'd take all the breaks he could get.

His client insisted this be a simple vape job with no fuss. Squib didn't care. One hole or a thousand holes, they still died. One hole saved on ammunition.

Simple sonic probes had provided the layout two days earlier. An easy commission—nipping in through the ventilation system posed no problem for someone of his diminutive size. He planned to drop in silently through the bathroom, the one room in any flat that nobody ever thought to guard. He lifted one of the faux ceiling tiles and looked down. A mottled orange animal sat on the toilet lid looking up at him. It let out a small sound, barely loud enough to even be heard.

Squib reached for his gun to silence the creature when he felt a burning in his chest. He crashed through the false ceiling to fall heavily to the floor, knocking what little breath he still had out of him. He couldn't seem to inflate his lungs. Looking down, he realized he no longer had a chest, only a hole where most of it had been. He looked up and saw his target, standing nude above him with his finger smoking. Squib could only think, as he died, No one alarms their bathroom…

* * *

Nothing smelled like a dead body—a mixture of iron, burned pork, and shit, in this particular case. Tony also couldn't believe the vast mere of blood. Vids never got any of the three correct. Mostly the smell creators for vids really didn't want to make their audience vomit. Twice Tony offered the contents of his stomach to the handy toilet. For the six hundredth time he missed the Body Removal of his former condo association.

While unpleasant, disposing of the corpse proved the easiest part of the job. A molecular blade cut through the joints very easily. In just thirteen relatively easy pieces he had all but the torso safely within the calorie reclamation bin. The torso took a bit of extra effort, and mess, but eventually it too, in several uneven chunks, followed the rest to be ground into protein paste. This just left Tony with five liters of red to decontaminate.

For whatever reason people just didn't understand how much blood pumped through a person's body. He scooped it up, sponged it up, mopped it up. He felt like the little Dutch boy of myth holding back the sea with a fork. The gradually congealing goo stuck to everything like honey and found the most devilish crevasses to penetrate.

Cin sat at the edge of the mess and looked on with ladylike disdain for anything as plebian as cleaning. Tony couldn't be angry at her. She was a cat, after all, and without her unusual warning—a rather wet, raspy tongue to his nose in the dead of night—it might be his blood staining the floor right now.

Tony didn't have any feelings for the poor bastard whose body he just dismembered, but the intruder's presence did cause him some concern in other ways. He didn't know who sent the criminal, but his tools weren't those of an ordinary robber, but rather a professional assassin.

Sitting up from his all fours position, Tony looked over the mottled pink floors. Before this was over he knew he'd be very happy for all the leftover bleach from his apartment's initial cleaning.

Who hired the bastard? Were the corps or Metros behind this attack? All questions for another time. Cin yawned. Tony fell back onto all fours to continue scrubbing like an ancient scullery maid. Someone should write a book: The Glamorous Life of an International Terrorist.

Implement — Phase Five

"When we agreed to this course of action, we knew there'd be a short-term increase in damage for a long-term payoff," said one of the nine eight-centimeter solidos on the stark obsidian desk. He didn't know the technology on how these conference calls were secured any more than he thought about tying his shoes. The corps bought security like one would buy a bag of potato chips, and with about as much thought to the purchase.

"That's all fine for you to say. None of your profits have been attacked. Nanogate, one of the crown jewels in our portfolio, is down seventy-eight percent and falling."

"It was your plan, Nanogate," Taste Dynamics said scornfully.

"Probably revenge-motivated," one of the other solidos stated. "The profile we shared shows a twenty-two percent chance of such retaliation."

"Nothing showed anything in such scale, however," offered another.

"The Nanogate Spire represented billions in lost opportunity cost, lost revenue in retained leasing, and redesign costs."

"Redesign?"

"Our polling shows we can't pin this one on the Greenies. They haven't publicly claimed responsibility. The masses think this was a design flaw causing an industrial accident, despite our media blitz to the contrary. They won't accept the same design. We have to start all over."

"Seems excessive. What about retaining your current headquarters?"

"We're already negotiating that point. We aren't in a strong bargaining position, though, and the owner knows it. He's holding us hostage with a ruinous penalty and will require us to purchase the current building at a twice or thrice inflated cost.

"But as costly as this is, it's a pittance compared to the other impacts they've been making. We've been able to keep the manufacturing plant disasters—all five of them—quiet with some well-placed bribes. The Loihi dome, however, caught the media's attention because of an ill-timed visit by some maintenance personnel. But the real point is that the cost to repair and replace will likely to be more than all of our combined companies' profits for this year. Worse, we may have a shortfall of product."

"Insurance?"

"How many of you buy insurance of this scale? We're self-insured as a shared risk across our entire corporate umbrella. Even if we did carry such a policy it'd bankrupt the company underwriting the policy."

"Any other damage?"

"Any other damage?! Of course there is, if that isn't enough. Nothing of that scale, however. Call it pricey vandalism: rewiring the powering station of our delivery vehicles so the batteries burned up; multiple costly supercomputer crashes despite all the ice we could surround them with; rerouting sewage lines into the fire-suppression system of one of our primary engineering facilities and then setting a small fire. There are more of the same, but they're swallowed in the larger problems."

"Total costs?"

"Our current estimate is one hundred forty point three trillion, give or take fifteen percent. Note that this doesn't cover the public opinion cost nor the stock impacts."

Even the normally nonplussed group fidgeted at the sum before one finally broke the tableau. "Stay the course. It isn't as if we hadn't expected costs. The computer analysis still shows this is by far the best course and it more than pays back in the long run."

One by one the other solidos agreed. He nodded in assent only because they expected it.

"One other item of note," ECM stated. "As we expected, the subject has changed his name, and databases have been modified to show the change. I'm sending details by separate carrier. This is the first confirmation that shows the subject is truly part of the GAM."

"Thank you for that clarification. Anything further?"

"I have one item," noted OldsTransport. "We discovered unusual market activity on all of Nanogate's holdings. Specifically, there were massive puts against the stock just before significant pieces of sabotage."

"Were we able to track the people doing the trading?"

"No. It was all done over the counter, in convenience stores and networked brokers in small amounts. Nothing traceable. Not only that, but innocents are getting involved in the frenzy as well."

"Does this really change anything?"

"No, except that they're now no longer poorly funded. We anticipate over six million just in the last week."

"I do ask that until this item is resolved, we meet weekly."

"Agreed."

"Yes, by all means."

The meeting ended as the communications links broke, one by one, terminating the images like soap bubbles landing in the summer grass.

Nanogate sat quietly for ten long minutes, ignoring the insistent flashing of his door and the neural rasps of his percomm.

* * *

"Jonah, Frances, and Colin, you don't happen to have your Metro uniforms still, do you?" Tony said, leaning back and picking his teeth after a group potluck.

"Frak, no. I left that life behind," Jonah said with the relaxed attitude of someone long away from such a painful memory.

"We still have our ballistics," Frances said for herself and her domestic and action partner. "They lojacked all of the bio-enhancement suits, so those had to go, of course."

The rest of the group stopped talking to listen in. Tony had become their number one planner, and if another epiphany struck him, they knew it meant a worthwhile mission.

"Yes, that's all I mean. So if we did some minor alterations, you could pose, at least for a short while, as if you were Metros."

"Yeah, but anyone doing a routine scan would find our badges deactivated, and our heads on the wanted list."

Tony ran his fingers through the thick brush of hair on his chest as he stared off in the distance. "And how do we make people careless?" he asked absently.

"Kill 'em quick?" Several people chuckled.

"Bore them silly. Let Andrew talk to them for an hour. They'd all fall asleep." Andrew pushed Jonah off the couch with a playful shove to the arm.

"Yeah, thanks for noticing me," Tolly offered, mimicking an infamous donkey's droll tones.

"Show them what they want to see?" Sonya offered seriously.

"Exactly. The great part of this plan is that in-depth scouting isn't necessary. This is a swashbuckling job. So here's what I'm thinking..."

* * *

"C'mon, you green bitch," the Metro said, pushing Suet's form ahead of him into the light of the security gate of Nanogate Storage Facility Sixteen.

"Stop!" called the security guard, drawing his sonic club, his hands already pressing the local panic button.

"We *are* stopped, you rent-a-cop," the second Metro said, his own pulse pistol in the green woman's back. "We found this number playing fast and loose with your fence about thirteen hundred meters down the way. She had this toy on her as well," the Metro said, tossing the man a small block of explosives.

The Nanogate security guard jumped, but realized, belatedly and a little sheepishly, that the device was little more than a featureless clay-like block without a fuse or detonator.

The facility's four other guards pelted up almost simultaneously from different directions, wheezing as they ran to respond to the panic button. With Greenies going after Nanogate facilities, they all looked tense, but they relaxed at the sight of the Metro uniforms.

"What the fuck?" their leader demanded between labored gasps.

"They found this one trying to cut through the fence," the first explained, poking at Suet, who just looked angry.

"OK, so what? Why don't you tote this bitch away?"

"Do you have the slightest idea how much paperwork is involved in an arrest?" the taller male Metro offered. "Look, I thought you might be willing to take this *punta* off our hands for the reward bucks. Make you look good. Hell, we even put a binder on her arm implants."

"Yeah," the shorter female Metro said. "This way me and my partner don't have to spend the rest of the night doing computer entry and booking."

"You could turn her in yourself. Why the free money?"

"You idiot! Metros can't get reward money. You a Nil or something? When did you get your private security license? Yesterday?"

"Oh, yeah. Sorry. OK. We got us a detention cell in here. Come this way. Mike, stay here."

"Y'all see the game last night?" Frances asked as they entered the building.

Suet waited patiently until they were beyond the gate's monitors and inside the structure. Excreting a lubricant from her pores, one tentacle slipped out of the wrist binder like it didn't exist. One of her arms wrapped around the neck of one security guard, lifting. The spine snapped instantly. Another arm swept the ground, catching one other guard unawares, taking his legs from beneath him. The first arm now did double-duty, lashing bloodily across the chest of the third guard with speed enough to crush a trough in his ribcage. Colin's and Frances's hand weapons, from their Metro façade, finished the standing cripple and the other stunned man.

"Jesus, Suet! Give us a chance for some fun, too."

"I nuke fas'. No s'ow up for you."

"Whatever. Let's plant these charges quickly."

Five minutes later they all gathered back together. "Can I do the honors?" Frances asked.

"By all means." Suet nodded.

Frances sent a coded signal. Detonators didn't need to be visible to work. The supposedly inert explosives in the guard shack vaporized the remaining guard, Mike, as well as a 30 meter section of fence and all the sensing equipment, leaving a gaping hole for the trio to stroll through before the real fireworks began.

* * *

Only a single light shining down on the desk held away the darkness. The corner windows showed only full night outside, one with no moon. Alone, late at night, Mitch Anson leaned back in his leather executive chair dictating a memo, eyes rolled up to the ceiling. His nostrils flared.

"It's clear that the ubiquitous nature of your failings proves you cannot be trusted at your current rank. Thus it is my duty to inform you that you are demoted two ranks, with a commensurate reduction in pay in the amount equal to eleven point four percent. Sincerely, Mitch Anson." His breath raced and a flush covered his face.

Orgasm was the only word to describe Mr. Anson's demeanor. Mr. Marks thought to himself that sometimes one's work truly delighted one. He watched as Anson's respiration slowed to normal.

"Excuse me," came Mr. Marks's quiet interruption. Anson, startled, sat bolt upright in his chair. He looked about wildly for the source of the voice, but found none. "Lights!" he demanded insistently.

"Unrecognized voice command," came a soft feminine voice. "The Portland Metropolitan Police have been notified."

"I'm very sorry, Mr. Anson, but I've already disabled your computer access."

"Who are you, you soon-to-be-unemployed Nil? This is not a place for practical jokes or hacking!"

Mr. Marks stepped forward into the arena of light around the desk. Anson's face lost its color. His mouth dropped open, only exceeded in size by the wideness of his eyes.

"Cancel emergency call."

"Call cancelled, Mr. Marks."

"I...er...I'm sorry," Anson stammered.

"Sir, I've come to deliver a message," he said in silky tones.

"B-but I didn't do anything."

"Sir, you needn't bother with the scatter-pistol built into your desk. This shouldn't be that kind of message. I do, however, have to inform you that Nanogate won't be needing your services in the future."

"What did I do wrong?" Anson demanded, slamming both palms down on his desk as he stood to face Marks. "I've given everything to this corporation and now you're firing me?"

"Oh, you mistake me, sir. I'm not going to fire you. You're going to resign."

"What?! There is no way I'll resign!"

"You will resign, sir, or we're going to go on to 'that kind of message.'"

Mitch sat back down. "Why? What did I do? I don't understand. I've done everything our corporation has asked for and more."

"It's the 'more' that's being objected to, sir. Your hiring of the bounty hunters to go after Mr. Sammis might've interfered with an ongoing corporate operation, had it not been caught in time. I personally removed all four of your hirelings." Mitch started almost imperceptibly. "Ah, there are more. How many more did you hire, sir?" Marks took only half a step forward.

"One. Only one more."

"Excellent." Marks didn't have an orgasm, but a smile crossed his face nonetheless. "Now, you can dictate your resignation while I watch. Then you will simply disappear. I suggest you remain off the net for the rest of your life. If you ever show up, one of us will pay you a visit...of 'that kind,' sir."

* * *

The group sprawled around a red and white checked linen cloth spread beneath one of the trees in an idyllic park. They carried a picnic basket and munched on fried chicken, even if the real chicken content of their dish equaled zero. As everywhere, protein contents were substituted interchangeably. Since very few foodstuffs still grew on Earth, and chickens never really took to space travel, they were on the endangered species list.

A gentle breeze brought the briny smell of a nearby simulated ocean.

"I always wanted to spend the afternoon in here but couldn't afford it," Tony said as he leaned back against the trunk of the tree.

"This seems obscene," Suet said clearly.

"It does seem out of place," Sonya offered quietly from her typical lotus position.

"I know," Tony offered, "but the best place to hide is in plain sight—purloined letter style."

"It still seems as if we're inviting the enemy to our meetings," Andrew shuddered, looking at the huge Nanogate sign hanging on the side of the building that enclosed the wooded acreage.

"Don't worry. Our cover as the Beaverton Bomber Bowling League went over perfectly. Many of the bowling leagues have buy-ins just for this kind of thing after the season's over."

"But the DNA scanners we submitted to?"

"We be nab' on the way ou'…"

"Not going to happen," Augustine interrupted. "With the information Tony supplied about the security on the low-risk areas, I easily rode into Nanogate's files and switched all our DNA profiles with those of some midlevel functionaries in other companies."

"Yeah, I can just imagine the visits they'll receive when this finally unravels, all thanks to our local net jock." Tony nodded at the elderly woman, his friend. "And before you ask, she's already masking our conversation—replacing it, actually, with bits and pieces of other groups of visitors amongst the trees."

"What about eyes?"

"The floating surveillance is also being similarly redirected," Augustine said in disgust. "You think I'm not thorough?" No one commented into her challenging stare.

"I think we can safely call this meeting to order," Sonya said. "I'd like to congratulate Andrew, Jonah, and Frances for their rather spectacular destruction of the Nanogate factory in Lusk, Wyoming."

"Grats!" several yelled boisterously.

"Agreed. The planning and execution rivaled perfection itself," Sonya said, adding to the praise. Frances blushed while Andrew just got more solemn. "The results speak for themselves. Our recruitment of operatives and the monetary contributions from anonymous donors is at an all-time high, even though Augustine's shrewd stock market moves have made the latter less important than ever. But even more impressively, despite the firm lid Nanogate put on all our deeds, their stock has plummeted to nearly all-time lows."

"As good as this is," Tony said in a prearranged tradeoff from Sonya, "it isn't enough. We need more. We need to drive Nanogate into bankruptcy, but frankly I'm running out of targets. Does anyone have any that we've missed?"

Augustine offered her opinion almost immediately. "I've done thorough research on all of Nanogate's properties, both those publicly disclosed and those that aren't. There's some small off-planet facilities and a few distribution points we might target, but that's about all. I might suggest we use the noobs on these targets. They're much higher risk now that everyone's alerted to our modus operandi."

"Good idea," Tony jumped in. "I was afraid Nanogate might be too narrow of a target."

"Too narrow? You're the one that told us we needed to narrow our targets," Linc said, sitting up from his semi-reclined position leaning on one elbow.

"Yes, but many of these companies are linked, if you'll pardon the pun. Other companies are funneling money to Nanogate to keep them afloat. We need to find these others and target them as well."

Linc said gruffly, "Want me to tail your cheating wife—fine. Want me to dig up the guy that stole your identity on the wire—fine. Want me to figure out how companies are interlinked—I'm lost."

"Oh, don't go being pessimistic, yet."

"Check other companies' stock prices against Nanogate's for correlation over time," Christine said in her normally empty tone. That she spoke at all kept the entirety of the group stunned and looking at her for several moments. Her eyes still held their near vacant expression. Tony wondered what went on behind those eyes, then decided he didn't want to know and shuddered visibly.

"I have correlations," Augustine said. Her surgical link provided nearly instantaneous access to data from the web. Her smile said it all. "Nanogate stock and the stock of seven, possibly as many as ten, other corps fluctuate as a single entity, albeit one to two orders of magnitude out of phase."

"Gentlebeings, I would say that we have additional targets."

* * *

Greysky scratched his left arm where flesh met synthetic as he leaned inconspicuously in the steel-irised doorway of the ground level slum. In the eight years since he had voluntarily traded his meat limb for one of plastic and metal, imbalances in the nerve-to-circuit junctions made themselves known as an itching sensation.

As a freelance artist, Greysky had been doing private enforcement work for nearly ten years. That his PE license expired the previous year didn't matter. A license meant eight hundred credits a day, in the wrong direction.

Over the top of his projected solido-paper he surreptitiously watched a tube hotel across the street, its garish pink neon sign at least forty years old.

"Sleeping tubes disinfected daily," crackled an almost incomprehensible electro-mechanical speaker. "A full half cubic meter more space than chain hotels." Transient quarters all over the world were the same. Put your credit into the slot and slide into a 2.5 meter long by 1 meter wide cylinder for twelve hours of relative insulation from the outside world. This particular tube sleeper even accepted coins and paper bills, catering to those who didn't even have universal credit.

Greysky snorted softly. He remembered having to resort, at one time in his life, to sleeping in one of those plastic coffins—and that's what they usually were, too, coffins. People live there and die there. They never lift themselves above a grinding level of poverty and their only purpose is to be insignificant monetary bits in an immense economic machine. Greysky's finances long ago warranted a home far from this place. He was the exception. But then he wasn't here to sleep—he was here to deliver a message.

Just as he started reading the story, "Pope Vows to Increase Heretic Deportations," the intended recipient of his current employers' missive walked into the lobby of the sleep establishment. The blond hair, a rare trait these days, gave him away.

Greysky leaned farther into the doorway, striking a coffee stick on the wall next to him and tucking the business end into his mouth. Watching through his magnifying eye, his target put coins into tube 312 and climbed in. The tube end went opaque, making it time for Greysky to deliver.

He angled across the street diagonally, not pushing people out of the way but blending into the rest of the destitute throng. He put his head down and shuffled along, the bulk of his body and the tools of his trade hidden amongst the people and his shin-length jacket. As the pink neon bathed him, he pounded on the end of 312.

"Message for Mitch Anson."

"What?" said a voice from beyond the door as it opened. "Who knows—"

Greysky released the tiny spoon of the implosion grenade. "This is a gift from your former employees." He flicked the fingertip explosive into the oval opening and slammed the door down on the surprised face.

Greysky felt the muffled explosion conducted through the street. He walked calmly away, already mentally spending his commission.

* * *

"So where are we off to this grand morning?" Tony asked brightly. For Portland at ground level, the day positively shined, with the barest of moisture drifting in the air and no clouds to speak of. The near silence of the time after night owls lay slumbering and the day seekers hadn't quite emerged gave a rare pleasant experience.

As nothing came without its polar opposite, the brightness highlighted the filth. Nearby, a discarded washing machine on its side rusted itself into oblivion as it spilled rotting garbage from its insides onto the cracked pavement. The quiet allowed Sonya to hear several insects vying for the muck. The smell of fresh sewage, free from the rain, wafted up. Sonya sketched a little frown with her mouth, not because of the smell but rather the question. An experienced terrorist wouldn't have even asked. He or she should trust their leaders and just follow. Despite Tony's exceptional ideas and directions for the GAM, he still avoided embracing the lifestyle.

"Have I said something wrong?" Tony inquired after she didn't reply right away.

As they walked along, Sonya ground off the burrs of her short fingernails along the walls of the ground-level masonry like some gigantic emery board. She chided herself for her annoyance. "No. I just sometimes forget. You're so sophisticated in some ways and so downy fresh in others. Remember the tired old line from the old flaties, 'I could tell you but then I'd have to kill you?'"

"Yes."

"Well, whenever you ask a question, you should think about whether you really want the answer." She watched Tony's face get thoughtful. He learned well, she thought to herself, when he learned.

It wasn't as if she ignored the trio of heavily modified muggers lounging in the inset doorway, she just didn't care. The three marched out, one drawing a modern variation of nunchaku, two short steel bars with a chain between. One sported an ancient police baton and the other a makeshift club. She knew they intended to kill. It didn't matter. Before Tony even noticed their approach, the trio, as one, found an overpowering urge to head to the local bar for a frosty brew, all thoughts of mayhem erased, for now.

Tony hitched the shoulder pack back up, prompting a plaintive mew from within. "Sorry, Cin."

"She travels better than most cats," Sonya said over the rather loud buzz of an ancient motorized bike that rushed by in a cloud of petroleum smoke.

"I guess she's still young. OK, if you won't tell me where we're going, can you at least tell me what we're going to do? I don't even have so much as a pea shooter with me."

"Good. Less to be found." A shiver of happiness ran through her. She took a childish delight in teasing him. Food vendors began to flock the early morning streets, beginning their raucous calls for customers in twelve different languages from Hebrew to Esperanto. Tony frowned. He opened his mouth as if to speak and then closed it. "We're off to meet the Family," Sonya said, taking pity on her friend.

"Whose family?"

"The Family, with a capital 'F'. At least that's how they stylize themselves again."

"Got it." Tony once again opened his mouth and closed it suddenly. He did learn. "Ever been married?"

"Married?" She snorted at the thought as much as the sudden change in subject. "Like any man or woman would have me." She turned into an arbitrary building and started up the steps. Long ago she learned that in their line of work randomness foiled more mishaps than it caused.

"Why not? You're attractive, in a lean tigress kind of way."

"Check six," she whispered back on the first landing. She felt no one, but that didn't mean they didn't exist. She faded into a doorframe, pulling her cloak tight about her to mask her presence. It didn't work against cameras, but living people easily let their senses overrule their common sense. Tony continued up the second floor chatting as he went. "Of course you aren't my cup of tea. I wasn't offering myself as a potential mate, termed or otherwise."

Tuning out her partner as he moved away, Sonya felt the building move gently beneath her feet and through the fingertips that she rested on the doorframe. The white noise of movement which engulfed her included eight different sexual escapades, three couples arguing about credit, one weapons discharge, seventy different breakfasts, a myriad of mice and insects, six aerobics classes and too many other things all too jumbled up to make sense of. What she didn't feel was someone tailing. No one took the steps coming up behind her. No one dashed ahead to get into a building in front of her. Flowing out of the shadows, she dashed up the stairs to rejoin her comrade.

"So?"

"No one following."

"No. Why not?"

"Why not what?"

"Why haven't you ever been married?"

"I guess I'm attractive in my own way, but I'm a hermit. Having someone around me all the time would send me off the deep end. My personal privacy is too important. I don't want anyone to have control over my life."

"It doesn't have to be that way."

Sonya snorted again. She stepped around a wino living on the fourth floor landing. "And you're an expert?"

"Well, no. But my parents managed to make it work."

"Without getting in each other's way? Without integrating themselves in each other's lives? I don't believe it," she snapped as shrilly as Tony remembered ever hearing her.

"Wow, the way you say it makes it sound like a virus or parasite."

She took the time for a cortico-thalamic pause, that brief moment between stimulus and response. In her case it took five floors, and two building transfers. Finally, she replied in her normal, mellow tones. "Sorry, but you hit one of my soap box topics," she explained, jabbing the call button of an old-fashioned elevator with particular vehemence. "I like my life. I don't want to change my life. Anyone I add to it would change it. I've watched friends get married and in almost all cases become miserable, or change into someone I wouldn't want to call a friend."

To her surprise, Tony said nothing. She entered the elevator and pressed the combination for the eightieth floor. "Like most witches, I suppress my urges for domesticity or other entanglements with the companionship of my pets."

"I wasn't trying to make you angry," Tony finally offered, somewhere around the forty-fifth floor.

"You didn't. It's just that assumption that someone has to have someone else to be a full person—well, it drives me crazy sometimes."

"I was just trying to make conversation."

She really didn't even hear him. "If I have one regret, it's that I won't have anyone to pass my gifts to."

The elevator door opened onto two imposing men in bodyguard yellow before Tony could continue digging into even more uncomfortable territory. One stood like a white, weathered mountain with an obvious Russie heritage, the other his polar opposite, slight and fast, with the cast of the southern Asians.

"Hi Greg, Tuan. We're here to see the Jamie."

"You're supposed to come alone," one barked. "You know the rules." The other guard stood at attention, holding his flechette gun in a perfect diagonal cross of his bare chest.

"Pish and tosh." Only one as massive and tall as Greg could stare down at Sonya. She locked eyes with him and didn't let them go. It took only a minute. She felt Greg must be slipping.

"Well, give us some warning next time," the guard said finally, giving up the staring contest.

"If you didn't have us spotted at least ten minutes ago, I'd be surprised."

"Whatever. Climb in," he said, pointing at the portal of a scanning machine like they use at spaceports for carry-on luggage. The entrance on this end fed into a blank wall and came out somewhere beyond. Sonya jumped up onto the conveyor belt and lay down without a second thought. She remembered her trepidation the first time and hoped Tony handled it well.

In the space of seven deep breaths, practiced with a calm meditation of the soul, the makeshift scanner dribbled her back out into the light. She rolled off the end of the belt to her feet with the grace of one of her cats. Tony, carrying Cin in his arms, provided a new definition of gracelessness as he fell hard onto his backside, his legs flailing in the air. Adding insult to injury, his head flipped back and banged against the scanner supports, drawing a scathing oath in a language Sonya didn't know but determined by its invective. Cin, on the other hand, landed on all fours on Tony's stomach as if this happened daily.

Sonya silently offered Tony a hand up. As he took it, not without a scowl, Sonya took the opportunity to examine his head. Just enough blood leaked from the scalp to eventually create a scab. It wound up in the category of painful and annoying, but nothing more.

She registered the new rich red paint since her last visit. It flowed in with the rest of the décor. Real crown molding and wainscoting in a style not seen for nearly a century accentuated the dark green velvet and the carved marble columns in the corners. Few countries on Earth or its colony worlds could've afforded even two of the six Maxfield Parrish paintings mounted to the wall. Yet only the Mob's reputation, and a few bodyguards such as Greg and Tuan, protected the art.

Invariably, any newcomer found themselves in front of "Daybreak." Sonya, on the other hand, preferred to immerse herself in "White Birches: Winter" at every opportunity. Placing Cin on his shoulders, Tony gawked at each painting in turn. Sonya sensed that Cin appreciated the works herself.

"Dian!" said a lean, red-headed woman in a long, blue velvet dressing gown to Sonya as she came into the room. Her long, well-toned legs, clad in stockings, garters and blue Pintera pumps, parted the gown and carried her over to Sonya. She gave her a pair of French-style air-kisses now regaining popularity with the effete. "I see you brought a pair of toys with you." The woman unabashedly examined Tony like a prize cow on the auction block, but with barely a fleck of interest in Cin.

"Jamie. Thank you for seeing me on such short notice."

"Always a pleasure, for the right price, of course."

"Naturally. Let me introduce Michael Durant, a new but very valuable member of my team."

"Nice to meet you, Michael," Jamie said, offering one of her manicured hands, complete with fingernails that changed color to contrast to whatever they lay against. Sonya watched Jamie's hard eyes, completely at odds with her pin-up body, as Jamie evaluated "Michael's" response. He gallantly took her hand in his and bowed deeply over it, but didn't kiss it.

"Oh, I see Dian's already got you under her thumb, and other places," the woman said with the faintest of smiles.

"No, not exactly, Jamie. I'm just not partial to redheads."

Sonya flipped Tony a glittering stare. A short silence filled the room.

"Touché. Well played, Michael, or whatever your name is."

Tony bowed again in acknowledgement.

"So enough games. Shall we sit and have some tea while we talk business?"

"Very well." Jamie snapped her fingers, and a small army of servants brought in an antique double-trestle table carved from a solid piece of granite, plus matching chairs, a silver tea service, and scones, perfect for a midmorning snack. Just as quickly as the servants appeared, they disappeared. Jamie poured generous servings for each, even a small saucer of milk for Cin.

"Dian, I remember you like yours with just a touch of milk."

"Yes, Jamie."

"And you, Michael?"

"I like mine sweet."

"Let's say two sugars, then. So what brings you here today," Jamie asked, proffering each their refreshment in turn. Tony let Cin down onto the table at her dish. Cin sat patiently as Tony pinched a small blueberry scone from the tray.

Sonya sensed Tony's decision to remain quiet and be subservient. A good choice, as he didn't know why they were here. "We're after a backdoor into any of these major corps' data-nets," Sonya said, sliding a small scrap of plastic onto the table. In one continued movement she lifted her cup and took a dainty sip.

Jamie didn't even bend over to look at the plastic or what it carried. "Really? Sure you wouldn't like some SLSA rockets? Maybe some Gunnison gauss guns? We also just recently got a shipment of Black Marionettes."

"Sorry, no. Information this time, not hardware."

"What you're asking for isn't trivial. I honestly don't know if we can deliver to any kind of timeline."

"What kind of price would be associated with this?"

"I couldn't even apply a price to such information," she said with the civility of a garden party. "Probably more than you could afford. It would be well into the millions."

"Please don't assume our financial status is burdened with the problems of the past."

"There were words on the street to that effect, but one can't always believe what one hears."

"Well, you can believe it this time."

"In that case, how about I investigate and provide you with a quote and a timeline?"

"That would be perfectly acceptable. This is excellent tea."

"Darjeeling. We have some being grown illegally in India and brought over. Another cup?"

Cin lifted her face from the bowl and proceeded to clean her face contentedly. "No, thank you. We really must be moving on. We have many other stops to make."

"Yes, we thank you for your hospitality," Tony offered.

"Well, Michael, if I'm not stepping on Dian's toes, I'll offer you even more hospitality," Jamie said in a voice both sultry and low.

Tony shook his head just a fraction. "Thank you, no. We do really have to be going."

"A shame. But come back any time."

Fifteen silent minutes later, Tony and Sonya walked side by side, back to the decay that was ground level. Both tried to speak simultaneously.

"Why didn't you take her up on it?"

"Why did we go there?"

They both laughed. "You first," Sonya insisted.

"Why did we go there? We didn't get anything out of her. And if you think she's going to come up with a quote for us, you're crazy. There's no way she can get that info for us. Despite her serene hostess façade, her inability to deliver was written all over her."

"Of course it was. That's what I was testing for, actually. Normally, she just quotes a very high price for something and we politely dicker. Even she didn't think she could get the information. And if she can't, no one can. That's what I needed. No backdoors for Augustine."

"Too bad. We could use the direct information."

"Yes, she's been asking for years. This is the first time we've had the resources to even pose the question. By the way, don't let her vamp attitude make you think less of her. She runs the most pervasive Mob family around."

"She did seem a bit casual."

"It's a defense mechanism. No one initially gives her the credit for her intelligence and her ruthlessness. Be that as it may, I had two other reasons for my visit. The easiest was to convey that our financial wherewithal has improved. That will get us better service and attention in the future."

"And the other?"

"To introduce you to her, of course."

Measure Performance — Phase One

Linc and Tony worked side-by-side in what passed for the militia's armory, an abandoned automotive service garage at ground level. Linc's bald head beaded with perspiration that also rolled down the side of his face. "Hot in here, isn't it?"

"Are you nuts?" Tony asked. "It's November, we had a high of ten degrees today, and I'm ready to set fire to this dump just for some heat." Tony watched Linc wipe a thick layer of moisture from over the top of his head with his forearm before preparing another explosive charge. Linc's face didn't have any of its normal healthful vigor, but instead wore a mask of white mottled with pink. "Maybe you're pushing too hard?"

"Don't worry about me. I can work the long hours. I want to win, and now that we can finally see some successes, I'm just a little eager." His outburst drained what little color remained in his face.

"Linc, let this one go. What is this, your ninth mission in seven days? I'll pick up someone else for this one. Christine's been itching to do something, seeing as we've all but nixed her specialty from further field operations."

"Well, I must admit I'm not feeling very well."

"You don't say? OK, sorry for the sarcasm, but I really think you should call it a day. You don't look so good."

"You sure you can do it without me?"

"Yeah. Walk in the park compared to the risks we were taking when I first started this show."

"Well, OK. Thanks, Tony. I'm going to go lay down."

* * *

Nine miniature solidos once again sat on the matte black surface of Nanogate's desk.

"We've heard enough of your complaints. These impromptu meetings are dangerous and costly." Several others nodded.

"We did agree to meet more often. We're meeting remotely only in deference to Tokyo Industrials and Unified Textiles, who could not alter their travel schedules."

"Yes, quite right. Taste Dynamics, please refrain from changing the topic. We shall now continue, with Nanogate having the floor."

"I've brought this to your attention previously, but now things are becoming perilous. All of those companies in my linked directorate have fallen under attack. Sixty separate incidents over two weeks. Our cash reserves are dangerously low. If it continues it may force us to close our doors…all of them."

"Your poor foresight is not our concern. Why are you whining when—"

"Gentlemen," CNI interrupted, "There is a perfectly simple solution to everyone's troubles. This effort was supposed to be a shared risk to us all. As it's been directly affecting only one of us, I suggest we all provide unsecured loans to weather these issues." Most of the quorum nodded.

"Passed by acclamation."

"A practical solution," offered Wintel, one of the more conservative of their group. "This will get you past the worst of it. If you'll refer to our simulations, you'll see the weapons should begin to be felt any time now. We'll see an easing of this area steadily for the next three weeks."

"I don't believe this body really understands the gravity of the situation. Two more weeks of this will cause a significant portion of our directorate to declare insolvency. Three weeks would completely destabilize not only my administration but also the corporate fold I control. This could easily cause a ripple effect that would impact you as well. My simulations show a fourteen percent chance of catastrophic failure, a twenty-nine percent chance of a system-wide depression, and a further thirty-eight percent chance of recession. My data is available to any who wish to examine the validity of the simulations.

"With these thoughts in mind, I would like to propose something more than just loans. Loans only temporarily prop up what has become a sinking ship. I propose we each assume an equal share of the losses. I ask for a vote."

Nanogate knew what the outcome would be before it even showed. The world of finance bred cutthroats, not altruists. They couldn't see or smell the danger to themselves for the blood in the water. Most of them were already deciding how they could snap up pieces of his company for the biggest profit.

Eight nays carried the vote.

"Thank you for your time, gentlebeings. I must prepare what I can and determine what loans I'll need from each of you."

Without fanfare he terminated the connection. His single button push summoned Mr. Marks in his yellow vinyl. "I have another job for you."

"Of course, sir."

* * *

"As we—I mean, Tony—predicted," reported Beth, "we've been experiencing a large influx of not only volunteers, but warmth from the community, where just a short while ago we were beginning to see signs of support erosion and in some cases even hostility."

"Excellent. With that and our next steps in place, I call for new business," Sonya said. As one the group remained silent. "Well, in that case, I have a new item. This one's a two-edged sword. We've been contacted by the head of the Nanogate syndicate."

"How did he find us?"

"There were two messages. Both found their way to me. The first Augustine ferreted out when she spent last weekend trying to break into another Nanogate mainframe level. There in the open for even the most moronic of icebreakers to find was a message addressed to the GAM.

"The second came to us from the brother of one of our current members. I won't mention who, as he or she would be embarrassed to admit they have a corpie as a sibling. Somehow, the Nanogate sent us a personal message buried as an implant in the man's brain. The details are lengthy, but after they fired the man he came to his brother for help. Our medical probes, the same ones you each were subjected to, discovered it easily. Both conveyed exactly the same message, word for word.

"He wants a percomm meeting at a specific time. He assures us there will be no attempt to trace the call. There's no reason for the call given. It's signed with the CEO's DNA."

Tony fingered a crack in the upholstery as he considered Sonya's words. "That really is a basket of snakes," he remarked after a moment.

"Why go 'o such 'engths?"

"Yeehaw! We got him on the run. He must be desperate."

"You think he might want to negotiate a peace?"

"Or buy'n time to fix his stuff."

"Or even it could be a trap."

"I congratulate you all," Sonya agreed. "I came up with exactly the possibilities you proposed."

"So why chew with him?"

"Well, he tipped his hand with this message," Tony answered excitedly. "He gave us info we didn't have before. He knows we've infiltrated his nets and he knows the people they're nilling are coming into our fold. And, perhaps even more interesting, he's contacting us in a clandestine manner."

"True. Hadn't thought of it that way."

"If you don't mind, Sonya," Tony said, waiting for her nodded approval. "Well, let's take each option in turn. Option one: We have him on the run and he wants to negotiate. If he is, he knows he has to offer something sweet to make us lay off. I think we'd be foolish not to at least listen to an offer."

"Yeah, righ'. We ge' more from him than we're sucking up now!"

"Agreed. Option two: We have him on the run and he wants to buy time. Again, I think there's no loss in listening. If it's a ploy for a stall, we can always ignore it."

"And we can shove it up his arse if it's shonky."

"Times two on that comment," Colin added.

"OK, OK. Option three: It's a trap. I think ninety percent of avoiding any trap is knowing it's there in the first place."

"And then we can shove it up his arse."

"Goes 'ouble for me."

"OK, Suet, I think we understand your sentiments," Sonya said.

"What about risks?" Jackson offered, almost as if scripted.

"Well, if we decide to go through with it, we can limit the damage by isolating the person making contact. Take one of the new recruits and limit their knowledge of our organization even further."

"Agreed, but then we'd limit our ability to have a dialogue."

"Not necessarily," Linc offered from his professional knowledge. "Have that someone, a cutout, physically tie two phones together receiver to transmitter. The person would only be needed to dial the number and put the phones together. Additionally, we could also use multiple cutouts before the call goes through. It's such an old dodge I don't think anyone would think of it."

"Yes, and I'm certain Augustine could monitor a trace. Even if successful, the manual percomm links would deny anything but a signal to process for comparison on other lines."

Now Sonya took her time thinking. "Any other risks?"

"We could put everyone on watch duty to make sure if someone does show up we have time to escape," Jonah offered.

"Well, then I call for a vote," Sonya said. "All opposed?" No hands showed. "I guess just as a formality…all in favor?" Everyone thrust up their hand.

"Carried. The call time is set for tonight."

"Tonight?"

"Better sooner than later. Set it up. Jonah, you set up security. Linc you handle the cutouts. Tony will be our voice."

* * *

At one time in her early youth, Sonya learned to isolate a single nerve in her body and heighten or deaden its input, a survival trait. She sat in a lotus, nude, in the center of her meditation room with her eyes rolled up in her head. She searched inside her body for groups of nerves to deaden to attenuate the pain. Her head throbbed in a way she couldn't seem to control.

One by one she turned off the nerve endings until she couldn't feel anything of the outside world, but the pain remained. Many years ago her mother had taught her how to encapsulate illnesses and since then she'd never been sick, but she remembered some of those feelings—the loss of control, the pain and the lack of well-being, just like her body's responses now.

She turned her sight inward. For a brief moment she just relaxed and rode on the flow of her bloodstream, trying to adjust her senses to her new state. The pulsing motion, timed with each pump of her heart, started to make her nauseous. She contemptuously turned off those neural inputs, an oversight and lack of focus.

It took several more seconds before she got her bearings and realized she now navigated through her kidneys. Everything looked in exceptional health. She flowed along out of the kidney. Ahead she sensed a foulness. As she floated further down, the blood pathway became clouded with necrotic cells, obscuring her vision. As she rolled into the liver, lesions spotted across its width, with entire branches clogged in an all-out war between her body's immune system and the cause of the damage.

Breaking her consciousness from the easy flow of the bloodstream she fought through tissue to worm deeper into the liver. She stopped next in one of the more virulent patches, visibly expanding before her. Healthy tissue and body defenses fought a losing battle as the invaders left naught but the dead and dying in their wake. She'd never seen anything move so quickly.

Sonya encapsulated the infectious patch in a gossamer bag, allowing new defenders to rush to the defense. In the past this gave her body the ability to not only defeat the disease but to learn from it and become protected for the next time, just as a body is supposed to learn. But this time she watched the new defenders die just as fast and her isolation expand like a balloon continuing to be inflated. The rate of expansion slowed to a crawl compared to its previous rampage, but it continued. Sonya put more of her personal strength into the enclosure. Still it expanded. She poured even more power into it. Still it expanded.

For the first time in many, many years, fear touched Sonya's mind.

Adjust Plan

Over the next hour, at a cost of hundreds of thousands of civilians, a single pony nuke or cyphod chemical bomb could've destroyed up to ninety-five percent of the GAM membership. They lounged inconspicuously in doorways, drank coffee in terrace bistros, drove lift-trucks in racetracks around city blocks, and even patrolled the street level. Not one felt comfortable in their role as lookout. Every one of them nursed second thoughts and fears about this mission. Each one put every other thought and effort into watching for the precursors of a trap. Reports from them all came into Augustine's neural net, every one of them comfortably negative.

"All clear, Tony. Make the call."

Pushing one single button engaged the complex network of blind percomm connections and duplicitous network jockeying. In an age of crystal clear audio connections, this one scratched and crackled with odd noises.

"It's your nickel," Tony said. While the elaborate system synthesized his voice, no one had any illusion that it couldn't be broken. They all agreed Tony should act as the GAM voice in this meeting. Only Tony and Augustine sat in presence even with all the precautions they had taken.

"What the hell's a nickel?" wondered the voice on the other end of the line.

"A historical unit of currency. Ancient slang for 'you initiated the call, so get on with it.'" Tony looked at Augustine, who shook her head. No tracing attempts hit the line or any intermediate connection.

"True. Thank you for your contact. I know the risk you are taking. My people have assured me that you are not tracing the line and I'm sure you have done the same."

"So we have the minimum amount of trust. Trace or no, we won't stay on line long. Spill it."

"Very well. I propose that you call off your attacks on Nanogate and its affiliates."

"Getting that close to shutting your doors?" Tony immediately regretted the jibe. It might limit his opponent's candor.

"Frankly, yes. Call me a survivor if you wish, but I'd like to go on surviving." Everyone listening, in person and remotely, took a brief pause at the admission.

"Well, we aren't going to just stop. Nanogate is a legitimate target in our eyes. What are you offering in return?"

"A new target."

"We've got hundreds of juicy targets."

"Not with inside information, you don't, no matter how good a wire jock you have."

"What specifically are you offering?"

"I will provide you detailed information that will allow you to take this attack to one of the other major conglomerates. This information will include areas of sensitivity, detailed intelligence, and aid in obtaining even more information to make your attacks safer and more pointed."

Tony's mouth gaped. "How do we know you aren't setting us up?" he counterpunched weakly.

"You don't. What assurances will you give me that you won't attack both firms under my care and these others?"

"You have a valid point. If we agree, what's the next step you propose?"

"I propose three future meetings that will provide you with the information I've promised. Each time I will provide more sensitive information, assuming I see the aggression against my companies cease."

"Agreed," Tony said, not even looking to his compatriots.

"We need a secure method of communication for these three meetings."

Without prompting, Augustine scribbled a notation on a piece of paper and handed it to Tony, who read and processed the information swiftly. "We'll each send the other a two-gig encryption key for each meeting. By using both keys in alternation, we can limit the attack to brute force only. The keys are to be hand generated. No computer—not even an isolated system—is to be involved. Send your three keys to General Delivery in Tucson, Arizona, in care of Jefferson Thomas."

"Agreed. You send your key to William Wenner, 1456 South Oscar Road, Beach City, Oregon."

"Our next call will be exactly four days from now at this same time. We will refrain from any attacks during that period."

"Thank you."

"I won't say 'You're welcome.'"

"I wouldn't expect it."

* * *

Not for the first time, Mr. Marks dressed in something other than his yellow tights. This time he wore professional overalls bearing the logo of Volt Electrical. Marks hummed off key as the Taste Dynamics security guard examined the work order Marks had fabricated just ten minutes before.

"Everything looks in place. Do you need an escort?"

"Only if you want to give me one. I've been here often enough they gave me my own key," he lied easily. "Seems your plumbing contractor screwed up the power lines again."

"OK. Report back here before you leave."

"No problem. Short job. I'll be out in an hour."

Mr. Marks walked along his memorized route to a janitorial door. Using the electronic key he had brandished earlier, the door opened to his touch. He calmly opened his bag and placed a thirty thousand gauss electromagnetic lock on the door to ensure his privacy. He extracted from his kit a fifty-centimeter, black-plastic stick. Flipping it open, once in each direction, he tripled its length. Expertly, he pulled it open, one section at a time. Each length popped up a perpendicular stick twenty centimeters long, each one on opposite sides of the pole from the previous. Once done, he leaned it against the wall, making a very serviceable ladder. Removing a laser saw from his pouch, he climbed up and began cutting a hole in the wall very near the ceiling.

Seven minutes later he took a visual network tester and played it over the grouping of cables he had just exposed. It took thirty-three minutes to identify the right cables. Selecting that one pair, he released them from the bundle, routed them out to a separate and exposed plastic trough, and then returned the remainder to their original resting place. With stolen Taste Dynamics sealing tape, he marked the hole he'd cut and the plastic trough, making it seem part of an official change and approved by security.

After sixteen minutes of miscellaneous cleanup and removal of the protective magnet, he dropped the last of his tools in his bag. Eight minutes later he walked out the gate with a wave to the guard, duty for another day accomplished.

* * *

"I therefore call this meeting to a close. Thank you all." Sonya nodded as they stood to depart. "Tony, would you mind following me back home?"

Tony's mind went immediately into overdrive. He'd never been asked to Sonya's home. To the best of his knowledge, no one had. She'd been kind, but never really friendly, nor did she ever seem sexually attracted. Anything she said to him normally would be said in front of the entire council. Why the change? At least eleven people looked at him with that same question in their eyes.

"Sure," his voice betraying just a tiny bit of confusion. When Sonya turned, Tony shrugged at the assemblage.

He followed her out to the slum of street level. She glided along the streets illuminated by the occasionally functioning streetlamp. Without moving in anything but a straight line, she seemed to dance amongst the fog and early evening darkness like a ghost, totally at one with the environs. Fearlessly, she walked past street level gangs and bands of whelps who routinely dismembered their victims for their two-credit implants. Less than a few weeks ago, terror would've overcome Tony at even the thought of escorting a young woman on a Portland street, other than those specifically patrolled and kept relatively safe for the nightclubs. Instead, he strode comfortably at Sonya's side.

While Tony tried to determine, unsuccessfully, if they were unnoticed or respected enough to be left alone, Sonya suddenly leapt high enough to chin her way up a rusted fire escape ladder four meters above the ground. It creaked ominously as she scrambled up arm over arm. Tony eyed the lowest rung. Sonya's panther-like jump outstripped his capabilities. Without undue stress he climbed up on a nearby blue dumpster, freckled with the ever-present corrosion of the Pacific Northwest, and with only a tiny jump managed the ladder. He unconsciously wiped the rust from his hand on his pants before entering through the window of her fifth floor apartment.

For their enterprise, fifth floor approached perfection—too low for anything but street scum, but high enough to keep out all but the most ambitious of the Nils and breakers. Tony wrinkled his nose at a pervasive musty smell. The single piece of furniture, an ancient leather sofa, held at least seven cats and four dogs. The heavily stained carpet held at least twice that number. Two of the cats came up to strop his legs. One of the small dogs chose that time to bark, but only a single yip broke his throat. Several of them came over to beg attention from Sonya, who managed to pet each of them and croon something Tony couldn't hear.

Despite the menagerie, Tony worried on that one-word question like a bit of steak caught between his molars. *Why?*

Instead of asking, he made idle conversation. "Nice security. Would they lick the invader to death?"

"Despite all appearances, they'd protect this home fiercely. That you're with me, and that you're an empathic person, makes all the difference."

"Empathic? Me?"

"Yes, even if you don't understand why you feel uneasy around some people and warm in the glow of others. Yes. Now come this way." She invited him into a kitchen strewn about with equipment of various missions, past and present. Oddly, the animals stopped at the doorway as if barred by an invisible door. They didn't invade the kitchen like they'd taken over the living room.

"I didn't bring you here for that discussion, however." She shoved out a padded chair with its stuffing peeking through the cracked vinyl for Tony. As he sat, she pushed away the parts on the table, many of which crashed to the floor, and assumed her customary lotus on the surface.

"You have to be overflowing with curiosity. Let me just begin by saying that I've not brought you here on a whim. You've become more than just another member of my organization, but really my right hand in planning and intentions. With fourteen extremely successful personal missions under your belt and the planning of many, many more, you've earned not only my trust but that of the entirety of the GAM. You know nearly everything I know about our organization. I need to bounce a couple of items off of you. Items that have me concerned."

Tony had learned the hard way that concern from the stoical Sonya usually meant a cosmic disaster. To have several such concerns meant nothing less than the end of the world. "Why not bring them up in council?"

"I didn't feel comfortable discussing such things publicly. Morale is a fragile thing. It's been so long since we've had any, I want to keep it going and not risk fracturing it."

"Sounds serious."

"Perhaps. Let me start with the most obvious. Did you notice that we had three members missing tonight?"

"Yes. I sent Linc home yesterday. Must have the flu."

"Hmm. I don't believe it's any form of influenza. He's running four degrees of fever. The other two are worse, with all the signs of dysentery."

"How did they get that? In this modern era? We don't have contaminated water. Even most of the barrios have good water here in Portland."

"They don't have dysentery. They have the symptoms. Each of the other two has been running at both ends for three days."

"OK, so we have a bug running around. Even those with full medical don't have a cure for the common cold."

"I agree, but I have a strong reason to believe that this isn't any common bug. You see, I have it as well."

"What?"

"Yes. I've had it for two days. You needn't worry. I've isolated my body with…well, you'd probably call it a spell."

"I hate to sidetrack you, but that's a question I've had hovering. I've seen you do some very slick things."

Sonya didn't hesitate. She must've anticipated the question. "My mother was a witch and her mother before her. For all I know, probably her mother before that. Just let it be said that I have certain abilities that are mostly personal or informational in nature."

"Can you elaborate?"

"I could teach it, but the training usually starts in infancy. Just say that I've usually got an ace up my sleeve in many situations that most won't understand nor comprehend."

"OK, but that still doesn't explain…"

"My illness started as nothing but muscle aches, but I knew there was nothing normal about it. I've not been ill since a bout of measles at seven years old. This made me obviously suspicious. I've tested my blood and it's positive for an unknown biological agent. It could be a naturally occurring mutation, but its targets seem a bit localized."

"I don't think we should assume anything yet. We should give it a bit of time. We're a small and closely knit group, after all."

"Well, I'm going to institute some quarantine procedures. All those that are ill will not be allowed to further mingle with the rest of our team."

"Seems logical no matter the cause. I don't mean to sound belittling, but this sounds like an overreaction."

"So be it. I find it all too convenient, but we shall see."

* * *

For their regular quarterly meeting, the cabal met in person in the heart of a private space station orbiting the Moon. That they alone occupied the station or had ever been on the station since its construction didn't seem to faze these ten wealthy individuals.

Living and sleeping in zero-gee, and the solitude no one ever got on Earth, rested one in a way no other relaxation could. Each had used it as a private retreat when the pressures of running a conglomerate climbed too high to withstand.

The tiny conference room would've seemed cramped in any gravity, but in zero-gee the group lay out flat nearly head-to-head in a formation that resembled the points of a three-dimensional compass. Each kept notes on an electronic stylus tethered to podiums that stretched out from the wall. Tokyo Industrials and CNI, both uncomfortable floating free, strapped themselves to the same solid structures.

"That brings us to the actions against the GAM," directed Wintel, the chairman for this quarter.

"Actions here have taken a radical change," said Taste Dynamics, who gently drifted away to the right from her notes.

"Agreed," Nanogate said. "The actions against Nanogate have ceased, but the damage has been done. We are a ghost of our former strength. Our simulations show eight to ten years to reestablish ourselves even without any further attacks."

"That's within the overall window of damage we predicted," claimed ECM.

Nanogate kept his face perfectly calm.

"Actually, the change I wanted to report is that we are now the ones under attack," Taste Dynamics explained. "As has been the norm of late, no one has claimed responsibility. Additionally, the attacks have been very severe and quite uncanny in their targeting."

"Please elaborate."

"We've lost seven shipments of a rare chemical required in the production of nanites, and even more importantly the new NAD, Neural Amplification and Disruption, weaponry. We've beefed up our security on these shipments, and miraculously no one made attempts on the last four we sent. This puts our finished goods deliveries to our customers behind by at least a full quarter, even if we reduce our own uses to zero. The cost in penalties alone is ruinous."

"Our original assessment of this was industrial sabotage, until someone succeeded in eradicating the formula for Pepsi. This formula is one of the most closely guarded secrets in my entire sphere of influence. Only three people, and one totally isolated and hidden computer system, knew the formula. All three of these people were killed within minutes of a large detonation which destroyed the computer system—a system whose location only three different people knew.

"I don't need to inform you of the magnitude of this loss. To hide this, we've started a spin on all the nets to get people ready for the new and improved Pepsi. However, every netwired pundit has plastered the real story over every black channel available. Sixty-three percent of the viewers believe the truth, not our spin coverage."

"Anything more?"

"Dozens of attacks on key industrial facilities. All of this has happened within the last week. Our stock, as I'm sure all of you have noticed, has plummeted to a mere thirty-four percent of its former value. My people are telling me that the word on the street is that the GAM has made Taste Dynamics its prime target. And as in the past, massive puts distributed across many over-the-counter operations again gave the perpetrators a massive infusion of cash."

"Why the change?" Nanogate asked with a straight face. High stakes poker players could take tips from him. "They could've finished us off completely with just a bit more concentrated effort."

"Lack of prime targets?" asked CNI. "A group like this feeds on morale and success. They don't have the will to follow through with their actions to completion. I venture they realized all they could pick on with Nanogate was crumbs and decided to go after more juicy morsels elsewhere."

"A plausible explanation," Taste Dynamics reluctantly agreed. "I remain concerned that the damage to our fiscal structure seems a little too precise and convenient. Could there be inside information?"

"That's definitely something you should investigate," said Bell.

"Wait a moment," Percomm Systems interjected. "Are you suggesting that someone in this room had anything to do with this?"

"I made no such implication," Taste Dynamics said with the blandest expression as she floated just a bit away from her designated place. Her body made gentle and unconscious movements to recover her podium and her notes, but her face didn't waver.

"That's good. Without cooperation, we would not be able to function nearly as effectively."

"Agreed."

"Yes."

"I suggest in the interest of continuing our support of those affected by the GAM that we extend our open loan policy to Taste Dynamics," offered Nanogate in a fine hypocritical glow.

Taste Dynamics glared but said nothing.

"Passed by acclamation."

* * *

"Grab her left arm...I mean, tentacle...I mean, just grab it!"

With a howl spawned from the deepest hell, Suet flailed again, throwing Tolly's huge frame across the bedroom with predictable results in the centuries old home built with old-fashioned sheetrock.

With the devastation left by a hurricane, the room bore holes randomly spaced about the walls, along with shattered lamps, torn bedding, and shredded bits of indistinguishable electronics littered about. One sliding closet door hung from a single point at right angles to its tracks, and the other had been broken roughly horizontally in half. The bed on which Suet lay only retained its two right legs, canting it to the left. The loose jade tentacle snapped across the top quarter of the battered but previously intact TriVid, shattering any semblance of form or functionality.

This time Tony and Andrew managed to grab and hold down Suet's right arm without damage to any party. The welts and bruises on everyone testified that they hadn't been so successful in containing the chaos previously.

"Augustine! Hurry up!"

"Cracking body implants isn't the easiest job in the world!" she snapped back from the other room. "Most of this is black market kludge. If I address the wrong command register, I could crash her completely!"

"I don't care! If you ain't smart, Sheila, we'll all be mush!"

"Andrew, get this arm lashed down so we can try and control the other one."

"P'ease shu' me off," Suet pleaded in a voice weak and cracked by hours of screaming.

"We're trying, sweetie," Tony said softly. "It won't be long."

"Oh, shi'! Here comes another one!" The screech of Suet's voice mimicked the intensity and agony of tearing sheet steel in a high-speed vehicle crash.

"Tolly, get up and grab that arm!"

He made it by bare microseconds. This time, her body rocked in jackhammer-like strokes on the bed. Her hips lifted nearly 30 centimeters before crashing down each time. The third oscillation took off the remaining legs of the bed with the report similar to a pair of gunshots, milliseconds apart.

Sonya, the newest arrival, bolted in from the front door. She chanted something as she ran full speed to the side of the bed. From one hand she cast a handful of dust at Suet's vibrating form. All motion stopped instantly.

"Augustine, that won't last long," Sonya announced as the others allowed themselves a brief moment to relax. "Get her implants shut down now!"

"Two minutes," came the slightly muffled reply.

"This is no cold," Sonya spat at Tony in the rarest display of temper.

Tony looked at her, stunned, unable to think of anything to say in response.

"What happened?" Sonya asked, forcibly calming herself down.

Tolly took up the description after two deep breaths and a brief examination of a dinner-plate-sized abrasion on his abdomen. "I got a ring from Suet's flat-mate, Sandy. Suet asked her to ring me up because she was having troubles controlling voluntary servos. I've meched for Suet in the past. I didn't think anything of it until I came in and found Sandy lying on the floor with her neck broken. Then I put out the all-points alarm per doctrine. You know most of the rest."

"You were right about the illnesses, Sonya," admitted Tony. "What's our next step?"

"Closest to this I've heard of is epilepsy, but gengineering cleared that up fifty years or more ago. When Augustine's done, I'll have her search the medical databases."

"What about the others?"

"Nothing like this. Jonah's symptoms seem to be that of radiation poisoning. Frances looks more like malaria. Andrew, Colin, and Arthur have each complained of fevers, but have no further symptoms. The only core members that I know of that don't seem to be affected are you, Augustine, and Christine."

"What about you?" Tony asked.

Sonya's composure momentarily slid. Deep lines showed out from under her eyes while the frown of her face intensified. A yellow pallor became visible under the olive skin. These images flashed for but a moment, and once again fell victim to her iron control. Her brows knitted tighter together in concentration.

"Mine seems to be focusing on my liver, similar to severe sclerosis. I'll be honest...I'm holding myself together with spells and little else at the moment."

"I think you made mention of a deeper probe into this. How can I help?" Tony asked.

"I brought my blood-drawing kit."

"I've always hated needles," Tony said with a shudder.

* * *

"Encryption enabled. Connection established," said the sultry computer-automated device. Tony often wondered if they chose those voices to make certain men, at least, would pay attention. This time he, Augustine, and about eighty kilos of computer equipment crammed themselves into a two-and-a-half-meter square women's bathroom in Benito's Fine Dining. Andrea, duplicitously garbed in bodyguard yellow, watched the door. Based on the two previous meetings, they didn't expect any danger, but they could take no chances.

"As we agreed, this will be my final call," Nanogate said without preamble. He didn't have to like what survival dictated.

"As agreed," Tony said as he watched Augustine's face for any sign of a trace, but it remained passive. While the last call, it also was the most dangerous in other ways—very little held the other from reneging on any promise.

"I hope by now I've given you enough evidence that I can be trusted."

"You've been very forthcoming thus far."

"As have you. My final intelligence is how to obtain a direct tap into the Taste Dynamics net."

Augustine's head jerked up.

"We have a tap into their network," remarked Tony casually.

"Not beyond their executive firewall you don't."

The lust in Augustine's eyes struck Tony harder than anything she could've said. "OK. You have our attention."

Nanogate allowed himself a tiny chuckle. "I thought I might. As before, I won't admit to any technical knowledge I don't have. I've been assured by a very good source that there is an old fiber optic link inside Taste Dynamics that passes through a low security janitorial closet because of a remodel this last week. You will find the schematics and pictures on the data carrier."

Augustine nodded.

"Apparently," continued Nanogate, "some contractor didn't know what it was and decided that for his ease of work, sliding it over a meter would be acceptable. I don't know how long it'll remain in place, but I expect until the inspection at the end of construction approximately one week from today."

"That's very impressive and seems complete. Anything more to share?"

"Just a question."

"Go on."

"How long will you leave Nanogate alone after this?"

Tony paused. It wasn't a question he'd considered. He could lie. He could make something up. It wasn't anything they as a team had remotely discussed.

"Assuming the information you gave us pays off, we won't directly attack any physical asset of your conglomerate for three full years."

"Acceptable. This finalizes our agreement, Mr. Sammis."

Before Tony could respond the line went dead. Augustine once again went wide-eyed, but for a reason that Tony didn't understand.

"Three years?!" burst Linc's voice over the alternate line. "How could you propose such a thing?! We've finally got them on the run and you throw it away?" Venom dripped with each word, but it broke when Linc began a series of wracking coughs that just didn't seem to end.

"I do have to agree with Linc's assessment, if not his vehemence," Sonya rasped in a voice that broke twice into a hoarse whisper.

"I had to come up with something on the fly," Tony snapped from fatigue. "Look, I don't see any of you sitting in the hot seat." Between missions and Suet's bedside vigil, his sleep in the last week totaled less than five hours, and that only because Sonya slipped a needle full of Doz into his ass.

"No one questioned your—"

"Yes, Sonya, they did. Before I drop this call, I want you to understand two things about this.

"First, we always have the option of NOT living up to the agreement I made. I don't like that option, but it exists. Second, if we work through the other major conglomerates, it'll take us at least three years, even with an increase in operational tempo, to get back to Nanogate."

"But we'd finish off Nanogate without a sweat in just a few weeks."

"True, but we'd be hitting lower priority targets when we need high visibility right now. We need to increase our recruiting to a point where we can run multiple operations every day all across the solar system. That's something our pitiful dozen can't manage, not even with the second cell that seems to be coming along so well."

He sucked in a couple of deep breaths, rubbing his eyes from fatigue. "I'm sorry, I'm so tired I can't be diplo."

"Go back to your flat. We can hold the fort. Aces!"

"Just one more thing," Augustine interrupted. "How did he know Tony's real name?"

* * *

Tony entered the ancient theatre, stepping around the worst of the mold and mildew on the floor. Nearly one hundred people milled about, not settled and confident as usual before an all-hands strategy meeting, but more like a disturbed anthill. They whispered, but with large spaces between them and their confidant. No one shook hands, or kissed on the cheek or patted on another's back. If any doubt remained, it erased itself as he moved closer. The stinging scent of nervous perspiration mixed with other less pleasant smells.

Sonya stepped around the puddles and the one large hole on the decrepit stage, bearing dark lines in her cheeks and creases in her brow. The ripped flatie screen behind her bore graffiti on top of other graffiti from several generations of tag artists. As she called the meeting to order, the team sat not in little knots as usual but spread wide, with no fewer than two seats between each listener. Tony found himself making a point to sit right next to Augustine in the front row as a show of confidence. Unfortunately for him, the seat upholstery held a vast quantity of water from the leaking roof and the moisture wicked up through his pants. He showed his solidarity by suffering the minor discomfort and not changing seats.

"I have two topics for our agenda, and then I'll open it up for new business," began Sonya. "First, Suet is doing as well as can be expected. Her seizures abated last night but she's still running an excessively high fever.

"The other three aren't doing as well." What few smiles Suet's condition prompted disappeared with the speed of a candle in a glass furnace. "Because of his high fever, Linc's kidneys shut down yesterday and he's being forced to suffer dialysis along with other treatments. I won't trouble you with describing Tolly and Jonah's symptoms. Just say they're dissimilar and life–threatening, and leave it at that.

"Additionally we have four other cases of people coming down with mysterious ailments over the last week. While we aren't sure they're connected in any way, we've drawn blood from everyone in this room. The testing we've done thus far is inconclusive. As I know more, I'll let you know." The group murmured. While she couldn't hear their words, Sonya felt their fear even more than when she had entered. "Are there any questions?"

"Are the symptoms at all similar?" someone called out.

"No, as I said earlier. The only common thing among all of them seems to be a fever. However, this is one of our body's standard defense mechanisms to most illnesses."

"Anyone outside of our group getting ill?"

"There's no evidence of any others, associated or not with our group, getting ill in larger numbers or with similar pathologies."

"If they're so dissimilar, is there any reason to believe these illnesses are connected?"

"The statistical probability that this number of a small group should come down with seriously debilitating disease within the same timeframe is vanishingly small. In fact, 'small' is giving it too much credit. That they're dissimilar actually makes it less likely, not more likely. When all factors are added in, the correct descriptive might be infinitesimal. If I covered this flattie screen behind me with zeros, it might not be enough. Any more questions?"

Sonya paused for just a few moments before moving on. "Item two: We have an opportunity for a coup in tapping into the corps' executive data nets. This isn't your standard icebreaker job, but rather a physical tap. Additionally, the data we may be obtaining could possibly be falsified, leading us into more than one trap. Any questions?"

"How did we find out about it?"

"We're keeping that tight to our vest at the moment. Let us just say our source gave us other information that allowed us to successfully complete seven other very profitable missions with zero losses."

"Why kinds of information are we likely to get?"

Augustine fielded this one. "Any new net we tackle gives us scads of useless information and a handful of gems. We feel this net will be the inverse, with a majority of the information truly valuable. Specifically what that information is, well, we can't tell right now." The auditorium fell silent except for the drips from the ubiquitous leaks from the ceiling.

"Normally, this type of decision would've remained at the executive action committee," explained Sonya, "but that committee is down by four members and this kind of action could decimate our action member ranks."

"Fuck that, we're being decimated now," someone called out from the back.

"In all good faith," Tony threw in, "I should let you know the executive action committee did discuss this. They recognized the risks and the potential benefits. We agreed to bring it to the membership as a whole, but we also took our own vote. Seventy-five percent felt it should be done, the lowest of any action taken by the committee in nearly its entire existence."

"OK, if there's no more discussion, I will call for a vote. All those in favor of continuing with this action." A mass of hands flew up into the air, covering most occupied seats. "Those opposed?" Exactly eleven hands went into the air, less than ten percent of the assembly.

"Passed. We'll go ahead with this mission. To do so, we need some help from you. We're in need of some specialized equipment. As I said, this isn't your standard icebreaker mission, nor is it a simple breaking and entering. Please avail yourself should you be called upon by the team doing the job. With that, I'll close the meeting."

For the next thirty minutes Sonya did the meet-and-greet thing. Tony watched from his seat as people came up to talk with her, but never too closely. Sonya slumped slightly between each new face and then stood up straight in alternation, like someone catching themselves just before falling asleep in class. Not only that, but her hair had lost its black luster, like the faded look of a billboard out during one too many rainstorms. As she disengaged from her final conversation, her right hand twitched nervously. She dropped unceremoniously into the seat next to Tony wearing a frown of concentration.

"You look exhausted."

"More than you can imagine."

"I've been doing some research on witchcraft."

"Research? The library, right?"

"Yeah. I read that some witches can draw energy from those around them. I'd like to volunteer."

Sonya didn't laugh, but the corners of her mouth did manage to go up. "Well, in this case your book learning didn't do you one whit of good. That one's a fable."

"It was worth a try."

"The only way you can help me is to carry me home."

"I will if you want. Not like you're large enough to make more than an armful."

"Thanks, but no. Besides, we have something else to do."

"Oh?"

Sonya scanned the room briefly, but no one lingered. "I dissembled when I said I didn't have any more information about the disease. I do. The blood work shows a common base virus in each of those affected. The same base virus is in the vast majority of those in the audience."

"Shit."

"In that you've mastered the understatement, Tony."

"So what's next? Who do you know in the influenza game?"

"Our organization is missing medical people. For whatever reason, we've never been able to recruit anyone significant in that field. I'm the closest. However, I personally have someone who owes me a favor. His Shih Tzu nearly died of a respiratory infection. I think it's time to call in that marker."

"I can't think of a better time," Tony said, his damp ass reminding him of another issue. "But can we stop by my place first? I have a wardrobe problem."

* * *

"It's a two," the tiny Korean said, looking at the virus projection on the wall. He flicked to yet another picture that bore similarities.

"Come again, Doc?" Tony said, sitting on the padded examination table.

"Sorry. Common name for one of the genetically engineered war viruses."

"A war virus? I don't think I ever heard of that."

"Probably not. It was a failed experiment in the ABC teams back some hundred years or so ago. The bio warfare folks were trying to create a plague that wouldn't wipe out the entire population, but rather stop after causing a bunch of damage. Best they came up with was a strain of influenza that would only be passed on by two generations of hosts, hence the name."

"Want to give an example, Doctor?"

"Sure. Let us say we give a two to patient A, also known as patient zero. He's the original host. Once the disease has spread to a certain point, he can pass the disease to anyone he comes into contact with—let's call them patients B1 through B20. Note that it passes just like any influenza, mostly large droplets or touch. All the B's are contagious when this disease progresses to a certain point. They pass it on to C1,1 through C20,20, if you can envision the matrix in your head. Note that the study I read showed a contagion rate of twenty individuals was nominal during normal activities, at least with an agent deadly enough to be effective for its original intent.

"By the time it reaches the C hosts, the virus has worn out its ability to replicate and is no longer contagious. The Cs can't give it to anyone. Note by this time A is dead and ninety percent of Bs are dying. The Cs will have about a seventy percent mortality. It worked out to an optimax of about four hundred total victims, with an overall mortality rate of seventy-one or seventy-two percent."

"Only four hundred people, eh?" Tony said sourly.

"Yes, sir. The risks weren't worth it. Bio weapons then, just as today, are only a good way to get the entire deploying country removed from the gene pool. They tried to work it up to a three transfers or higher, but it never scaled. Anyway, they passed it on to the black ops folks. Never heard of it being used."

"You do now."

"Really?"

"Those are all blood samples from people I know," Sonya said quietly. Her eyes barely changed when she heard her own death sentence.

"Are you…" The doctor looked up to hear the continuous—and, in this case, reassuring—whisper of a decontamination particle flow coming down from the ceiling.

"Yes."

"I'm sorry, Sonya. It'd take months to work out something akin to a vaccination. Note I said vaccination, not a cure, and any vaccine has about a two percent disease rate. It would just restart a disease that'll die out after two generations on its own."

"I know. Still, can you explain why it would manifest differently in each host?"

"Maybe because of the catalyst. Ah, your look reminds me I forgot to share that bit. This disease requires a trigger to start its actions. No catalyst, no disease. It'll lie dormant for years waiting. Some catalysts can be gengineered to be as common as oxygen, but others can be quite complex, such as the specific ethanol combination that makes up Bailey's whiskey, but not Jack Daniels. Others may be just any alcohol. If the catalyst possessed the latter's broadness, each set of symptoms would depend on the type of trigger."

"Doc, I have just two more minor requests and then I'll consider our debt wiped."

"Ask away."

"I need to know which of these samples shows patient zero and what catalyst this particular strain would trigger on."

"Give me two days."

* * *

Tony sweated despite the November chill. He huddled further under the active-camouflage cloak. His right hand flexed spasmodically around a machine pistol, chosen because its larger slugs were more effective against any of the possible armored targets today than those of a flechette gun. Two pairs of footsteps closed on his position and approached within a meter of his position before veering off along the fence line.

The GAM members knew they all remained undetected by the simple fact that no cries of alarm pierced the chill night air, nor were any weapons discharged. When Tony could no longer hear the footfalls, he risked lifting his poncho just enough to see the guards at over 100 hundred meters and moving away. The aerial purr from a hover drone caused Tony to freeze in place. Drone visuals focused like some primitive predator, mostly on motion. While he couldn't see it, he could hear it pause and hover in place.

"Just move on," Tony thought. "Nothing here but a patch of grass."

The drone's sounds finally receded. Tony risked another quick look to see it floating back the other direction, ignoring the patch of grass that his cloak imitated. Three clicks on his mic sounded the all-clear.

Martin and Andrea both came up from their nearly invisible positions. Despite the advances in electronic surveillance and visual aids, night remained a playground for the professional thief and saboteur. Tony's team wore black garb under their active camo, either of which offered little for the natural or electronic eye to focus on outside the brightness of day.

Without talking, the three walked slowly but cautiously over to the nearby building and began climbing up the patterned stone face. Mechanical tools, designed specifically for this mission, gripped the patterns themselves, allowing the trio to scale the building confidently, if slowly. They opened and slid through an unlocked, nondescript fourth floor window. Despite always being lit, bathrooms seemed to offer themselves as perfect points of entry with no surveillance, and often less than zero physical security. The GAM actively sought them out as entrances and exits.

Tony pointed at the stall second from the end. There they set up a dummy on the toilet and stored several sets of emergency equipment. Andrea wired an explosive to the stall door so that if it were forced open, the smoldering ruin would announce a compromised escape route. Martin changed clothes while Tony stood guard.

Martin, now wearing a business suit and a badly faked employee badge, walked brazenly out of the bathroom, just like a corpie who belonged. Tony and Andrea waited until the three clicks over their comms told them the camera outside pointed away. Almost as one they sprinted across the hall into its blind spot. The camera blithely spun from one side to the other, allowing the pair to sprint down the hall to an unmarked door just twenty meters from the bathroom. All this took place as Martin continued to walk up and around the next corner.

Andrea gave three clicks on her mic as she opened the simple lock in less than four-tenths of a second. After they raced in, Tony mostly closed the door, watching the camera through the crack in the door. The mindless Cyclops tracked back toward them and then away again. Tony clicked thrice and Martin sprinted around the corner and through the door.

The janitorial closet, like most of its ilk, measured three meters deep and two across. A drain sink hunkered down in the far corner sporting a faucet that leaked just one drop every few seconds. An automated floor polishing bot silently occupied its charging cradle. Two meters of industrial shelving neatly displayed bathroom and cleaning products. Seven meters above their head, a plastic network trough clothed in Taste Dynamics security tape hung next to the exposed ceramcrete supports from the fifth floor.

Andrea pointed at an exposed bolt near the ceiling, probably left from the construction of the building a dozen or more years ago. Tony nodded and formed a cradle with his fingers. The tiny Andrea ran with a jump into his hands. Tony flung her upward, where she latched onto the support with one hand much stronger than that of most Olympic gymnasts. She quickly fastened her climbing belt to the bolt as a working point to hang from. Tony bent over and let Martin climb up on top of him. Andrea and Martin worked with the smooth and steady speed of seasoned professionals, with every move rehearsed. The trickiest part of the operation involved nothing more than two trinkets eight centimeters long, bearing an official Taste Dynamics seal, artificially weathered to look more than two years old.

The two devices must simultaneously cut each of the unidirectional security optics, in two precise locations each. "In place," Tony heard whispered through his earpiece from his crouched position.

"In place here. Cut in three, two, one, cut."

"Augustine?"

"Good link on both devices," she replied from her far distant location. "No apparent deception from Nanogate. Definitely high-level information and controls. No direct connection to security except a one-way lockdown function, so I can't poll to see if this link compromised itself."

"Mission complete. Wrapping up and returning." Tony grunted quietly as Martin shifted his weight. Martin gave him the thumbs-up as he dismounted. They created a cradle of their arms and Andrea disconnected and dropped from her perch into it.

Martin cracked the door and watched for the camera to swing away before exiting. As a group they bolted back to the eye's blind spot and just moments later off to the bathroom. Reversing their procedures, they climbed down. The moment their feet hit the ground, their good luck came to an end.

"Excuse me. May I have your DNA, please?" The security bot trained a variety of weapons on them, but spoke in the most deferential of tones.

"My name is Tony Meyers, Manager Optical Systems, sixtieth floor," Martin said, trying the bluff they had rehearsed for an interception inside.

"Thank you, Mr. Mey—"

Andrea struck first. Her machine pistol tore into the optical sensors on the robot's head as she dove to the side. Tony and Martin both fired simultaneously and with equal ineffectuality at the armored body.

"Must disable before its control gets picked up by human intervention, or the mission is blown," Martin called out.

Lightning bolts of pain struck along Tony's nervous system. The bot's Neural Amplification Device caused no physical damage, but Tony felt his body tear itself apart. The agony made him wish it literally tore him apart to limit his pain. He shook violently in place, unable to move from his position. While the torture limited his curiosity, his mind processed Martin and Andrea in similar straits.

After seemingly an eternity of electrical impulses that felt as if they were charring blackened pathways through his body, a tiny white man, his lower body encased in skintight lemon yellow, appeared behind the security bot. A single, deceptively slow swipe of his katana removed its head. Another swing split the body vertically in two, and the sword lodged itself a full meter into its massive motive mechanism.

As suddenly as the pain had begun, it released. Tony gasped as the cessation hurt almost as bad as the source. Andrew and Andrea lay on the ground next to him. It took him several moments to regain body orientation enough to even realize he also lay prone.

"I know you're in pain," the little man said with a precision in his voice. "The pain was nerve inducted only. You must go before the security force arrives. You have thirty-six seconds."

"Thank you…" Tony gasped as the trio wrenched themselves off the ground.

"My name is unimportant. Nanogate, however, sends his regards. Now, please go. You now have twenty-eight seconds."

"But what about you?"

"Unfortunately, I've been seen. Your faces are known. I, however, must erase my DNA to prevent implications. Fifteen seconds." From out of nowhere the man produced a pair of nova grenades.

Tony wasted none of the remaining time on the horror he felt as he sprinted for their exit. Moments later, an ultra-brilliant flare of light announced that everything in a 60 meter radius of the small man ceased to exist. Tony wasted a brief glance back. He mentally sent a "godspeed" to their immolated savior.

* * *

The Portland rain caused the theatre to leak even more than during their last meeting. The rain always lifted Sonya's spirits in the past, but now it dragged her down even more into the gray oblivion she faced. In some places, the noise of water cascades covered up even nearby conversations like the sun overpowers a tiny penlight.

Saddened, she watched Tony converse with Carl and Andrew down in the front row. In a few moments everyone would share her world, a world that had diverged from the others since yesterday afternoon. Selfishly, she wondered if she should allow them to keep the gift of ignorance.

One of the constant aches in her side increased in intensity to something just shy of a burning brand. She couldn't continue to hide her own infirmity much longer. They must know the truth.

Even through her pain, she laughed at herself. She wore the pride of keeping the spies from her organization like a cloak of gold. In the end, avoiding her mental abilities involved nothing more than ignorance. "You could be wrong," she remonstrated herself. "He could still be guilty." Shaking her head, she cocooned herself in his innocence.

A waterlogged piece of the ceiling chose that moment to drop, hitting the floor with the sound of a gavel. Time to deliver the bad news. Time to expose their weakness. Time to break her dream in two.

"Follow me," she said, not even looking at her muscle. She walked with dignity to the forward edge of the stage. Per agreement, Greg and Tuan, the Mob enforcers she'd hired, fell in behind her. They weren't here for her protection.

Sonya looked out at the faces that proved, if not their friendship, then at least common goals. In spite of this, she knew over half of them would try to rip apart her vision once she shared her news. She hoped to be able to sway them with logic, but emotion hefted a much larger stick with many of these visionaries.

She wondered what they saw in her now. She knew what stared back at her when she had checked herself in the mirror earlier—dark, rheumy eyes, shoulders hunched in tension, and a face creased in constant pain. Her future seemed so insignificant in comparison to the rift she foresaw. She had to find a way to keep them focused on the mission. To do that she willed away her pain and her fatigue one last time.

"I've called all of you executive members to this meeting for several important announcements, and for us to make at least one critical decision," she began, pausing while the others quieted down and turned their attentions to her.

"First, you may have noticed that Colin is not among us, but Suet, Linc, and Tolly are online."

Augustine nodded that the link operated normally.

"We'll start with the fact that Colin exhibited frank symptoms last night and is in critical condition. His internal body temperature dropped to life-threatening levels. I could do nothing more for him, so I took the drastic step of putting him in the hands of medical professionals to save his life. Be certain that Augustine helped us forge full medical and a new identity for him. It'll be months before the bureaucracy correctly sorts it out. I have no prognosis on his condition. Because of the risk, I'm declaring him off-limits to any visits."

"What?!" Frances erupted.

"The reason for the ban is as most of you have probably already suspected. I can now confirm that we have a bio-weapon targeting our group."

Several people nodded and others looked somber. No one felt the need to say anything.

Good, Sonya thought. They hadn't recoiled from the danger and the fear. "The weapon is of degrading capabilities and probably won't spread beyond our tiny community. I've learned that the catalyst for this disease is explosives. It's triggered by any number of explosives, from gunpowder all the way to the newest molecular putty."

A minor ripple went through the assembly as some who never handled explosives sighed in relief, and others who procured or prepared them took a greater anxiety.

"Naturally, anyone outside our group wouldn't know an explosive from a toilet and have never handled them, so they're safe. We deal with them daily, so you can see why the ban is necessary. The perpetrators know this disease's shape and its parameters. I may have saved Colin only to put him in the hands of the corps, but his condition forced my hand. If he lives, and that's a huge question right now, we'll mount a mission to bring him back."

"If they haven't executed him first!"

Sonya didn't see who spoke, but she felt she missed more and more lately as she concentrated on the mere process of staying alive each minute longer.

"I can't stress how narrowly he missed death. I may have only postponed the inevitable, however. This disease has over a seventy percent fatality rate."

This fired through the tiny body of people like a taser. Murmurs loud enough to drown out the water rippled through the staff.

"Please let me go on, because our time is limited." In respect, the group settled and quieted. "Along the same vein, I've been hiding a secret and can't postpone sharing. I really shouldn't have hid it this long anyway. As some of you may have guessed, I am also ill with this disease."

"NO!" three people shouted in unison, jumping up from their seats.

"Please, hush," Sonya said, using both of her hands to wave them back to their places. "Denying the obvious won't change the outcome. I've been holding off the ravages of this with my own force of will, but that hasn't changed the fact that I am dying."

This time four people jumped from their seats, but refrained from any verbal outburst. She watched as Tony turned his head away, failing to cover the tears dripping down his cheeks with one hand. He snuffled and tried to put up a brave face, but the bright red streaked circles around his eyes spoke volumes. A vain part of herself felt gratified that not even Christine's eyes exempted themselves from at least welling up with tears.

"My liver has been severely compromised and it is only a matter of time. I suspect I have between one and two weeks left. I'll last as long as I can for the good of our cause. This brings us to the obvious requirement of choosing my replacement.

"But, before we get to that, I don't want anyone accusing me of skewing the outcome of picking a successor before I release the piece of news that will shock you all."

Puzzlement didn't quite replace grief on some of the faces lifted up toward her. The question in their minds etched itself in their non-verbal communication—*how can she shock us after telling us she is going to die?*

"This message is the reason I've violated our long-standing rules of having outsiders," she pointed back at the hired bodyguards, "and using a meeting place twice."

She hesitated, gathering her strength before continuing. "Research discovered patient zero, the means by which we have all been attacked. Before I reveal this person I have to emphasize what I just said: 'the means.' Please do not confuse the source with the intent." Sonya paused.

"Who is it?" someone demanded.

Sonya gave a tiny nod to the guards, who sauntered down into the audience to flank the person, to even his surprise. His eyes questioned hers and then his shoulders fell at the response.

"Tony Sammis."

Every eye turned on him.

"I don't expect this can be a bad joke, can it?" Tony asked.

"I'm sorry, my friend, but no. I ensured all tests were run thrice. Only I knew the random identity codes for each of the blood samples."

"It seems I've been a fool," he said quietly.

The room exploded in a mishmash of conversations, most of them yelled. All the while she experienced Tony's eyes locked on hers. She read a wealth of communication in those guileless eyes. Her faith in his innocence restored itself.

"I told you we should've vaped him!"

"He's killing Sonya. That must've been his real mission!"

"With all the help he's given us, we are so close!"

"We're close, all right...close to extinction!"

"No, I meant winning, you nitwit."

"How did that corpie know Tony's name?"

"How could he have done this?"

One voice finally cut through the rest with the power of a bull in rage. "SHUT UP!" Andrew wavered as he stood defiantly. "Now sit the fark down." Slowly, the group settled. "I know why Sonya did this. Think about it, people. If she hadn't told us, we would've overwhelmingly voted Tony in as our next leader. Am I right?"

A few grudging and a few enthusiastic agreements answered him.

"You should know I've got this farking disease," he went on, using one hand to hold himself upright. Andrew's normally swarthy skin paled to the color of a pear's flesh. "Yes, that's right. I was hoping it's just a cold, but now I know better. I've got a rash covering about half my body and a high fever, so I'm probably dead already.

"All that being said, you need to think about this long and hard before you decide to pass judgment. I still believe in Tony. I don't think he could've done this knowingly."

More than one person tried to speak next. Sonya silenced them all by starting to talk quietly.

"I agree with Andrew. Some of you know of my skills and capabilities. They all tell me that he's not the culprit here, but rather a victim himself."

"Why isn't HE sick?" someone demanded.

"Why kill off your weapon?" Sonya asked. "Whoever gave this to him made him immune. Worse, he'll continue to carry this disease, threatening everyone around him for the rest of his life. Not so confident about him being the villain of this piece now, are you?

"Think on everything you've heard here today. We'll vote next week," Sonya said weakly. "Please go home."

Several people glared at Tony as they left. Gregori glared back. Tony seemingly ignored this byplay, instead keeping his eyes fixed on Sonya. As the group dispersed, she flopped down into the seat next to him with a heavy sigh.

"Why are things always so hard?"

"You don't believe…"

"Tony, if I did, I wouldn't be sitting here with you. From what I know with my skills, there are only two options: they infected you without your knowledge, or you agreed and they deep-hypnoed your memories. In either case, your current persona is not to blame."

"Thanks, I think."

"Don't fret, it'll play out as it will."

Tony turned three shades of crimson before turning toward her, his mouth tight and his forehead furrowed. "Do you think I give one good goddamn about becoming the next leader of the GAM?"

Sonya stopped herself before answering. "I don't know, do you?"

"Fark, no!" His face softened. "I worried about losing your trust and faith…and your friendship."

She laughed lightly but found it brought on a cough that wouldn't stop. For the better part of five minutes she coughed until a thick plug of mucus, tinged in deep red, hit the floor.

"Are you all right? Actually, that's a silly question. Sorry."

Sonya opted for a smile this time. "I'm as all right as I can be. And to get back to your worry…never at any time did I feel you did this deliberately. I'm proud to be your friend.

"Before this turns blubbery, I do have to say I've taken the liberty of booking you into a suite at the Seattle Grand Hilton. In the end, you don't want your home known to these two stalwart champions of your safety, and I don't know how this will play out with the rest of the team, so you will need their protection."

"Thank you."

"No, thank you. Despite everything said, you've given us hope that we'll win, despite everything. May I exact a promise?"

"You have but to ask."

"Even if this goes badly and our team breaks up, please start another group to finish what we're so near to accomplishing."

Tony sat quietly for nearly a minute. "I won't let your dreams die…any of them."

* * *

The holes still dotted the walls, but an enterprising person had cleaned up the broken debris. Tony perched on a director's chair and mopped Suet's jade-colored forehead with a cold cloth. The artificial skin still needed to perform all the normal functions of what it replaced. Sweating profusely, her body desperately tried to lower its core temperature. Even from his chair he could feel waves of heat roiling off her, like a space heater accidentally left on maximum.

Her tentacles and legs twitched feebly as they tested the Kevlar straps like an outclassed boxer who refused to throw in the towel. She regularly moaned nonsense words in her delirium.

On previous visits, Tony had brought Cin with him. She spent the time circling Suet's head, licking the overheated ears and head-butting Suet's tentacles. When tired of this, Cin would lie between Tony and the patient, showing concern with a constant purr. He thankfully didn't have the help of his furry friend on this impromptu trip.

After sixteen hours this session, Tony formed a system that made the chore of tending Suet somewhat mindless. Soak the washrag in ice water and mop her brow and hair. Repeat three times. Soak again and wipe down her entire body: her face, each tentacle (taking care around the glucose/saline IV), each leg, and her torso. Rinse the washrag and do the groin. Rinse again before each armpit. Finally, take the other iced washcloth and run it over her cracked lips, making sure to squeeze a little moisture into her mouth.

Repeat. Once every tenth repetition he'd loosen one of her restraints and wipe under there as well. Tuan, the second bodyguard provided to him by Sonya, proved useful here by holding that limb down until Tony retightened it. This seemed to be the bodyguards' sole usefulness. One would relieve the other every twelve hours. They never spoke except in whispers to one another.

At one point Tony asked to try the tub, but the pair of them couldn't control her enough to keep her from hurting herself or them, so she remained in bed, a prisoner of her own failing body and some low-tech bondage.

Most of the time Tony thought of his promises to Sonya. Of course she could be wrong. She may not die, he thought optimistically. A little voice in his head warned him he might as well wish for the moon to be green cheese.

He couldn't break out of the circularity of his thoughts, matching the repetitions of his bedside ministrations. "How can I possibly keep this promise? There are too many unknowns. How many would live through this thing?" he said, pointing at his friend bathed in her own sweat. "How many of those would feel that being shot is too good for me? How does one go about starting a guerilla organization from scratch?"

Four repetitions later Tony finally kicked his mind. "Break it down, Nil. The best choice would be for me to take over the current organization. Our action group is being decimated, but the support organizations will remain intact. To do this I would have to, at minimum, prove I had no knowledge or complicity in this. As Linc would say, 'I smell a lot of footwork.'"

The nurse, Susan, came in to check the IV and to take vitals. She shook her head at what she got from the body beneath her.

"Thank you for letting me help," Tony offered, just glad to talk to someone who'd talk back.

"I feel kinda silly just sitting here when you're the one doing all the work," she replied.

"Oh, I doubt she even knows I'm here."

"Not true. Her reactions and restlessness are far worse when you aren't here."

"Really? I guess I'll have to take your word for it. It does make me feel better." Tony paused. "Does she have any chance?"

Susan lowered her head and turned away.

* * *

"But why should we even vote? How can he lead us when he's the source of the disease?" asked Andrea, the spokesperson. The small congregation sprawled uncomfortably on the floor while the cats imperiously controlled the couch. The Pomeranian yipped at anyone other than Sonya speaking or anyone with the temerity to move more than an eyelash—that is to say, almost constantly. The Chihuahua walked amongst the four visitors looking for attention. Frances petted it absently. Only Christine seemed more interested in the animals than the conversation.

Sonya heard sound come out of her throat as a croak rather than words. She soothed her broken voice with a careful sip of water. It burned like alcohol on an open canker sore as it went down.

"If I could, I would insist. He did nothing wrong." Sonya forced herself through each painful word. So many things going wrong with her body all at once. Not much more time to put things right.

"We don't know that and can't prove that," Jackson interjected.

"Look, I know I can't force you to do anything after I die, so doing anything other than trying to persuade you would be foolish. It would be equally foolish to let you destroy our team."

"We aren't trying to do that."

"Whether you're trying or not, that'll be the end result. You will drive out Tony. Those who believe you're acting hastily and without proof will rally to him. He won't have enough to create decisive actions, and you'll be left with the empty shell that was the GAM."

"But we can't vote him to the leadership," Andrea said, crossing her arms and scowling. "He could be working for them. Hell, we know he worked for them, wittingly or not. I don't know which is worse."

Sonya knew better than to reach out to Andrea, the most stubborn and set in her hatred of Tony. Once her mind formed on a course, nothing could get it off except a very painful lesson. But the others…if she might sway even one, it was worth the effort. Sonya took another swig of liquid fire.

"I don't think we'll solve this here. The proper place is to debate it and vote."

"We *have* been debating, but we—"

"No, Andrea," Frances interjected, calmly but firmly. "We haven't been debating, but rather heterodyning off one another's fears. Sonya's right in her form. I'm not sure if she's right about Tony."

"Thank you, Frances. I won't live to know if I'm right or not, but I believe it here," she said, thumping her chest. Mistake. She knew at once as the coughing began. Despite the body-doubling whoops, she caught the horror in Jackson's eyes.

"Afraid?" she choked out as soon as she could manage.

"Yes."

"Why?"

"Because I've been having muscle aches and really bad headaches that over-the-counter meds do nothing for."

"I sympathize. Talk to Linc. He may be able to help you with the pain and the fear. To my surprise, our friendly bartender is quite knowledge-able in many of the religious areas—an oddity considering his previous line of work. I've already made my peace with this life. You might want to investigate yours."

Jackson looked possibly even more frightened that he did before. The drain on Sonya left her unable to comfort him any further.

"I'm sorry," she went on, "but I'm going to have to ask you all to leave. First, though, let me give you just one more thought."

"What's that?"

"How often have I been wrong…?"

* * *

A line of corpie couples stretched back and forth through a velvet rope maze, waiting for the venue to open. Their outfits would've gotten them arrested in most restaurants or on public transportation, but here at ground level in the club district their sensuality and erotic nature fit in with the rest of their kind.

Tony focused on one couple, trying to remember life in those con-fines. The man dressed only in maroon see-through tights and a purple dinner jacket. His companion wore nothing but a pair of iridescent panties, matching heels and a 30 centimeter diamond chain dangling from each of her oversized nipples that swayed and bobbed with the tiniest of her movements.

Tony listened in but couldn't make heads nor tails of their conversa-tion. Somewhere over the last few weeks, he'd lost the ability to speak and communicate with corpies. He couldn't decide if he should be happy or sad. Before he could make up his mind, the reason for his visit exited the door.

The massive arms reflected the glaring light of the dying rose solido high overhead. As his usual practice, the doorman-cum-bouncer looked over the crowd to get an idea of the patrons before he invited any in. As usual he'd ban any troublemakers before they nerfed the guests' evening of fun and the club's profits.

"Hello, Mr. Tony," Jock said without turning as Tony walked up behind him.

"How do you do that?"

"Do what, sir?"

"I believe it's called situational awareness. You knew I was coming up behind you even though your attention is focused on the crowd."

"I always could. Wouldn't be good at my job if I couldn't. Canya, take over for me, I'm going to break for just a few before we open."

"Yar."

"Oh, and watch the Brazilian couple in the third rank. He usually carries a molecular blade in his boot."

Jock turned and walked over with Tony to sit down on a planter sporting a trio of artificial arborvitae. "Oh," he added with a grin, "I also have rear-facing visual prosthesis. Saved my life more than once. I have it programmed to ignore things unless something approaches on a near-collision course."

"Interesting. Maybe I should think about more prostheses."

"I wouldn't, sir. If I had to do it all over again, I probably wouldn't have made the modifications to my body."

"I never would've taken you for a naturalist."

"I'm not. I don't see any problem with cybernetics or implants where necessary, but augmentation? Naw. But that was then, this is now. You didn't come here to talk about implants, sir. I still can't let you into the club. Miss Carmine has that wrapped up tighter than a Martian kohlrabi in winter."

"No. I wouldn't want you in trouble. Besides, it's not my scene anymore, Jock."

"OK, then why?"

"It was something you said last time we met."

"Uh-oh, I don't have the greatest memory."

"Not to worry. I only wanted to know about Carmine."

"Mmm. I'm not supposed to talk about our customers, but seeing as you're going to be the head of the GAM . . . "

"Where did you hear that?"

"Oh, c'mon, man . . . er, I mean, sir. It's on all the wires. Pick any toast and you can read about it."

"All over the web?"

"Just about every single one."

"OK. Well then, let's see what it gets me."

"OK. Carmine is grinding money. Everyone's toadying up to that coupon and she's loving it."

"How much money?"

"At least five, maybe six."

"Tens of thousands, maybe hundreds? Wow. I know she doesn't or didn't have that much."

"And that doesn't count the five she paid off Tito to keep you out of here. And it ain't run out yet. She comes here with an entourage and Tito can't wait to sell her and her 'friends' overpriced drinks and other goodies. Her tab on a typical night is four."

"You know if she's still living in the same place?"

"Don't know, sir, but I can find out."

"Please do," Tony said pulling out a roll of bills.

"Sir, I ain't your doer. I'll do it for you, but don't insult me with money."

Tony nodded, understanding he had more of a friend in Jock than he ever thought. "If I wanted money, I would've capped you before the price on Greenie heads disappeared."

"Huh?"

"Yeah, just after you dropped out, the corporate bounty on known Greenie heads just evaporated. It had been sizable, in the high fives. Now it just doesn't exist. Hey, Canya's waving me over. They must be about to open the doors. I should get back."

"Thanks, Jock. Here's a way to contact me with Carmine's address and anything else you can think of."

Measure Performance—Phase Two

Nanogate noted with dismay the smooth, confident way that Taste Dynamics strutted into the meeting, just a few seconds late. Days like these he missed the cool confidence and skills of Mr. Marks. Taste Dynamics wouldn't be so smug if he released Mr. Marks correctly.

"My apologies for my tardiness," Taste Dynamics announced. "I needed last minute data to report."

"Don't let it happen again," Wintel reprimanded. "Now let's get started."

As part of his personal training, Nanogate long ago cured himself of fidgeting in boring meetings, but the patience behind the calm façade he never managed to cultivate. The meeting dragged into two full hours of routine matters—forcing legislation change of employee taxes in the US, lowering the basis on EU coinage, raising the mortgage rates on Io and a planned strike on the Ceres mining colony. Nanogate took no notes. He barely noticed.

"Now to the action against the Greenies. Taste Dynamics, you have the floor."

"Since our last meeting, there have been no actions against the assets of Taste Dynamics. I spent the extra few moments before the meeting to double-check my data. It's confirmed that in the last week we haven't had a single act of sabotage or assassination attributed to the GAM throughout the entire corporate network."

"That is exceptional news," Nanogate mouthed mechanically.

"Yes. I believe we should continue our higher meeting frequency for another month to be sure this danger has passed."

183

"Agreed. Any opposed?"

"Before we move on to another topic, I want to announce an added bonus." Taste Dynamics all but twittered with excitement. "As we know the unique RNA sequence of the disease, we've kept a covert surveillance on all of our internal nets and as many external nets as we could. It paid off in a big way. We located a doctor doing work for the GAM. Through him we can squeeze whatever remains of their organization."

"Excellent work. The eighty percent solution we originally proposed may end up being one hundred percent."

* * *

"Body Removal. I'm not getting your video."

"That's because I'm not transmitting, Adriana. This is..."

"I recognize the voice, Tony Sammis." The liquid nitrogen in her voice came through clearly. "You have no further business with this condominium organization unless you wish to pay the balance of your forced sale. I believe the amount is..."

"That's not why I called."

"Then this conversation is ended." She hit the cutoff button.

"But I'm not done," Tony said, sliding up behind the fat black woman in her closet-sized office. Shifting her weight in surprise caused the chair to creak. "I wouldn't turn if I were you," he added, putting the tiny machine pistol against the rolls of fat where the back of her neck belonged. "Just keep facing the screen."

"How did you..."

"Get in? Come now. I feel hurt. I've been defeating the deadly in-depth defenses of corps lately. You don't think I can break into the security office of a condo complex?"

"You're a Greenie?"

Tony remembered something out of an ancient flatie. "Smile when you say that."

"Huh?"

"Never mind."

"You know I c-can't give you back your condo," she stammered desperately. "I don't have any c-cash and..."

"Oh, fark, Adriana, I don't want any of that. I just need the answers to some questions."

"Ask away," she said with an overabundance of nervous cheerfulness. "I'll answer anything you want. I don't have a death wish, and you do have the upper hand."

"Oh, by the way, if you're waiting for the fast response from the emergency signal you sent out, I'm afraid I'll have to disappoint you." Tony watched the huge expanse of her shoulders slump in resignation. "I've layered your office with an old-fashioned Faraday cage—a metal lattice that blocks all signals.

"Now, I really don't want to hurt you. I really only want you to answer questions. If you play your cards right, no one will ever even know you answered them."

"OK, what do you want to know?" she conceded in a much more surly tone.

"Who put the nab on my flat?"

"Miss Carmine."

"You wouldn't do it just on her say-so."

"No. She came in with some corp bodyguard..."

"'Bout 130 centimeters, white, whipcord muscles, and wearing only yellow liquid latex?"

"That's the vaper. Anyway, she handed me a notice of lawsuit against you."

"C'mon, Adriana. We both know that wouldn't have quite done it either. What tipped the scales?"

"A rather nice roll of bills and the threat of a vape against me."

"That would do it. I know how difficult a price on your head makes life. OK, I think that's all I need. By the way, just how much do I supposedly owe the association?"

"Giving bad news to a man with a gun isnnnnnt..." Because of the bulk, her head barely tilted. The contact agent on the muzzle of his gun should keep someone of her bulk out for no more than five minutes. Tony didn't waste a second, slipping out through the hole he'd cut in the water closet wall. His own bodyguard stood patiently in the hall waiting for him and fell in behind Tony as he walked.

"Bathrooms again," Tony said. "Such an obvious security failing. Glad I put security in the commode long before this."

"Augustine," Tony went on, calling on an open line through his percomm.

"You get what you went for?"

"Yup.

"Carmine?"

"Yup. Carmine again, although this time we had a corpie escort."

"Bodyguard?"

"Yup. Same vaper. I think it's time to move on my ex. Pleasant thought. I'm sure not too many get the chance for such revenge. Any word from Jock?"

"He called not ten minutes ago. She moved, but he doesn't have her new flat."

"OK, Augustine, you're the ice jockey. Follow the money. It must've left some trail. It should lead right to her."

"Bloodhound on the trail."

* * *

The small pump room reeked bitterly of raw crude oil and mold. The defunct Alaskan Pipeline's abandoned pumping station offered a safe meeting place. Prior to the GAM scouts who found it, not a single person stepped foot inside for the better part of two decades. The dampness clung to every surface, and the tiny 60 watt incandescent bulb barely cut the gloom.

"We're here to discuss..." Sonya stopped to take a breath. Her words were extremely labored. Her breath capacity fell off each day as the disease now fully involved her lungs. This environment helped her not at all. She knew her time measured itself not in weeks, months or even years, but days...maybe even hours. She took as large a breath as she could before continuing. "...the future leadership of our organization. I choose not to vote...as a veto. My vote will count exactly...the same as everyone else.

"Just so we're clear...Suet, Martin, Tolly, Colin, and Jonah are all too ill to vote. Linc, Andrew, and I are all showing frank symptoms...but are clear-headed enough to cast a valid vote. "Discussion?"

"Shouldn't you speak first, Sonya?" Linc asked weakly over the telecomm.

Sonya leaned back against one of the smaller pipes in the room, rusted and far larger around than she. "I'm reserving my right to speak last."

Augustine spoke up first. "Tony has performed every function that Sonya has. His plans have passed every test we can throw at them, especially those that really count. They work. He directed us down a path that has us looking at victory. I nominate Tony for leader."

"Victory?" Andrea took the fight up instantly. "We're all dying...all except Tony. I've got the disease now. According to Sonya I have less than a thirty percent chance of living through it. I don't want the man who killed us leading the rest of the team right into the corporate maw. I think he should be vaped, not elected leader. I for one won't let this team be in any more jeopardy than it already is. I suggest Frances for our new leader. Her combat and planning experience in the Metros makes her an ideal candidate."

"I really don't want this opportunity," Frances rebutted. "And while I don't feel quite as vehemently as Andy, I have to agree with her opinion of Tony. I personally don't care if Tony is guilty or not. Even if we rebuild our cadre, I don't know how he can lead us without making us sick."

"Even if I were to live," Linc said, "I wouldn't go back to our old, sloppy, hit-or-miss tactics. That isn't any reflection on Sonya, but Tony has put us on the right path. Can Frances implement Tony's direction? Possible. But I don't feel comfortable that she can improvise or adapt to changes."

"I haven't spoken up much because I understand and respect all of your feelings." Andrew grimaced in pain. "I'm afraid of what's ahead of me, but I believe in Tony. He saved me more than once. I'm not likely to forget that."

The conversation died with the sides clearly drawn. Sonya's fears found their way up from her soul and spilled in this room. The pain in her body manifested in her dream torn asunder.

"Tony, do you have anything to say?" Augustine prompted, her eyes widening and her face attentive.

"I don't."

Sonya gave the tiniest of smiles, knowing Tony couldn't resist the opportunity to talk. Pain in her abdomen wiped the pleasure in less time than it took to experience.

Despite his claim otherwise, Tony spoke anyway, just as Sonya knew he would. "Those against me feel I'm a menace, whether I acted with malice or not. Despite their feelings, I intend to prove to all my friends here, not just those behind me, that I never intended to do anything but help this group to its objectives. I never aided, planned, or agreed to be some kind of biological bomb.

"And one last thing—I never wanted to be leader. I'd rather have all your good will…your friendship."

A long pause followed. "If there are no more comments…" Sonya waved for Augustine to continue as she bent double, wracked in a coughing fit.

"Aren't you going to speak, Sonya?"

She violently shook her head back and forth as she bent over, hacking like a fifty-year smoker of the old tobacco sticks.

"Sonya is calling for a vote. This vote is to be secret. I would've made it electronic, but people might've thought I'd hacked the election. Instead, you're each being provided a bag containing one each of three different colored marbles." Augustine wrote in chalk on the least abused of the ceramcrete walls as she talked. "Here I have a bag. I will come by and each of you can drop one single marble into the bag: red for Tony, blue for Andrea or a clear marble if you abstain. Linc, I've got a mechanical arm here programmed to drop a marble for you. Just push one for Tony, two for Andrea, or zero for abstain."

Augustine moved quietly around the room collecting the marbles. With each, a sharp click echoed through the room as the glass orb hit one of its brethren in the black velveteen bag. When the last person dropped their marble, Augustine rolled them around and dumped them into a dish for all to see. Four red, four blue and two clear balls rolled around.

"It appears we need more discussion," Sonya said optimistically.

Three hours and six votes later, they still needed more discussion. The vote changed to five red and five blue, but the debates didn't cause any other alterations.

"Linc and I are too tired to continue. We'll resume in two days," Sonya said stiffly as she barely kept the pain from lashing out at her friends.

* * *

Tony started, awake in a strange bed as his percomm shrilled its urgent tone against his skull.

"Good morning?" Tony said, craning his neck around to find the time in the massive room of the Seattle Grand Hilton. The clock proclaimed him correct by a little over seventeen minutes.

"All right, Tony, I have what you were looking for," Augustine said without preamble. "Carmine went up."

"Sorry, I'm still groggy. Not too much sleep in the last few days."

"Yeah, I've been on dazers myself for over a week."

Tony realized why Augustine's abrupt manner seemed more like a burn when he talked to her lately. "OK, I think I've finally got my head screwed on straight."

"Carmine went up."

"That's what money will do for you. Where?"

"Denny Towers, Penthouse Two, Seattle."

"Figures. That bitch loved status. Denny Towers. Rubbing elbows with all of the who's who of the government, film industry, and business. She has to be wallowing in that lifestyle."

"One more corpie wannabe."

"I think she may have bypassed the corpie stage and gone right to owner, but we'll see. Denny Towers, eh? How convenient for me. That's only about one TriMet hop from here."

"I thought you might feel that way. Security codes to the building and her flat coming on separate line to your handheld."

"Thanks. Talk to you later when I have something."

"Time for a late night visit?" Gregori asked from the darkness.

Tony flipped on the light to find one of his bodyguards sitting in a chair on the other side of the room. "Where did you come from?"

"You don't think Sonya just pulled two people at random out of the woodwork, do you? Can't protect someone from another room."

"Yes, you are quite good. I expected you were, or you wouldn't be welcome in the Family. But I'm off on Greenie business now. Why would you want to stick?"

"Two reasons. One, we were hired to protect you, whatever you were doing. And two, while we work for the Family, our sympathies lie with your organization. Who do you think introduced Sonya and Jamie initially?"

Tony smiled. "OK, Greg. Are you up for breaking some laws?"

"Just tell me which ones, sir. Will we need my partner, Tuan?"

"Doubtful. For that reason I'll probably not need you, either, but always nice to know I have some backup."

"Yes, sir."

"First stop is an all-night bowling alley," Tony said, getting up and dressing, so intent he missed the odd look he got from Gregori.

* * *

"How can we come to a compromise?" Augustine asked before Andrea and Frances even got seated.

Sonya thought a meeting of the key members of both sides might break things free. She vowed to herself not to speak. Even as she did she hacked hard enough to cough up blood.

"You do know all we have to do is wait," Andrea said as sweat rolled off her brow. She mopped it about every three seconds with a damp towel looped over the back of her neck.

"Wait for what?"

"The first one that dies will break the deadlock."

"That's gruesome."

"What the hell, I've got it too. Besides I don't see that there's any middle ground. You want Tony to lead. We don't."

"Even if he's innocent?"

"We're split on that, but there's no way he could possibly prove it."

"Actually, we have a source that may prove it."

"No chance!"

"He's after it tonight."

Frances held up an arm to interrupt. She got it in spades. Her long-sleeved shirt slid up exposing pox covering a good portion of her arms. Sonya reached out for the diseased limb, but Frances flinched away.

"That puts a new spin on things," Augustine said. "You want us to choose someone to lead us who's likely to die?"

"Who doesn't have some symptoms?!" Andrea barked. "Martin came down with a fever and muscle aches last night, and Jackson is in his bed shaking with chills. That only leaves you, Augustine, and Christine that haven't shown any signs."

"I have a suggestion," Sonya croaked. Her voice wouldn't stand the strain. As it was she could taste the blood at the back of her throat. She scribbled something down on a small whiteboard and handed it to Augustine.

"She says for us to pick someone without the disease as interim leader. If Tony can prove his innocence, then we have another vote."

"Well, we aren't going to vote in a lunatic, as much as I love Christine. That only leaves you, Augustine."

Sonya nodded profusely.

* * *

The laughing outside the door announced their presence long before the electronic chirp approved entry. Carmine and a couple staggered in, wearing as little as the public would tolerate. Carmine's tiny blue crochet dress made 6 centimeter-wide bands down her body until they met at her crotch and then flared into a tiny skirt. The other two wore less.

"Noth mush of a housekeeper are ya, Carmine?"

"What happened?" Carmine looked around at the contents of her living room strewn around the floor.

"I guess that would be me," Tony said from a chair in a still-shadowed corner of the room, like something out of an old dime-store novel.

"Tony?"

"Whoz t'is Tony fella? Thought we was going to have some fun," the drunk man said, slapping Carmine on the ass.

"Shut up."

"For once I have to agree with her. Why don't you both just be on your way. I have nothing I want from either of you."

"You Nil," the other woman screeched. "Get outa here!"

Tony slowly revealed his hand from around the edge of the seat to show his flechette pistol. The couple disappeared faster than free food at a mission. Carmine edged her way over toward the door as well.

"Don't, Carmine. I don't mind killing them both to get at you. I also don't mind cutting your legs off to get at what I want." Her eyes met his as if searching for a cue. Tony heard the ding of the elevator. It opened and closed before Carmine made her choice.

Her emotions opened up like a flatie to him. The thought of seducing him discarded itself almost immediately. "You've grown tough, Tony."

"A lesson you taught me."

"Likely true. So if you want to kill me, why haven't you?"

"I'll be honest with you, Carmine. I only want information. You give me what I want and I'll walk out and never come back."

"Do I have much of a choice?"

"Well, you could keep me talking, hoping your bodyguard will come in here and protect you, but you'd be waiting a long time."

"Killed him, eh?"

"Nope. He's just incapacitated. You don't have to worry about your deposit on him. Since he's not around, I suppose next you might think about edging over to the cupboard for the shotgun or maybe the laser behind the bar."

"No chance, eh?"

"I don't think so, but you might surprise me. You did once before."

"Well, can I at least sit down?"

Tony tilted his head in assent. Just as she started to sit on the couch, Tony spoke. "Not there. Over on the Windsor chair."

"Boy, you don't trust anyone, do you?"

"Yes I do, Carmine. I just don't trust you specifically. Trust is earned." The seductive way she stretched her legs reminded him of other times.

"I'm dead if I tell you, Tony. These aren't the kind of people you metro on."

"If you tell me, you can run. It can work."

"And return to living like a Nil?"

"Or I can start torturing you now. I could just kill you outright, but that doesn't get me what I want."

"I can't turn and you know it. Isn't there any way we could make some kind of deal?" Her hands sensuously stretched down her fishnet stockings and back up, lifting her tiny skirt. Tony's gun went off almost before the dull glint of the ballistic plastic barrel came out from underneath her skimpy clothing. Carmine's body reflexively jerked, firing off a single shot as she died, gouging a hole a meter in diameter in the ceiling.

Gregori slammed through the outer door almost in time with the shots. Tony watched as it took several seconds for him to gestalt the room. Finally, the shoulders loosened, and his stance became more dignified and less professional.

"Damneditalltohell," Tony said all in one breath, idly waving the end of his gun around. As bad as Tony's aim had been, he had put thirteen separate tiny projectiles through her torso. "I thought I could convince her to give up the information. I guess we'll have to try it the hard way. Get the cleaver from the kitchen."

* * *

"Jesus, Mary, and Joseph! You carried that thing all the way from Seattle?" Augustine remonstrated as she stared at the decapitated head lolling around inside Tony's brightly colored bowling bag. As a devout Catholic, she added the murder to the growing pile of sins to confess.

Assuming the GAM actually were close to completing their lifelong quest, she might have to finally fulfill her promise to Mary and return to the confessional for the first time since she took up the terrorist mantle. It scared her in a distant way. But, like anything, first things first.

"What if a Metro or TriMet pig decided you looked suspicious?"

"Two normal guys on their way for a bit of bowling after a hard day in the factory?" Tony said. "No Metro would've bothered to stir off their lazy ass."

"Even a random sweep."

"They didn't."

"Obviously. You're still here."

Having done the net raid to get the information, Augustine knew the woman looked somewhat attractive before Tony's ragged job of decapitation.

"Tough-necked bitch. Just like when she was alive. It took six blows with a cleaver and another few more with the butcher knife."

Augustine shrugged. Murder was murder no matter how grisly. She only needed the brain intact. The brutal treatment by her friend bothered her not at all.

"So what can you get from her?" Tony asked.

"About sixty years, if I remember my criminal code correctly. Of course, decapitation might be considered special circumstances, in which case we're probably looking at life."

"Augustine, I'm not joking around here. What kind of neural reconstruction can you give me?"

"She...it's been dead less than an hour?"

"'Bout seventy minutes," he said after consulting his chronograph.

"Remember that neural reconstructions aren't terribly detailed even when done at death," she cautioned as she draped a fine gossamer net, whose every junction glowed brightly, over the top of the head. "Over an hour? I wouldn't go looking for the magic bullet here, especially as this isn't the Metro Crime Analysis Unit."

"Some chance is better than none."

"OK. By the way, Tony, we need to talk about something else."

"Can it wait? Every minute those neural pathways degrade."

"OK, but as soon as I'm done."

Tuan and Gregori both sat stiffly on her sofa, taking care not to recline against the homemade afghans that covered the back. As she worked, Tony paced around her net cradle. At one point Augustine wondered if he'd wear a track in her Berber or accidentally smash into her antique Crate and Barrel coffee table.

While three of her mental tracks sorted the milky and broken images into something usable, one track watched as Tony examined the solidos of her family—five children and eighteen grandchildren at last count, although Millie was pregnant with twins.

Tony frowned at the family reunion solido they took at Mickey's Grove. He waved his hands over the prayer candles lit in front of each picture as if he couldn't believe they were real.

"The last of the images drained out of the skull. Here's what I have." Tony raced back into the stark world of direct wired electronics. "I know you don't care about the techno-babble, but I did manage to arrange the neural memories into a visual image similar to a solido and do a probability fill on those parts that can be deduced from previous or past frames." Augustine typed in the air with her eyes rolled back in her head. "I have to warn you that this is still pretty crude."

The images of the dead woman's memory blossomed into the room around them, magnified significantly. They skipped and shook like a bad memory string.

"I've downloaded everything I could get. As usual, the storage required for such a download in all sensory dimensions is bloody huge.

I've taken the standard measures of ignoring smell, taste and touch and have focused in on parts you might find relevant, from the first meeting of you two to present."

Tony rubbed his nose like it itched. "You can fast forward through most of that until mid-October, when they betrayed me."

With her right hand, Augustine turned a pseudo-control in the empty air. The former life he sometimes shared with Carmine flew by at a phenomenal rate.

"She kept another lover," Tony said. He reacted less than a computer memory bank to a random datum. Augustine recognized the Wilted Rose.

"Slow down." She once again manipulated her pseudo-controls with her right hand, and the images slowed to only double speed. With her left she synched and engaged the audio.

"Her apartment." Tony said as the speed became really watchable.

Through the images they heard a knock at the door and Carmine went to open it. Tony gaped as a short whipcord man in lemon yellow tights stood in her doorway.

"Carmine Peligran?" the voice squealed. Augustine again dialed down the speed as Carmine's vision nodded in the affirmative. "Did you know your boyfriend has an animal in contravention to the law? And he practiced medicine without a license?"

The picture faded to black but the audio continued. "Come in, please," she said. They heard the door closing but the visual faded into a blurry and milky paste. It cleared enough to discern the slight body-guard leaned back into a big black armchair.

"We want you to spurn Tony Sammis and we're willing to sszzzrk to do so. I'm sure you'll find solace with your other partner and a wad of credit slips."

"Why?"

"I'm not exactly at liberty to say, although I'll tell you truthfully I do not know."

"OK. I know what you are and who in general you represent." She held up a hand to ward off the protestation. "I don't know specifically, but you've given me enough to guess. You don't ssss about Tony's pet or that he saved one old frump, now do you? .. you? ..you? .. you? .. you?"

Augustine frantically attempted to compensate but the bodyguard's response got covered completely. "Then what are you after?"

"My instructions are that we wish to drive Tony completely out of his ssssurroundings and into the world of unlicensed and unrecorded individuals."

"You want sssssssssskr a Nil. I grok it." While only seeing it out of her eyes, they could tell she leaned back on her divan like some Egyptian princess. The point of view showed that she rolled her eyes up in her head for a few moments. "I want one hundred eighty thousand a year plus level two medical, three years' minimum."

Augustine actually looked at Tony, but he didn't flinch as he watched his former lover pull a Judas on him.

"Miss, we're looking at a one-time payment of say sssjjjjkrr…his simple act." The video became less blurred and the clarity returned with a vengeance.

"Oh, I'm sorry, I didn't quite explain. You will find me useful in a number of ways. First, given the right funding I'll torpedo Tony in several ways. I know the right people to pull his credit, auction his house, and snub him at all of his hangouts, some of which you may miss. I might even be able to get him arrested."

"No, thank you, miss. We don't wish him arrested, although based on my instructions, all of those other items could have value. Would you be able to reject him so effectively and completely?"

"For one eighty, I sure would. Sure, he was handy. But what is any one man? I can get those by the truckloads."

"Remarkable attitude."

"Then do we have a deal?" she asked, thrusting out her hand to seal the deal.

"As I said, Miss Peligran, I don't have the authorization for such an extravagant change in plans. However, your forthright attitude and embellishment to the request might have some future value to my employer. I will pass them on."

"But not with your endorsement."

"That's not my decision. I leave such matters to my employer."

"Very well. When will I hear from this person of substance?"

"Before the day is out, miss. If you will excuse me, I have other arrangements to make."

Augustine snapped up the speed as Carmine spent a good portion of that day pacing around her living room. Tedious to watch. The memories snapped back to normal speed when Carmine's percomm went off.

"Carmine here."

"Miss Carmine," came a smooth baritone voice. Augustine grabbed Tony's eye as they looked at one another at the same time. The educated tones held their own distinction, one familiar to both of them. "Your offer tested my curiosity. I will be honest in saying I'm not often intrigued."

"Tony can be just the first of many assignments I can help you on."

"All right, I agree to your terms. I'll give you a drawing account for each, umm, client I send your way, based on its difficulty. Any of the account you don't spend on the job is yours. I won't offer any additional sum, except in cases of extreme opportunity or a mistake in my judging the difficulty of the case. For Mr. Sammis, I offer an additional fifty thousand. Welcome to the payroll, Miss Peligran."

The rest of Carmine's memories showed nothing they hadn't already determined, although Tony watched Carmine's last moments intently. It was like watching oneself be murdered.

"I don't know if this will sway the rest of the GAM, Tony," Augustine said, snapping off the recording. "It's convincing, but not definitive."

"I know. By the way, you mentioned you wanted to talk to me about something."

Augustine adjusted something on her computer mainframe that didn't need adjusting. Then, for good measure, she wiped off the dust accumulation. She didn't know how to share what she absolutely had to share.

"Sonya reached a political compromise about the leadership of the group," she finally managed.

Tony sat down on the arm of the sofa, facing her. There was no rancor in his face. It seemed more tired than anything.

"Not unexpected. Who got the bag?" Augustine cocked her head to one side. "Oh, come now. I'm not naïve," Tony continued. "After that session yesterday, I knew there was no way to put me in without the efforts you and I just did, assuming they paid off perfectly. They didn't. Even if they had, some of them wouldn't accept it."

"An incredibly astute judgment."

"Worse, I don't even want the farking job."

"Huh? You've been fighting like you wanted it as soon as Sonya announced she was ill."

"Do you want to know why? I personally hate the political in-fighting. The thought of taking the job makes me want to puke. But I made a promise to Sonya. She sees me as some kind of super weapon that will bring her dreams to fruition. Between you and me, though, her dreams of open fields, rainforests, and free-roaming bison is a world of the past. There are too farking many people. We can't wish them away."

Tony's statement almost pulled Augustine from the net completely. She furrowed her brow as she refocused on the six different tracks her net-self worked down. "Then what are we fighting for, Tony? You've always known. I think the rest of us have lost our way. I don't even know anymore."

"Simple. We're fighting for representation. Our government—no, not the one in Washington, but the one that really runs things—is an oligarchy. It's a group of people making decisions over the lives of all of us without our input. Everyone in the world knows the corps run things."

Tony, warmed up now, wasn't about to stop. "The United States broke away from the England of several centuries ago for taxation without representation, for the right not to be seized either economically or bodily at the whim of a tyrant. Take what happened to me as an example. The corps decided it. They planned it. They did it. Was I asked? No. Did I do anything wrong? No. They did it to silence the people, the Greenies, from actively protesting their rule.

"But it's a moot point. I doubt I'll ever be the leader unless a good portion of the opposition dies, in which case there's no group anyway. It's never easy to prove what's in one's heart. So who got left holding the bag?"

"I did."

Tony gave her a genuine smile that encompassed his entire face. "I'm sorry for you, dear."

"I have to admit I didn't expect that reaction."

"Posh. You're my friend. Leadership is never an easy thing, but I'll help you with it any way I can."

An attention-interrupt:percomm broke up the conversation. "Hold that thought. I have a percomm coming in." Augustine lifted a pseudo-control of an imaginary old-fashioned percomm receiver to her ear.

"Augustine," croaked Sonya. "I need you to link me to the entirety of the membership."

"Hold one." Augustine reached for a pseudo-control of an old rolodex and plucked cards out, pressing them into the percomm. One by one those cards lit up. "Go ahead, Sonya, I've put you on percomm with the entire GAM."

Sonya's voice cracked roughly. "Suet died last night at twenty-three thirty. She died quietly and without any additional pain."

Tony stood abruptly. Snuffling, he paced as tears leaked gently from his eyes.

"Preparations are underway and the ceremony will begin promptly at noon tomorrow."

Tony's legs gave way beneath him and he dropped to the floor in a sitting position. The slow leak turned into a cascade over his cheeks.

Augustine ignored anything else. She unhooked and went down to him, wrapping him in her arms. She thought to comfort him until she realized her own vision also blurred. They sobbed together in one another's arms.

* * *

"Few of you knew Suet's burial wishes," Augustine began, dressed in a black floor-length gown with a high neck of white lace. It made a perfect background for the puffy redness of her face and the trail of fresh wetness down the sides of her cheeks.

Tony threw six kinds of fits when Augustine told him part of the political maneuvering required him to remain away from all funerals excepting Sonya's, if that came to pass. He sat in a tiny room watching everything via solido. Sonya sat in the front row, a bloodstained handkerchief covering her mouth.

"I was one of the few who earned her trust enough for her to share," Augustine continued. "She ran away from her humanity because of the pain it inflicted upon her. She feared moving to her next life forever being the machine even more. She exacted two promises of Sonya and me.

"First, to ensure her body was rehumanized with its original parts. She stored the original ones in cryo for this very purpose. She rests here now as before she became more than human. When I'm done I'd appreciate it if you would all pass here and say your final farewells to the woman you never quite knew.

"Second, she didn't wish to be shoved into the nearest calorie reclamation bin. She wished to be buried. I know this ancient custom isn't practiced anymore. However, some years ago, Suet purchased this actual plot of land for her ever after. I don't think any of you can imagine the cost involved. Even with our relative riches now, any one of us would be hard-pressed to come up with that amount. She worked twenty long and hard years to come up with the cash.

"I once asked her why she did it. She told me of the peace it gave her, knowing where she'd rest. Knowing that there'd be flowers or grass or even weeds left of her when she passed. So insecure in her place in life, she took comfort in what the next life might bring." Augustine finally faltered. She cleared her throat as she wiped the tears away. With a white linen handkerchief she blew her nose.

"Suet was a solid friend and rock in our sea of constant change. She will be missed."

Tony panned the camera over to the casket just as others began to file by. He never would've recognized the plain, mahogany-haired girl cradled in jade-colored silk. She was the iconic girl next door. She was the one never beautiful in a sophisticated way, but still wholesome. Through his watering eyes, Tony managed a laugh.

"Wholesome! What a description of Suet. She would've roared laughing if she heard that." Tony remembered some of the less than wholesome activities they had shared. He remembered her breaking the neck of one security guard with her fast-as-lightning tentacle by wrapping it right on around and lifting. He remembered her tender lovemaking. The strength and ruthlessness of her body rendered gentle and tender, even if it was just friendly fornication.

He also remembered her attempts at bowling. She couldn't decide whether to wrap her tentacle around the ball or try to bowl with just a tentacle in one hole. But either way she had fun trying. Tony lay down on his bed and consciously gave in to one final fit of self-pity. Even though it would be his last for Suet, it wouldn't be his last with so many more friends left who wouldn't live another two weeks.

"Goodbye, my friend," he managed through the sobs.

* * *

"Colin just passed," Augustine told Tony over his percomm.

He barely reacted. Jonah and Beth yesterday, Tolly this morning and now Colin. Numbness overwhelmed him. So often did he now remotely attend services he didn't bother removing his black suit.

"I also have found the proof you and I have been looking for," Augustine added, almost as an afterthought.

"Really?" Tony made an effort to come out of his lethargy enough to care. Too many of his friends dead. All his dreams shattered.

The front door to his suite opened. Christine entered.

"Hello, Christine. Welcome. You want a drink? I'm thinking about getting drunk myself."

As usual the slight woman said nothing, but sauntered right in like she owned the place.

"Tony, how did Christine know where you were staying? I don't even know that," Augustine whispered over the percomm.

"Don't know." He turned his attention to his guest. "If I remember correctly, you drink Dewars on the rocks, Christine." Tony poured.

Christine walked over with her left hand cupped to receive the glass. A twinkle in her eyes made it look like she was laughing. Tony didn't understand mirth with all the emotional pain they shared.

"Tony, I don't like this," Augustine commed. "I'd be very careful if I were you."

Tony caught only one glimpse of ravening silver as he handed over the drink. He felt the blade bite in his gut. His breath stole away. The pain radiated outward. The glass fell. He gasped.

Time slowed to a crawl as ice cubes and orange liquor spilled from the tumbling glass. His own blood sprayed all over Christine's front like red dye bursting from an overfull balloon. Slowly her arm withdrew the blood-coated knife. An intellectual side of Tony's brain managed to be detached enough to find the knife fascinating. He'd seen its like—only two centimeters wide but a full seven long, faintly curved and sharp on both sides.

More random thoughts filled his head as the smell of his own bile filled the air. The glass hit the carpeted floor and bounced slowly like something out of an off-world film. The liquid shot off to either side, denying that it could be absorbed by the fabric.

"Christine!" Augustine shouted as the link between Tony and Augustine suddenly included the assassin's percomm. Tony couldn't understand Augustine's anxiety. Christine's second thrust caught him just between the first and second rib. The knife, so smooth and sharp, didn't grate on his ribs but rather slid smoothly between them like they were two tour guides.

"Christine, he didn't do it! I have the proof!" Augustine shouted.

Nerves pounded Tony's brain with emergency messages that it continued to ignore like an ostrich with it head in the sand.

A new voice began playing over the percomm.

"Summation of minutes of meeting October. New plan to use and discard an unwitting employee to destroy Green Action Militia approved."

Christine looked puzzled, withdrawing the knife, her hand coated in a red glove of blood.

"That's from the personal log of the chairman of Taste Dynamics. No doubt. One hundred percent proof positive. I just found it today."

For Tony the pain couriers finally found their destination. Time exploded to normal speed as he fell over into the arms of his attacker and friend.

* * *

From her medi-chair Sonya looked down into the room where a doctor performed brutal and ancient invasive surgery on a covered body. "He has to make it," Sonya said, her voice harsh and barely over a whisper.

"He's a fighter," Augustine said.

Sonya could see her own dark, rheumy eyes reflecting off the gallery glass, wondering how long she could continue her own losing fight. "I hope he's tough enough," her voice rasped again. "What did you do with Christine?"

"I have her locked up in the new safe house we were just setting up. No one knows about it except me and Linc."

Sonya just nodded. "He has to make it."

* * *

The message, almost as old as computers itself, "Are you sure? Y/N," blinked on Nanogate's desk terminal in the dark. He'd waited until everyone cleared the building before doing his own bit of corporate sabotage, this time to himself.

His finger hovered over the Y button on his terminal. Just one stroke away from erasing any proof of his collusion with the Greenies, and yet he hesitated.

He couldn't remember how many years it had been since he felt good about anything he did for a living. His personal credit numbers soared. His power over those around him grew. He gained satisfaction from these things, but they didn't make him happy or feel good. Smug was the closest emotion he could really compare.

In fact, he couldn't ever remember being happy about anything, except his brief work with the GAM. At the time he thought he felt relief that he'd saved Nanogate. But it was more.

He resolutely smashed the Y key. Personal survival. Feelings came a distant second.

Snarling, he shoved everything from his desk, ignoring the crash of the irreplaceable Chihuly lamp.

* * *

"She must not have liked you, Tony-boy," Augustine said to Tony as he struggled to regain consciousness.

He looked around to see Sonya lying in the bed next to him, Linc sweating profusely in an overstuffed chair in the corner, and the remains of the action committee crammed in, standing or sitting around in a bedroom he didn't recognize.

He tried to say something but no sound came from between his chapped lips. Christine handed him a cup of water. He hesitated only a moment before taking the rose-colored plastic cup. He'd already be dead if she'd wanted him to be. He nevertheless watched Christine's eyes as he drank.

"Sorry," Christine said.

Tony started at this. Christine didn't apologize for anything to anyone.

"Yeah, Christine's an artist with a blade. She never misses her target," Augustine expounded. "One thrust to the heart or the liver and the target is done. She only tortures those she really hates. She caught you through the intestines and into the kidney, but you were lucky—the damage didn't require an organ replacement. Her second thrust punctured your left lung."

"Sorry," Christine repeated. Every head in the room turned toward her.

"Grrrk," Tony croaked and sipped the water again. Carl chuckled. "Thank you for coming. What's the occasion? I'm sure I'm not nearly in as bad shape as some of you."

"We collectively, as a group, owe you an apology."

"I should think so," Tony said mockingly holding his hand over his wounds and medical incisions. Everyone laughed except the normally aloof Christine.

"Not quite, but close," Andrea continued. "I meant that we should have never doubted you. The one damning piece of evidence in my eyes, Nanogate knowing your name, makes sense, now. We won't doubt you in the future. I hope you'll accept our apology and leadership of the team, what's left of it."

"I accept." Tony looked over at Sonya and smiled.

She smiled back as she closed her eyes. Her head settled back against the pillow and her chest rose one last time. What had been the background chirp of her heart monitor became a shrill whistle prompting the pounding of medical feet.

Adjust Plan for Desired Results

"Sonya left this special message to be viewed by all of us prior to her funeral arrangements," Augustine said to the assembled throng from the pulpit of the hospital's church. She wasn't happy with the security arrangements, but they were the best that could be arranged on short notice. The lights dimmed as the solido began.

"Welcome, my friends," Sonya said in a cheery voice that didn't match the crowd's mood. "I know you're all saddened at my passing, but let me assure you I went with my heart cheerful and knowing the hope I leave behind. Carry on the battle. Don't let it end, not for me, but for yourselves.

"If I have any one regret in this entire world, it's that I never produced an heir to pass on my teachings. Not enough time or temperament to suffer a life partner.

"I do request that you don't put my body through the city's recycling. I'd rather be recycled into pet food. Please let me feed my pets rather than the multitude of people I've already given my life to protect.

"I want to thank all who contributed to my wonderful life! Without you it wouldn't have been nearly so great! Until we meet in the next world, farewell."

Sniffles and outright sobs could be heard from the audience. Tony, from his levitating medi-bed, wiped tears from his eyes and nothing could hide that fact. Augustine's own vision blurred and she blew her nose loudly.

To Augustine's amazement, Tony stood up carefully, with one hand on the wound in his gut. She hoped all the biodegradable staples and quickheal they patched him up with would hold.

"Sonya gave me a life when mine ended," he said firmly. "She gave me a home when I had none. She gave me a family I never knew I was missing." He shrugged off Tuan as he tried to hold him up on one side.

"Sonya did this for all of us. We were strays she brought into her home, just like the menagerie of pets she kept, who, by the way, Augustine has agreed to take care of."

She nodded to the group, managing a smile.

"Sonya wished us to carry on our fight," Tony went on. "I want to know how long each of you have been fighting? Augustine?"

"Six years."

"Jez?"

"Three years."

"Peter?"

"Eight years."

Augustine wondered where Tony was going with this. It didn't take a vernacular semanticist to feel the pitch coming.

"I've only been at this a few months, and frankly I'm tired of it already. I've already lost six of my dearest friends and likely will lose even more. As your new de facto leader, I don't want to fight this war any longer."

It took several moments for this to sink in. Augustine's venom at the bare statement burned in her gut. The grief turned to rage. All she wanted to do was get her fingernails into his eyes. But then she saw the grief on his face and she forced down her emotion.

"No, I don't mean I would let what we've accomplished die," Tony continued. "I want this as much as any of you. I mean I see an opportunity to leave Sonya a successful legacy. I see an opportunity to end this war by the end of next month…in Sonya's name. I think all those we have lost will rest easier if we succeed."

* * *

"Jock! Good to see you again," Tony said affably, though the tone didn't come through well as he had to shout over music so loud you could almost see the ripples in the air.

"Mr. Tony. I see you got the establishment to let you back into the Rose."

"Just a little emotional blackmail. Then again, it might have something to do with the head I left in their office. C'mon in. I need to talk to you."

Jock looked uncertainly at Tony and his two companions. Tony saw him hesitate just a moment before swiveling into the booth next to Christine and letting the sound barrier fall back into place. He gave Jackson's heavily sweating brow a look.

"The management already told me to come down and talk to you, or I'd still be at the door," Jock said in preamble. "I don't need no trouble, Mr. Tony." Jock tapped his ear. "I like you, but I do have to look out for number one."

Tony laughed. "Jock, I'm not stupid, and I don't want to get my friends—you, in this case—into any trouble. I'm certain the management is listening in on this conversation—if they have any brains at all, that is. The oversized owner of this establishment was mercenary and slow, but stupid never entered my mind. If nothing else, having Carmine's head staring at him from his desk would have been enough to make him wary."

Jock looked at Christine and Jackson as if to try and verify the gruesome story. Jackson nodded.

"Look, I need to confirm that you work for Protection, Inc.," Tony asked.

"Yes, sir, I do. But I work for them under the table. No records. Remember, I'm…"

"A Nil. Yes, I remember, Jock. Hopefully that won't matter too much longer."

Jock tilted his head with questions in his eyes.

"Can you get me into a meeting with your senior officer?"

"Maybe."

"Would this help?" Tony said, sliding a 3 centimeter-high stack of plastic credit slips across the table.

"That would do it."

"I thought it might. Also, do you know anyone that works for Vape Security?"

"Yes, sir."

"I need to talk to their head officer as well." Tony slid over another stack of bills.

"I can make those things happen, sir."

"I knew you could," Tony said sliding over yet a third stack of bills. "This is for you."

"You don't have to do that, Mr. Tony."

"Yes I do, Jock. Here are two notes, each with the time, date, and location of individual meets." Tony handed over three slips, two stuck together as if to appear as just two passed hands.

"Thank you, sir. I'll make it happen."

Tony walked out, Christine and Jackson at his side. The moment they reached the outside air, Jackson turned with eyebrows raised. "What was on the third note?"

"What third note?" Tony asked.

"I was dealing seconds before you were born," came the reply. "You weren't bad, but not good enough to make a living at it, though."

"OK, you caught me." Tony shrugged.

"Are you going to tell us anything about what's going on? The rest of us have been on edge waiting for the last two weeks while you healed enough to move about."

"OK, I'll tell you this. The first two were just as described. The final card bore only the line, 'Purchase as many puts on major corporations on next Friday as you can.'"

"We move on Friday? What's the target?"

"You will find out next Wednesday, just like all the rest. I need to talk to the heads of those security firms, and one other, first."

"If I were childish, I'd say that Wednesday is still ten days' off."

Tony smiled as he pushed through the street level crowds. "You're right, that would be childish."

Christine, as always, said nothing.

* * *

Nanogate sat quietly in his study in a 1960s leather wingback chair. No one kept him company. He clutched the report on the acquisition of Marineris Mining in his left hand, unread. His eyes tracked only the dance of lint specks in a shaft of sunlight through his skylight.

Not a single GAM incident had marred his daily reports in over a week. His corporate espionage reports told him his competitors weren't circling around the lamed Nanogate as he expected. He didn't know which report worried him the most. The lull reminded him of the quiet of a six-year-old coloring on the walls, a teen with his first narcostick, or that calm just before a squall's first gust.

His sense of self-preservation, honed over many years in the cut-throat world of the corporations, screamed at him to do something—*anything*. He couldn't think of a thing to do about either of the negative reports. Picking up the single malt scotch, he sipped it gently, brooding over his lack of choices.

It was times like these he particularly missed Mr. Marks. Marks and Nanogate existed in symbiosis, where Mr. Marks's advice often complemented his own. It was a rapport he didn't share with his new bodyguard.

Staring off into space, he noticed the sudden dimming of the light just before he simultaneously heard and felt a drop in air pressure signifying his floating home was no longer airtight.

An impressive man, clad in canary yellow tights, dropped rapidly through the perfectly round hole in the skylight to a rough landing three meters in front of him. The muscles bulging on muscles, so typical of steroid replacements, made the bodyguard a caricature of a human. A tiny Adonis-like face perched between massive shoulders reaching all the way up to his ears. On top of all that, the intruder wielded a wide-field gauss gun with apparently expert skill. Before he finished standing, he leveled it directly at Nanogate's chest.

"Ah, a visitor," Nanogate said, not moving from his chair. "I do have a door and an appointment secretary, you know."

"I've come to deliver a message," the unknown bodyguard said in a tone intended to cow any victim.

"Percomms work, too." Nanogate nonchalantly took another sip of his scotch.

"This one requires your death."

"So melodramatic. So who wants me dead? No, wait, let me guess. I like guessing."

The bodyguard said nothing.

"If it were the Greenies, they wouldn't have bothered to talk. They would've just planted a bomb or shot me from some distant window.

"If it were one of my underlings, they'd be too terrified to confront me, and even if they got the nerve, they would've just shot first and asked questions later.

"If it were one of my family, I would've expected poison, or perhaps electrocution in the bath—I hear that's very popular now.

"Hmm…that only really leaves my contemporaries. As I'm guessing, I would say you represent that bitch, Taste Dynamics."

The bodyguard inclined his comicly malproportioned head. "Well, she did say you'd probably figure it out, so I'm not concerned. She offers you a bargain."

"Oh, goodie," Nanogate incongruously said, bouncing up and down like a kid who just got a surprise present.

"Tell her how you set up Taste Dynamics, and she'll leave your fortune to your family. If you don't, she'll strip them to Nils. You, of course, die either way."

"Hmm. I'll have to think about this one."

"You have ten seconds."

"Oh, I won't need that long. It figures your oversexed boss would pick someone that looked like Adonis with the subtlety of a wounded buffalo. Tell your boss 'piss off.'"

The gauss gun didn't hesitate. It showered innumerable fragments of metal outward at just short of the speed of sound. Not fast enough.

Almost instantaneously, a cylinder slammed down, ripping a hole in the ceiling plaster, crushing an antique end table and indelibly compressing the carpet in a circle less than a meter around Nanogate's chair. The weapons fragments buried themselves in the ballistics barrier's impenetrable skin.

The bodyguard looked stunned. Belatedly, he fingered his grav belt, but ceramic composite shutters, stronger than any metal, slammed closed over the skylight.

A thick mist started to rain down into the room as trillions of nanites cascaded out of nearly invisible sprayers. The bodyguard writhed and wiped frantically as his skin took on a metallic sheen. He took another wild shot at his target, with predictable results.

"I'll send your remains to Taste Dynamics," Nanogate said as the nanites continued to eat the intruder, from the neck down, one molecule at a time.

* * *

That one of the highest members of the American Mafia chose such opulent surroundings still gave Tony pause. Knowing his host, the brilliant gold of the new wallpaper may have been just that—true gold. Priceless works of art replaced the previous priceless works of art like some sale gallery's rotating stock. The previous Roman theme had been replaced with a Louis the Fourteenth sunburst in the carpet and boulle woodworking in the walls. Even the chair bore fantastic marquetry within its simplistic, straight wooden lines of the period.

"Welcome back, Tony," Jamie said, sliding onto a lounge chair wearing only a long, flowing dressing gown that left no illusion as to her natural red hair.

"Ah, you learned my real name."

"Not difficult with the newly elected leader of the GAM. Sonya was a naughty girl. She led me to believe you were less important than you are."

"You knew Sonya's real name also."

"She knew that I knew. It was a game we both played."

"Hmm. In either case, my notoriety seems to be preceding me."

"Fame, not notoriety."

"Whichever. Both can be dangerous for a guerilla."

"I won't debate that with you. The corporations already know your name, so what's the harm?"

"Good point."

"I'd offer you something for brunch, but I can tell you're a man of action and not one to be put off by the civilities of life," Jamie said, stretching out her long legs to be admired.

"Perhaps in the future we can investigate those civilities, if you're so inclined. However, right now I beg your pardon in that I'm short of time."

Jamie sketched a Marilyn Monroe pout on her face. "Well, if we must. Pray tell, what business can be so pressing?"

"I'd like your organization to delay any of the Portland Metro responses to a specific area for a period of two hours."

She looked at him almost incredulously before she threw her whole body backward on the lounge and laughed in a deep, throaty way.

"Have I said something funny?" Tony inquired in all seriousness.

This seemed to only cause the young woman more mirth. The new bodyguards in the room even took notice of their employer's antics.

"Yes, quite. I can see why Sonya kept you around. You're quite an amusing fellow."

"I can assure you I'm quite serious."

"Then in that case it would cost…say, twenty million," Jamie said, throwing out a number in such a way as to make it obviously out of reach.

"Let's make it twenty-five million instead to cement a new friendship," Tony said in a declarative tone. "Would you like cash or a cashier's credit?"

The mirth instantly left Jamie's face. "You're serious, aren't you? Where would you get that kind of credit? We used to have to discount to Sonya just to keep her armed."

"We've come up in the world. Looks like your sources aren't quite as effective as you thought."

Jamie sat looking deeply into his eyes, all hints of the siren gone from hers. Her eyes now only held hard, cold business.

"Tony, remind me never to play poker with you," she remarked after a moment.

"As you say, miss."

* * *

Tolly died late Tuesday night, bleeding out through every orifice. Fortunately, he had suffered a major stroke first thing in the morning, so the mental release came long before his body's gruesome death. Fear and anticipation warred with one another Wednesday morning when Tony brought the team together in Sonya's apartment.

"Why are they here?" Andrea pointed at the knot of four Greenie members who normally didn't sit with the action committee. "Mark only does supplies and Susan is in fundraising…not that we need much of that anymore."

"Wait," Linc noticed. "They're the rest of the members that are sick. Let's see what Tony has to say."

"Good morning," Tony said as cheerfully as possible. "I won't beat around the bush. You've all come here to hear the plan I have—a plan that could end this war. It isn't the perfect solution, but then I don't believe there is such an animal."

All eyes focused on him. His words held magic. They would listen to their witch doctor.

"Our objective is the council of CEOs." The eyes of his audience offered no clue to what they thought. "They meet two days hence, Friday, at fifteen hundred right here in Portland's own Powell's Tower. This council doesn't even give themselves a name, so I certainly can't think of one, unless you want to borrow 'Axis of Evil.'"

A smattering of chuckles proffered themselves. Andrea's hand went up.

"Yes, Andrea?"

"We can't get to them. We've examined such a plan long before you pointed us to fiscal targets rather than executives."

"Minor correction to that, Andrea. If I recall, in the past the plans were nixed because the cost would be too high. I read your own write-up on that proposal. You said, 'While possible from a theoretical sense, the cost would devastate the ranks of the GAM action committee. This makes it infeasible.'"

"That sounds about right."

"Well, I'm here to tell you that the cost hasn't dropped. The plan will require every operative we have and then some. Worse, I anticipate there will be two teams of three and a lone individual who'll be in this on a suicide mission basis."

"Seven lives lost? Are you insane?"

"Yes, seven lives plus incidentals. I anticipate the total cost at considerably higher myself. I'd say more like nearly twelve. And to answer your question, yes, I might be insane, but please listen to my plan. I'll accept your judgment."

"One other question. Why are we going after executives again? Won't others just fill their place?"

"That is a recognized feature of the plan. The security on these men is fierce. They're guarded by a phalanx of army droids posing as innocuous security bots and by a squad of fast-attack dragoons always on standby during one of the council's meetings—not to mention the Metros themselves.

"All the security and alarms for this meeting place are run off an isolated system, not touching the net in any way. It's an isolated system, so it can't be hacked. In addition to this, we have the physical security. The only access is through a one-person grav portal. To use the portal you must give a visual, DNA, and electrical characteristic scan. The grav portal won't function for anyone but the head executives. If you do somehow succeed, at the top are both automated weapons and live guards all programmed to shoot anyone who doesn't belong. In addition, there are two private security firms, rotated among seven on a random basis, who are on speed alert to any incursion in this area. They're authorized to use deadly force.

"Now, through the help of Augustine's capabilities, I've learned which security firms are on protection detail Friday. I've dealt with each of them individually. Neither knows what our target is. One will have a mysterious power outage Friday at fifteen-twelve. The other will have their receiver sabotaged. I've also found a way to deal with the Metro response.

"There's only one way we can take out the on-site security teams, both live and robotic. They must be ambushed just as they deploy from their bivouacs. The robotics can only be stopped with an EMP. We have a pinch that'll do the job. It can't be done remotely, so the problem is whoever sets that pinch off will likely die in the ensuing conflagration. With the right equipment and explosives, the live group should be killed easily—however, their location is such that it's doubtful the team could escape before backup can arrive.

"That leaves the grav lifts. We can rig it with the right combination of hack and illusion so that we can get past it, but there's no way we can take down the guards or the robotics going up individually, unless one of us is a suicide bomb.

"Once on the grav platform, we're effectively at the meeting room. Just a couple of locked doors. Did I mention that all of this has to happen within seconds of one another or the guard teams will seal the top of the building and jettison it into orbit where the leaders will be removed by another fast response orbital craft?"

"It is an expensive plan," agreed Andrea after a moment's consideration. "As you said, it's suicidal in many phases. You still didn't explain how this will end the war, though."

Tony smiled and explained for two short minutes. Before he even asked, the eyes of every person, sick or not, volunteered for the suicide missions.

* * *

"Ma'am, this package was delivered addressed personally to you," the security guard said, holding out a nondescript cube-shaped box, 40 centimeters on a side.

"So? It can't wait?" Taste Dynamics snapped.

"Ma'am, per standard protocol we scanned the box. It contains no explosives, no active electronics nor any molecular technology. It does, however, contain a human head."

"Really? I'm intrigued," Taste Dynamics purred. "It isn't every morning someone delivers such a unique item. Is there a return address?"

"No, ma'am. It was mailed from a branch office of the actual US Post Office that doesn't even have surveillance cameras."

"Curiouser and curiouser. Who belongs to this head? Did I know him or her?"

"We couldn't make that determination without opening the package, ma'am. It's addressed to you."

"Well then, open it up."

The guards snapped the imperv loktite strips and popped the lid off. The box held Adonis's face, captured in mid-scream.

* * *

Tony kneeled next to the grav chute as Augustine wired into the local computer. He reached over and shook Linc's hand. Linc, wearing a suit of molecular explosives, nodded and smiled. He gave Tony a thumbs-up sign and smiled even wider. Tony had picked carefully for the three suicide missions, not taking anyone who didn't show frank symptoms of the two virus. Even knowing this, he regretted sending any of them to die.

Augustine gave an OK with her fingers and pointed to the grav tube. She then gave two innocuous clicks over the mission frequency. Linc closed his eyes for a moment. He took a deep breath, pulled out his automatic and walked into the entrance. Tony watched as he disappeared up the tube at blindingly high speed. Tony spared enough time to hope that Linc would shoot that quickly up to heaven, or whatever eternal reward he deserved.

* * *

"Which brings us to the excellent news of our actions against the GAM," Taste Dynamics said, her face twisted into a sardonic grin. "For another week we've had zero actions against our facilities or people."

"Our projections tell us why this is happening, but do we have any intel?"

"The operatives we do have in the field report hearing rumors of key GAM members dying, including their leader. Even better, the rumor on the street is there's a power struggle among those left."

"This is excellent news."

"This means that the number of actions from the GAM in the future will be reduced?"

"Perhaps even eliminated," she said, sparing a cold look at Nanogate. Nanogate didn't even flinch. Hers was not the first assassin to fail against him.

"I suggest we keep this on the agenda…"

"Advisory," came a pleasant computer-generated voice. "Stocks of all major corporations experiencing significant drop in value based on broad sell and put activity." That program would only activate in the case of a ten percent or more drop in all major stocks.

"What?"

The room echoed with a resounding boom. Dust filtered down from the ceiling and one window cracked afterward with a loud report.

"This facility is under attack," said the same soft, but obviously artificial, female voice. "Please remain calm."

* * *

Tony counted on his fingers. Before he reached eight, the building shuddered and flame licked briefly down the tube. Ignoring the incendiaries, Tony jumped into the grav tube just in time to hear two almost simultaneous tremors. One would be Andrea setting off the pinch. The other would be the opening blast against the response team.

His guts sank to the floor as the grav tube flung him upward. They then slammed into his mouth as his ascent slowed. Even before he arrived, a sweet stench of burnt flesh mixed with the acrid odor of smoldering plastic filled his nose. Tony scrambled for a perch as a black gaping maw, partially obscured by smoke, replaced the customary landing ledge.

Several small fires that had been computers, notepads, or even a table burned fitfully. Nothing else remained of the room except heaps of smoldering biologic. One of the mounds moved slowly, crawling in a seemingly random direction. Tony walked up, put his gauss carbine to the indistinguishable mound and pulled the trigger. The lump stopped moving in a sickening splash of something between liquid and solid.

Christine landed from the grav chute one second behind him and Augustine just seconds after that. Arthur brought up the rear a few seconds later. Tony had already moved toward what had been the doorway. The door itself lay askew halfway down the hall. Tony wouldn't need the explosives he brought to gain entry.

The four of them marched in an open diamond formation, with Tony leading, into the meeting room. Seven of the ten most powerful people in the solar system already stood, looking for something to do, or some way to escape. The other three just gaped.

"What are you—" one of them sputtered.

Tony interrupted with a blast from his gauss gun into the ceiling. Christine and Augustine stood beside him covering the council.

"I beg your attention, ladies and gentlemen. Sorry for the theatrics, but I needed your attention. It's time to change your little cabal here into a positive force."

"Welcome, Tony," Nanogate said. "You were very effective."

Christine shot the man in the fleshy part of the arm. His scream and subsequent whimpering stifled anyone else from making comment.

"Oh, quit whining. She only nicked you. Trust me when I say she could easily have chosen to remove a single testicle had she taken it in her mind."

Completely out of character, Christine smiled.

"Now that we've settled that, I want you all against the window, facing out at our fair city. And before you think you're only buying time until the cavalry arrives, we've neutralized everything, including the Metro response. If you look out, you might just see the police involved in a riot at the Main Metro complex itself.

"Now that I've taken hope from you, I will give it back. Behave and your families will live."

One woman half turned toward Tony, but froze as Christine's weapon swung about to point at her head.

"That's right," Tony went on. "We have each of your families ready to be vaped. We have trigger teams shadowing all of them, including yours, sir, on their holiday on Io. Now, I want you each to announce which corporation you head."

Each went in turn from one end to the other. Wisely, none of them hesitated or protested.

"Good. Now I'll answer the question put to me earlier by Nanogate. Yes, I was a very effective weapon for this council. Your plan worked, after a fashion. You've decimated the ranks of the GAM."

"So this is revenge?" Percomm Systems spat back.

"No. If this were revenge, I'd have tracked down how to hurt each of you the worst," Tony said as he paced up and down the line. "Torture your daughter, maybe?" he asked one executive. "Or maybe make your grandson a vegetable?" he said walking by another. "How about removing the genitalia of your lover and giving it to your wife? Bottom line, this is the start of something new…perhaps tainted by just a smidge of justice."

"So you want to kill us and take over?"

"Hell, no," Augustine laughed as she answered.

"I have to agree with my colleague. First off, we don't have the experience to run your companies. Your successors would soon oust us. Even if we could, we don't want this kind of power. We do, however, want those who exercise supreme power to be answerable to the people."

"How are you going to do that?" Wintel asked. "You can't post a guard on each of us twenty-four/seven to make sure we behave."

"True. We can't. But then our actions against your corporations have made each of us very wealthy. So wealthy, in fact, that we'll be funding multiple independent watchdog organizations, each with enough capital to start a small army. Remember how easily our small organization got to you. Think of how easily someone could do it with military hardware."

"So you're going to let us live?" CNI asked.

"Well, that depends. We obviously can't kill you all, or we lose our object lesson here. But then letting you all go would lose its impact. You'd eventually think it was a fluke and try to do something stupid."

"So what *does* it depend on?"

"This pretty young lady here is going to draw lots. Those drawn will be killed outright. It isn't a perfect plan, but then none is. I honestly don't know how to restore full public responsibility. I leave that for you to decide, knowing that we, and many like us, will be watching. Note that some of them won't quite have our patience."

"Why would we just stand still and wait to be killed?"

"First of all, do you think even the ten of you, unarmed, could overcome four trained, armed guerilla fighters? But, more importantly, if even one of you resists, we will kill each and every one of your families. That includes any wife, parent, child, lover, friend, pet, or bastard within two generations."

The executives fidgeted but said nothing.

"Christine, if you please. Oh, and did I mention, we'll be drawing eight names…exactly eighty percent."

Author's Note

I want to thank you for reading *An Eighty Percent Solution*. I truly hope you've enjoyed it! Because of the curse or blessing of my creative side, I not only write, I also game master roleplaying games and undertake many other activities where I invent to entertain. It's unlikely that in my lifetime my creativity will wane. Because I write to entertain, I must also take this occasion to drag out my podium:

/*soapbox begins*

It's been my sad fate to have been in one too many classes, through my high school and college years, where some teacher of literature attempts to draw out some secret, hidden meaning to novels I've loved or tales that were just that.

I'm perverse enough to want to make it clear to my readers and fans that I write stories to entertain—full stop. My books, short stories, and other creative pieces are not being used to pass on some hidden message. I'm not obscuring political parallels in the background. I'm not offering a secreted religious message. Yes, I have many opinions—political, religious, and sexual—but I won't use my novels as a medium for expressing them.

I conceive of an idea and try to flesh it out so it's logical, believable, and most of all, entertaining to you, my public. You're the ones who determine my success or failure, and I won't make you work harder by veiling something critical. While I may have reduced my potential sales by not allowing some gung-ho teacher to force scads of students to use my work to illustrate parallelism or some other concept, I will be true to you, the readers.

/soapbox ends

Now, I'll give you some insight as to where the kernel of an idea for this first of the CorpGov Chronicles came from. It started, as many of these things do, with someone else's work—to wit, Sir Arthur Conan Doyle and his well-known detective, Sherlock Holmes. I watched an episode of their story just as I took a corporate training class on management practices. Sherlock's addiction to a seven percent solution came on the screen just as I was dealing with the concept of "eighty percent of a problem can be solved with twenty percent of the effort."

It took all of about seven seconds for my twisted mind to come up with the rough outline of this book from the title I envisioned from merging the two...and *An Eighty Percent Solution* was born.

As a shameless plug, I hope I've entertained you enough to interest you in the next installment of the CorpGov Chronicles. I've envisioned and mapped out several sequels to *An Eighty Percent Solution*. I won't ruin either your anticipation or my ability to make adjustments to the stories' flow by going too far into the future. Instead, I'll whet your appetite with a brief blurb describing the next CorpGov novel, *Thinking Outside the Box*:

After replacing the evil business cabal with a responsible government, the terrorist organization known as the Green Action Militia thought their job was finally done. Instead, the newly formed CorpGov calls upon them to help prevent another coup, this time by the Metro police bureaucracy. The Metros want nothing more than to keep their lives of privilege and power in a world that drowns in the blood of injustice.

To this explosive situation, a previously unknown power block begins to forward their own agenda. Tony and his decimated crew of guerillas must dig deep to avert the chaos of a three-sided civil war.